She was touching
wanted to.

The simple purity and comfort of a human connection, a touch that didn't involve menace or pain.

Yes, it had to be that, she told herself.

The hand was warm as it cupped the flare of her hip bone. When the hand slid across her belly and curved to her waist where she lay on her side in the bed of the pickup, she didn't resist an automatic movement to relax into the heat of his body, curled behind her.

In the humidity, it was only moments before she felt the hollow of her spine grow damp with perspiration, but still the heat was welcome. To be close to another body, without fear, without trembling...it was both all she had wished and more than she had dared to hope for in the past year.

His hand slid, as if in sleep, gently along her rib cage. Abby wondered if he could feel the sudden slamming acceleration of her heartbeat, or the manic trembling that was turning her insides to liquid.

Dear Reader,

The idea for this book seized me one afternoon as I exited a convenience store with my purchases. Outside the store was a car, door standing wide-open, keys in the ignition and the engine running. There wasn't a person in sight, and as I stood there wondering where the car's owner was, I realized that just about anyone could walk up, get in that car and drive away, never to be found again.

Now, I don't know about you, but I don't know a woman over age twenty-five who hasn't had at least one moment where she imagines walking away from absolutely everything and starting a brand-new life. Because I'm a storyteller, my brain began chasing that idea. What would drive a woman to steal a car and vanish? Could I justify such a desperate act?

I'm a romantic at heart, so the dark seed of the story—a woman fleeing domestic violence—began to grow into a love story right away. The hero turned up promptly, but it takes more than a good man to save a woman—it takes a strong woman, too, willing to participate in her own salvation.

I hope you'll join me in a suspenseful ride with Abby and Cade and Mort, the K-9 dog. Let's tell ourselves stronger stories, as women and as humans, and begin to make a difference.

Mel Sterling

LATIMER'S LAW

Mel Sterling

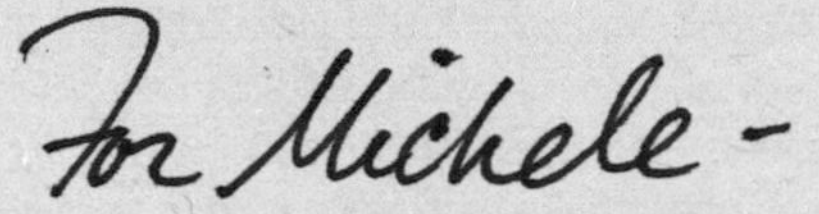

Enjoy & thank you!

Mel Sterling
May 2014

ISBN-13: 978-0-373-27872-5

LATIMER'S LAW

This edition published by arrangement with Harlequin Books S.A.

For questions and comments about the quality of this book, please contact us at CustomerService@Harlequin.com.

Printed in U.S.A.

Books by Mel Sterling

Harlequin Romantic Suspense

Latimer's Law #1802

MEL STERLING

started writing stories in elementary school and wrote her first full-length novel in a spiral-bound notebook at age twelve. Her favorite Christmas present was a typewriter and a ream of paper. After college, she found herself programming computers and writing technical documentation. A few years ago, she rediscovered romance writing during a prolonged period of insomnia and began to indulge her passion with a vengeance. She lives with her computer geek husband in a quiet happy house full of books, animals and ideas.

For my husband, the best and most honorable man I know. Thank you for giving me the freedom to run.

Chapter 1

The last straw was a single, ridiculous button.

Abby shifted the paper grocery sack in her arms as she stepped out of the convenience store. The hard plastic cap of the orange juice nudged at just the wrong place, the curve under her biceps where the bruises had never quite faded in the past few months. No bruises where they couldn't be covered. Long practice brought skill. She moved the sack again, and a button burst from her worn chambray shirt.

She followed the button's freewheeling path across the concrete sidewalk until it plummeted off the curb. It bounced across the white stripe of a parking space and into the black shadow beneath a pickup truck. With a sigh, Abby went around the half-open driver's door, looking apologetically into the cab. How to explain she needed the driver to move the truck so she could find a button? She couldn't come home from the store with that particular button missing, right at the shadowed hollow between her breasts—well. It was unthinkable. Her mind raced ahead, picturing the scenario. She could drop the button on the floor when she put the sack on the kitchen counter, as if it had come loose at that very moment. The trick could work, but only if she had the button.

The pickup was empty.

Empty.

With the keys in the ignition, and the engine running.

The shimmering brilliance of an impossible, desperate solution forced all the air out of Abby's lungs.

Escape.

Abby didn't glance toward the store or look around for the truck's driver. She dumped the grocery bag into the passenger seat and hoisted herself in behind the wheel, feeling the soreness in her arms and back. She yanked the door closed and settled into the seat.

Three pedals on the floor, gearshift in neutral on the column, parking brake set.

Her heart lurched. She couldn't let herself think beyond the physical mechanics of making the truck go. She stretched her leg to stomp the clutch, studied the gearshift a moment and worked it into reverse. Maybe six years since she'd driven a manual transmission, and months since she'd driven at all. The bank repossessed the car when she couldn't make the payments, but before that there'd been a series of repairs that consumed the meager savings she and her husband, Gary, had scraped together. What didn't go into the adult day care business went to the mechanic.

Fate was kind. Abby managed not to stall as the truck groaned into reverse out of the parking space. She rode the crow-hopping lurches into first gear, pulling herself close to the steering wheel because the seat was too far back, but there was no time to adjust it. Something heavy fell over in the covered bed of the truck and Abby felt a gut-punch of guilt.

She was stealing a truck.

This wasn't in the same league as keeping the change she found in the washing machine or behind sofa cushions, or filching a five from the grocery money when she thought Marsh wouldn't notice. This was a felony. *Grand theft, auto,* her rap sheet would read.

Was she out of her mind?

How fast could she get out of sight? It wouldn't be long before the truck's owner called the police—minutes, maybe.

How bad could jail be, in comparison with her life?

Left turn from the parking lot. Left again at the four-way stop, hands jittering on the wheel, stomach churning. Then straight on to the interstate, heading north, grinding gears as her speed increased.

A few miles past the town line, still hunched over the steering wheel, Abby realized the roar she was hearing was the truck's engine under strain. She was pushing ninety, screaming to be noticed by the highway patrol, followed by a ticket if she were very lucky, more likely arrested when she couldn't produce insurance and registration. She stood out like a white gull on blacktop, in the red truck on the mostly empty road. She had to calm down, think about what came next.

She rolled down the window to catch the breeze, too stressed to decipher the air-conditioning controls. The Florida summer heat was making her dizzy. She needed to get her heart rate down. Try to still the shaking in her hands and stop jerking the truck all over the lane, another attention-getter she couldn't afford.

First things first. Get off the interstate, travel the secondary roads. Keep moving. Head for Gainesville, maybe, a bigger town than Wildwood, where she could ditch the truck and use public transportation. She wondered if there was a map in the glove box. She was so overwhelmed by what she'd done that she couldn't remember the names of towns in the county where she'd lived more than half her life.

Money would be an issue immediately. She didn't dare use the credit card—it would give her away. In the hip pocket of her jeans there was only the envelope of fifty-odd dollars, whatever she'd managed to scrounge in the past fifteen months. She had the change from the two twenties Gary's brother, Marsh, had given her for the market. Whenever she left the house, she always carried her stash with her. She knew Marsh went through her room. Any day he might find the loose baseboard molding in the back of the closet where she had cut a small hole in the drywall and hidden her hoard.

Marsh.

How did he know she needed the anchor of his touch when he tucked her hand in his elbow? The reality of his wool suit jacket. The faint humidity Abby could sense there at the bend of his arm, with her fingers gently covered by his free hand. She'd thought she was done with tears, until the motorized hoist began to lower Gary's coffin into the earth. It seemed somehow sterile and impolite for a funeral to be such an automated and regulated event.

Marsh understood. She heard him draw a harsh breath as the casket's top slipped below ground level. His hand tightened on hers. How could they just put Gary into the earth? How could they cover him up with foot after foot of dirt? She couldn't breathe, thinking about it.

Thank God Marsh was here. She'd still be dithering uselessly about whether red or white satin should line the box where Gary would lie forever, never turning his too-hot pillow to the cooler side.

Marsh. Damn his rat-bastard-needed-to-be-shot hide.

And while she was at it, damn her own stupid hide for skidding down the slippery slope that had led to this moment, careening along the interstate in a stolen pickup, in the middle of the hottest summer she could remember, roasting in the long sleeves that covered the bruises. The only positive was that the tears, so quick to spring since Gary died, were nowhere to be found.

A green marker sign grew in the distance, and Abby recognized something at last: Micanopy, an even smaller, more backward town than Wildwood. She recalled a narrow road winding through pecan orchards, the occasional orange grove and state forestland. It would eventually lead to Gainesville. She eased her foot off the accelerator and signaled for the exit. Only a mile down the narrow road was an intersection with a numbered state forest road. She paused, checking for other cars, thinking hard. From a camping trip in the early days of her marriage to Gary, Abby recalled a campground several miles into the state forest. If nothing else, its location next to a tea-dark river would help calm her. Flowing water always did. She had to get control of herself before she did something even more stupid.

Abby downshifted and turned the truck off the paved road onto the graded gray marl of the forestry access. The tires raised clouds of silty dust in the heat, and she slowed even more to leave less of a trail, as if Marsh could see her from Wildwood. Best to get out of sight altogether while she took stock of her situation. And maybe, just maybe, leave the truck behind and make her way back to Micanopy. She could hitchhike into Gainesville. It wouldn't be safe, but at least she wouldn't be caught in a stolen truck.

The unpaved road was in poor condition. Summer downpours had rutted it from crown to edge, jouncing her, jarring her torso and tossing the heavy things in the bed of the truck around again. Twenty minutes later she located the loop drive of the tiny campground and circled it, glad to find the place completely empty. With a shuddering sigh of relief, Abby circled a second time and angle-parked the truck into the most secluded of the eight campsites to conceal its license plates. She turned off the engine. For a long moment she stared at the river flowing past thirty feet away, watching a water-darkened stick curl downstream. Then she put her head on the steering wheel and gave in to the shakes that had threatened to overtake her for the past hour and a half.

She, Abigail McMurray, former straight-A student and all-around good egg, had stolen a truck.

She'd run away from home, what little remained of it now that she'd given up so much to Marsh. A giant bubble of guilt welled and burst in her chest. Those poor people, the adults who came to the house for day care and respite for their own caregivers. Only Marsh was there now. She was horrified to think he might take out his ire on one of the sweet people who trusted her to shelter them, feed them healthy meals and make sure Rosemary didn't hog the DVD remote during Movie Hour.

She should turn around, *now,* and go back.

She *couldn't* turn around now and go back.

But she could. After dark she could go home, leave the truck in the drugstore parking lot a mile from the convenience store where she'd taken it and sneak away. After wiping down the interior to remove her fingerprints. She could leave a note of apology and money for gas. The police would find the truck soon enough. It could all go away. It would be as if it had never happened.

Except for Marsh's anger. His anger, and his fists.

Abby's stomach clenched. Her mouth was dry. She'd been gritting her teeth for miles and miles—a monstrous tension headache throbbed at her temples. Maybe some juice would help. She started to reach for the jug, but it only reminded her of the impetus for her flight.

She bit her lip and grabbed the jug anyway, wrenching it open with fierce determination, and downed several swallows of the juice. It was only orange juice, after all, not an enemy, not a symbol, not Marsh's grip. When she had capped the jug again, she got out of the truck to stretch her legs and face what she'd done head-on. Time to be practical about it all.... If she wasn't going to take the truck back, she might as well see if anything in the pickup bed could be of any use to her in her new life of crime.

The fork, covered with mayonnaise and bits of tuna, clattered into the sink with a noise that hurt her ears. Abby felt the familiar black wave of grief submerge her. It was all too much. Tuna. Peanut butter. Sandwiches. Tomato soup. Toast. Apple wedges. Cheese. Celery sticks. Wheelchairs. Adult diapers. Tantrums. Seizures. Without Gary, it was too much.

"What is it? What's wrong, Abigail?"

"I can't. I need Gary. I can't do this."

"You can. We *can. Look, I'm here. Just tell me... how many tuna sandwiches?"*

Abby slid down the cupboard doors by the sink and sat on the floor with her knees drawn up and her head pressed against them. "I don't know."

Marsh put a warm hand on her shoulder. "Then tell me who gets peanut butter. I can manage that, I know. Come on, Abigail. It'll be all right. All we need is time." His voice was serene and placid. When he spoke, she could think again. Maybe it would work. Maybe all it took was time. Maybe he was right. He smelled like Gary. She wiped her eyes against the knees of her jeans.

"Rosemary. Rosemary gets peanut butter. Joe gets tuna."

"Good, good. The older guy, is his name Smith? What kind of sandwich does he get?"

The old red truck had a white camper shell over the bed of the pickup. Tinted windows prevented her from peering in, so she went to the back of the truck and turned the handle, lifting the hatch…

…and found herself staring into the unwavering barrel of a pistol, held beneath the grimmest, bluest gaze she'd ever seen, a blue gaze bracketed on one side by a starburst of corrugated scar tissue, and a smear of blood on the other. Standing at the shoulder of the man with the gun was a German shepherd, teeth bared and hackles raised.

When his pickup lurched into motion, Cade Latimer toppled from his crouch, striking his head on the big green toolbox. He had left the K-9 training facility outside Bushnell a few minutes ago and had pulled off the interstate at the Wildwood exit only to get a bad cup of convenience store coffee for the road and give Mort a snack and a drink of water. He'd climbed into the bed of the truck to tend to Mort before they got back on the road to head to the northeast corner of Alabama for some decent hill country hiking, fishing and camping.

His first reaction was to right himself and lunge for the back of the truck—he must have forgotten to set the parking brake, and the truck had slipped into reverse. He had a vision of his truck rolling slowly out of control and into the street, causing the sort of stupid accident he had always hated to see while on patrol duty in the sheriff's department. Before his undercover days, how many times had he lectured drivers about putting on their thinking caps before getting behind the wheel of a two-ton killing machine? But then he got a glimpse of someone in the cab of his pickup, behind the wheel, and realized something else was going on. Something illegal.

For a moment Cade couldn't believe it was happening. Surely no one in this Podunk, backwater, stuck-in-the-Depression town would steal a truck. Weren't small-town folk supposed to be as honest as the day was long? A second lurching hop sent him flat again. Mort scrabbled uselessly, claws squealing against metal as the truck fishtailed onto the road. Cade reached out to steady his dog and spoke the command for the German shepherd to lie down. Warm wetness trickled down from Cade's scalp. He'd cut himself on the metal toolbox.

One last bump, then the truck's motion smoothed and Cade ventured to look out the side window.

Interstate. Passing swiftly.

Damn it.

He peered through the darkly tinted camper shell window into the cab of the truck and wished—not for the first time—that he'd had the cab's window replaced with a slider. Most often he thought about that when he wanted to check on Mort while the truck was in motion, but now he wanted the slider so he could strangle the jerk who'd stolen his truck.

With Cade in it, no less.

Cade expected to see some punk-ass kid, maybe two, with cigarettes hanging loosely from their lips and leaving ash all over his vintage bench seat, out for a joyride with a six-pack of cheap beer. Instead, he saw the clean profile of a woman, light brown hair scraped back in a bobbing ponytail that brushed her back below her shoulder blades, and in the seat next to her wobbled a sack of groceries.

Groceries!

Some redneck soccer mom had stolen his truck. Maybe she was drunk already, though it wasn't even ten in the morning, and confused which truck in the parking lot was hers.

Blood dripped from his jaw onto his neck. Cade reached into his back pocket for a bandanna. Blotting, he looked at the cloth and saw the bright blossom of red there. Scalp wound. A tentative probe with his fingertips showed the cut was neither long nor deep, though it felt tender and was already swelling.

The woman had caught him completely off guard. It shouldn't have happened. His personal radar should have been better. He was a K-9 deputy, for crying out loud. It was his job to pay attention. Just because he was on vacation was no reason to check his brain at the door.

What was worse, he knew not to leave his keys in and the engine running, even if it was only going to be for the two minutes he was feeding Mort. Talk about putting on his thinking cap.... He'd grown soft in the two years since he'd had to leave undercover work at the Marion County Sheriff's Department after his accident. It was disturbing to realize how much he'd come to depend on Mort's alertness to supplement his own training, awareness and common sense. Cade glared at the woman impotently, peering past her at the speedometer needle as it crept up and up. He watched her hands shaking on the steering wheel. She was all over the damned road. Drunk, high or terrified by what she'd done?

Staying low, not wanting her to glance in the rearview and see even a shadow of him crouching in the pickup's bed, Cade shifted toward the tailgate again, edging past his camping gear and fishing tackle, cooler, bedroll and tools. He leaned out cautiously, studied the concrete of the interstate flashing by at high speed beneath him and brought the flap of the truck's canopy down. He latched it securely to shut out the boil of the truck's slipstream, then glanced over his shoulder to see if she'd noticed. Her face was still turned toward the front, and she was scooted toward the wheel as if she hadn't bothered to pull the bench seat forward to accommodate her height.

Still at the back of the bed, Cade settled low and opened his zippered duffel. The 9mm Beretta waited there in its pocket holster, safety on, with a full clip and a bullet chambered. He stuck it in the back of his jeans, and slipped a couple of heavy-duty cable ties out of the same bag. He formed them into a two-link chain before settling low again, in case she pulled another thank-you-ma'am across the roadway. Not much he could do at the moment, but by God, when she stopped—he'd be ready.

She'd stolen the wrong truck.

Chapter 2

"Hands up, lady."

Abby's shocked gaze traveled slowly up from the menacing dark little mouth at the end of the gun barrel to the blue eyes behind it, and locked there. Peripheral vision showed her the shiny, puckered nightmare flesh of an old acid burn fanning out from the edge of his left eye toward his hairline and ear, and spilling down the side of his neck to vanish beneath his clothing. A vision of splattered melted red candle wax flashed through her mind. It took her too long to look away from the damaged skin, and the man's eyes narrowed in irritation at her visible shock and revulsion. When her gaze finally hitched away from the terrible visage, she barely noticed the rest of his appearance. He wore jeans and a T-shirt, and a khaki fishing vest full of pockets. Her hands rose slowly on their own, the truck keys dangling from her left. Her own terror and guilt made her babble.

"Oh, God. Oh, God. I'm sorry. It was a mistake. I didn't mean to—"

"Shut up. Turn around. Drop the keys. Down on your knees."

"You ought to be down on your knees to me, Abigail. It isn't every man who'll take on his brother's widow and his business and make it all work."

"I know. I know. It's just that...it's the checking account. It's the last thing with his name on it. It's so hard to let go."

"It's been six months. Gary's not walking through that door ever again."

"Stop it! Just...stop."

"Ah...I didn't mean to make you cry. I don't want to hurt you. Why do you make me say these things, Abby? Why?"

"I'm sorry. I know you don't mean to..."

"Come here. Dry your eyes. It won't look good at the bank when we change the names on the account if your face is puffy."

Abby stared. With one hand the man reached out to open the tailgate while the other held the gun pointed at her. "I said on your knees, woman!"

Some final anchoring cord of rationality snapped inside Abby. "You can't speak to me like that!"

His unbelieving laugh was deep and rich as he slid off the tailgate and stood. "This, from the nutjob who stole my truck with me inside it? Mort, *fass*." At the single command, the dog leaped out of the truck and put his nose against Abby's thigh, growling. "Turn around. On your knees. Do it now."

Abby's heart pounded. In her head she saw herself at dog-level, her bare throat torn and bloodied by the teeth of the menacing shepherd. Or her brains splattered on the sand of the campsite by a single shot from that beast of a gun. She turned slowly away from the tall, blue-eyed man, dropped the keys in the sand and went to her knees. The dog's nose shifted to her shoulder and the growling continued.

"Hands on your head."

She obeyed, lacing her fingers. "Please don't let him bite me." She could hear the trembling in her own voice. Fear spiked sharp and bitter in her mouth and she thought the orange juice might make a reappearance. She had the same feeling of horrible dread when Marsh was displeased.

"I'll tell you when you can talk." His foot nudged her ankles apart and then the sole of his work boot settled lightly on her calf.

The man grasped Abby's left forearm and brought her hand behind her back, then joined the right to it with a grating ratchet. He had shackled her—not with handcuffs, but something else. Her heart pounded even harder and then the juice did force its way out of her throat, spraying the earth before her. With her hands behind her back, there was no way to wipe the sick from her mouth. Judgment upon her for her crime. Even while she wept from fear and dread, some freakishly alert portion of her brain noted that the man's grasp, while firm, was not angry or brutal, and he didn't wrench her arms painfully when he pulled them behind her.

A shameful part of her felt she deserved harsh treatment, expected it—perhaps would even have welcomed retribution. But the rest of her was pathetically grateful for small mercies. With a snuffling sob she tried to clear her nose. She turned her mouth against the shoulder of her shirt.

"Oh, for crying out loud." He took his weight from her leg and grabbed her arm just beneath her biceps to help her rise. "Get up." Abby could not hide her gasp, nor the wince that contorted her face when he gripped where Marsh had bruised her arm. "There's a picnic table. Sit on the bench, and keep your mouth shut." He hustled her over to the table constructed of concrete posts and bolted-on planks. "Stop that crying, too. You're well and truly busted, lady. Tears won't make me go easier on you. Now turn around and face the table." The man grasped her shoulder to balance her as Abby obeyed—the black mouth of the gun was pointed her way again, though the dog had backed off a few paces—and swung her legs over the bench. There would be no leaping up and running into the scrubby woods. He knew what he was doing, impeding her without physically restraining her beyond the cuffs.

He stood back from the table, lowering the gun at last. "What's your name?"

Abby gulped and shook her head. She stared at the man. He wasn't someone she knew from town.

He didn't recognize her, she could tell. She tried to think, but a moment later he spoke again.

"Mort, *fass*." The dog bristled forward and pressed his nose against her again. Abby couldn't stifle a fresh gasping sob.

"Your name."

"I can explain—"

"I don't want explanations. I want facts. Your name."

Abby's gaze dropped from the scar to the glinting barrel of the gun held at his side. Its latent menace dried her mouth, and try as she might, she could not summon enough moisture or breath to speak.

"Fine. We'll do this your way." He glowered at her and stepped forward. Abby flinched back instinctively, and then froze when the dog growled and breathed hot, moist air over her arm. She felt the prickle of his whiskers.

"I—I—" Fresh tears started. Abby feared they would only aggravate this man. "Please don't make him bite me."

"Then don't push me." He moved behind her and she craned her neck to watch him. "It'll be best if you stay still and don't give him a reason to attack. I'm going to take your wallet out of your pocket."

How odd. He's courteous, even when he's demanding information. His hand went smoothly into her pocket and withdrew the thin bifold wallet—Gary's, which she'd used since his funeral, a way to keep his memory alive.

The man put the table between them again. He

laid the wallet on the plank surface and pulled out the contents one-handed. Her driver's license, the solitary credit card, photos, cash. Abby stared up at him, noting that the blood on his face was dried and smeared, but the cut in his hairline was still moist and fresh. It needed attention. She supposed her wild driving was the cause of his injury, and bit her lip. He'd been hurt because of her. He had close-cropped straw-colored hair and the tan of an outdoorsman. He was muscled and fit, and he handled the gun and the dog with familiar ease.

"Abigail McMurray. 302 Carson Street, Wildwood." His gaze flicked up and caught her own. "Well, now, Abigail, what have you got to say for yourself?"

Abby swallowed hard and faced her own crime. "There isn't much to say, I guess. I stole your truck."

To her everlasting astonishment, the man threw back his head and laughed. She could tell it wasn't forced. He was honestly amused, and it startled her to see such confidence and poise in a man whose truck had been stolen, and who had the thief sitting right in front of him. She half expected the Phantom of the Opera to emerge from that awful visage, something rough-voiced and vengeful. The juxtaposition of the terrible scarring and his careful demeanor kept her off balance. "No kidding. I'd never have guessed if you hadn't told me. No, Abigail...what I want to know is *why.* What makes a soccer mom like you jump in a truck at a quickie mart and drive off? Where's your minivan, your Beemer? Start talking."

"I'm not a soccer mom. I'm a…" Abby's voice trailed off as she realized she'd just risen to his bait. She flushed. "Just call the cops and get it over with. I know I'm a felon."

He gestured around them. "Nice of you to confess, Abigail, but just where might there be a phone in these parts? I've checked my cell—there's no coverage here." He straightened, reached to tuck the gun into the back of his jeans, and then bent forward, knuckles on the table. "And if there's no cell coverage, that means we're pretty remote, doesn't it? No one to hear you scream when I make you tell me the truth. I'm more interested in the truth than in calling the cops."

No one to hear you scream. Don't grunt like that—what would the neighbors think? It's so hot outside. I don't want to wear a long-sleeved shirt to wash the car, but what would the neighbors think if they saw my arms? I'm not ready for those kinds of questions. I'll never be ready for those kinds of questions. If only Marsh wouldn't grip so hard. Abby pulled herself away from the dismaying flicker of memories. "I don't think I should talk without someone else here. A cop, or a lawyer. Someone."

"Your husband, maybe?" His fingers flicked Gary's license so that it spun toward her over the tabletop. She watched Gary's cheerful face come to a smiling stop. Who ever looked happy in their driver's license picture? Everyone else looked startled or stoned or fat, but Gary just looked like Gary, ordinary and plain until he smiled. "Is he going to meet you here, maybe?"

"He's dead." Why she felt compelled to say that much, Abby didn't know. She wedged her tongue between her teeth to remind herself to keep quiet. Sweat trickled down her face and the ridge of her spine.

"That explains why you're carrying a man's wallet and license." He gestured with his left hand, and the dog sat. Abby turned to look at it, expecting to see wild eyes and froth at its lips, and instead was startled by the lolling tongue as the dog panted in the day's glaring, humid heat. The shepherd looked as if he was grinning. He looked between Abby and the man continually, alert to each slight movement.

With the dog's muzzle away from her arm, Abby was able to relax the slightest bit. It was clear the dog would obey its master. She gained an odd respect for the man. He controlled the dog without force—or, rather, with only the force of his will. It was a concept she hadn't thought about for months. All men had been painted with Marsh's brush, despite the years spent basking in Gary's gentle love. One bad apple.

"Wait here. Don't try to run. My dog will stop you." The man went to the pickup and opened the passenger door, reaching in for the bag of groceries. He brought the sack to the table and started taking items out of it one by one. When he was finished, he surveyed the goods before him. The orange juice. Potato chips. Two cans of chili. A half gallon of milk. Grape jelly for Rosemary's sandwiches. Emergency rations because she hadn't had a chance to ask Marsh to drive her to the supermarket last evening.

Of course she hadn't. She'd been busy doing other things. Busy collecting the latest set of bruises on her arms, and elsewhere. Busy taking pills to knock back the pain. Busy wondering if this time he'd slip and mark her face. Her stomach clenched; how long would it be before Marsh came looking for her? Had he called the cops because he couldn't leave the day care while the clients were there? Or was he simply sitting, wondering what had happened to her, his anger growing? Had he fed the clients lunch?

Or…maybe…Marsh was afraid. Afraid she'd gone to the hospital or the cops at last. She hoped he was afraid, as terrified as she herself every time she saw the edges of his nostrils whiten or his hand reaching for her, or, what was worse, the look in his eye that signaled something less painful but more humiliating. She could picture him now, in one of his button-down short-sleeve shirts that brought out the green in his hazel eyes, watching her from where he sat in the living room while she folded his clothes—

"Did you steal these groceries? Was that why you were running away, because you were afraid someone at the store would catch you? Hardly seems worth the trouble for twenty bucks in junk food."

"I'm not a thief!" Abby flared, realizing how stupid that sounded when his eyebrows shot up and he looked at her with a gaze of blue disbelief and a twisted smirk on his well-cut mouth.

"Surely you're joking."

Abby bit her lip, mystified. Unless her perceptions had been skewed by the time spent with Marsh, the man was honestly amused. He was angry, too, but about the truck and not her responses. "I mean…I… had reasons why I…"

"Why you took my truck?" He came around the table and loomed over her. Abby shrank away as far as she could without losing her balance. It wasn't easy with her hands behind her back. "Come on, Abigail. Just give me the truth and this will go better for you. Why'd you steal my truck?"

"I'm sorry about that. Really, I am. It was a mistake, that's all. An error in judgment." She could hear herself babbling, and sought to divert him. "You're bleeding, did you know?"

"Your fault."

"I know. I'm sorry."

He tilted his head and studied her for a long moment. "You know, Abigail, I believe you are."

Marshall McMurray looked at his watch for the fifth time. What was taking Abigail so long? She hadn't managed to get herself to the grocery store last night, though she knew they needed several basic things to be able to serve the clients lunch. But even if she'd decided to buy more than the few critical items on the list Marsh had jotted, she should have come home from the corner store by now. It was only a few blocks away.

Marsh's gaze roved the large living room, where most of the people Abigail and Gary took into their home each day were playing board games. Rosemary, who should have been seated with Stephen playing checkers, was roaming the room looking for the television remote, which Marsh had in his pocket. She loved to get possession of the remote and blast the volume, hooting with excited glee when the others moaned in reaction. Abigail let her have it far too often. Marsh saw no need for such indulgence, not when it resulted in only more noise and agitation for the other people. He was in charge now; Gary was gone.

Marsh missed his brother, but he knew he was better suited to Abigail than Gary had been. Gary had always catered to Abigail's whims, which meant the business floundered. Small businesses, and women, required steady direction and a firm hand on the tiller. No wonder the adult day care hadn't been delivering much more than a basic living for his brother and his brother's wife. Together Marsh and Abigail would fix that, though. It wasn't Marsh's first choice for a living, but it was a start.

All the clients seemed quiet enough, but Marsh knew they'd be asking for Abigail before too much longer.

He went to the window and pulled aside the curtain that shielded the clients from the nosy stares of passersby and blocked some of the summer heat. The placement of the window didn't give him much of a view to the street, but Abigail wasn't walking up the driveway.

Behind Marsh, someone was slapping wet clay at

the art table. Over and over. The flat sound reminded Marsh of the noise of skin on skin, the noise of two bodies in bed. And just like that, his brain revealed the explanation, the reason why Abigail hadn't come home yet.

She was meeting someone else.

His gut knotted. His fingers knotted in the fabric of the curtain, and he yanked it closed, sending the wooden rings rattling along the rod. Behind him the slapping continued. His fists wanted to knot, too.

She was probably sleeping with the man even now, leaving Marsh to deal with everything by himself, when she knew perfectly well state regulations required a minimum caregiver-to-patient ratio. She knew they were violating those very regulations, with only Marsh at hand to tend her clients. She knew it was nearly lunchtime when she left. She knew they'd be getting agitated, hungry and bored.

She'd told her clients she'd be right back.

Abigail had lied. Bald-faced lied. *Lied to him.*

Marsh turned from the window, glaring at Joe, the middle-aged man with pimples, who was slapping the clay mindlessly while he rocked back and forth in his chair, his eyes roving back and forth at high speed. Any moment now Joe would start moaning, overstimulated by whatever was going wrong in his neurons.

Abigail had left Marsh to cope with her pack of misfits, while she was off doing God knew what, probably with the idiot clerk at the store, maybe in the back room, maybe behind the store, up against the concrete wall where she could be seen from any passing car—

Rosemary bounced up to Marsh. "Lunchtime!"

Marsh gritted his teeth. "That's right. Almost lunchtime, as soon as Abigail comes back."

"I'm having peanut butter and grape jelly!" Rosemary said. Joe moaned a little, but Marsh could tell Rosemary's outburst had settled Joe in some way, opened a pressure valve. That was a good thing—Joe was damned strong, and without Abigail's soft voice and hands to calm him down, it would be a problem if Joe acted out his disturbance and became physical. Joe's eyes slowed their frantic flicking.

The old guy, Smith—Marsh never remembered his first name—who varied between utter stillness and manic activity, looked up. "Tuna fish. Tuna fish."

"Peanut butter!" Rosemary said, her mouth tightening as if Smith's preference would overrule her own.

Joe moaned again. His eyes started to flick.

Stephen joined the general ruckus, sending a hand across the checkerboard and scattering the game pieces. "Abby, Abby, where's Abby, where's lunch, where's Abby to make our lunch and pour the milk, lunch and milk, lunch and milk?"

Damnation, how all of them repeated themselves. It made Marsh nuts. If only he didn't have to put up with them—if only Abigail were here, as she should be. Next time he'd go and do the shopping, since she couldn't manage to get it right. Couldn't get herself home to feed the people she was responsible for.

"Shut up, Stephen!" Rosemary scrabbled after the checkers on the floor. "You messed me up. I was winning. You messed me up!"

Joe threw the pancake of clay at Rosemary, who shrieked in fury. Smith got out of his chair and started to walk in a circle in the center of the room, coming too close to Rosemary. Marsh was just in time to get between the two of them before Rosemary decided to slap.

"I know what, we'll all have popcorn for lunch!" Marsh said, with false cheer. He cursed Abigail silently. She had a lesson coming when she did get home, after causing all this mess. "Let's go in the kitchen and put a bag in the microwave. It'll be special, real special." Just like the special words he'd have for Abigail later that night, once everyone had gone home to their families.

"Special," repeated Joe, getting to his feet.

"And a movie. I get to pick!" Rosemary chanted. She stepped on the pancake of clay and ground it into the short-loop carpet. Marsh closed his eyes for a second, not nearly long enough to count to ten, but enough to allow him to ignore the newest mess. Then he got hold of Smith by his elbow and brought him along to the kitchen. The only way to stop Smith from walking in circles for the rest of the day was to completely change the scenery and give him a new focus. No way was Marsh going to let Rosemary pick the movie, though. He was damned sick of *Finding Nemo,* her latest favorite.

The afternoon wore on, full of countless exhausting and infuriating outbursts from the entire group. Marsh's patience thinned with each passing minute that Abigail didn't arrive. Rosemary and Stephen both had meltdowns ending in tears and thrown objects, events that wouldn't have happened had Abigail been present instead of shirking her responsibilities, wherever the hell she'd gone.

Marsh couldn't shake the idea that she was with another man. Where would she have met someone else? The produce aisle at the grocery store? It wasn't like Abigail went very many places without Marsh. He could hardly think. He tried to keep himself from going to the window every few minutes, because the clients were starting to notice his own agitation. He popped more bags of popcorn and got out crackers and cheese, and settled the group for a long afternoon of movie watching. It was easier than doing art projects or baking cookies in the kitchen, though both activities were favorites with the group.

Finally, at four in the afternoon, just ninety minutes before family members were due to retrieve their grown-up children, Marsh dug out the telephone book and wetted his finger to flip through the yellow pages. God help Abigail if she was still at that store.

Marsh dialed, keeping an eye on the group, who were quiet at the moment, engrossed in the umpteenth repeat of *Finding Nemo.* Stupid film.

When someone answered on the third ring, Marsh had to swallow down a growl of anger. "I'm looking for someone who was headed to your store a little while ago. I…uh, forgot to tell her to get a gallon of milk. She's about five feet six, and she has a long light brown ponytail. Wearing jeans and a blue cotton shirt. Is she there?"

"Store's empty, just me here right now."

"Has she been there?"

"Not since I came on shift."

"Well, when was that?" Marsh couldn't believe the idiocy of the clerk.

"Coupla hours ago. Look, is there a problem?"

"No. There's no problem. Is anyone else there, your supervisor maybe, someone who was there before you?"

"No, man. Wish I could help you, but like I said, haven't seen her."

"Thanks." *Liar. You're probably the man she's run off to meet. She's probably there now, listening to you answer my questions, laughing at me.* Marsh clicked off and put the handset away, in the cupboard, where it was out of Rosemary's view. That woman had a real thing for anything with buttons on it, telephones, remotes, controls for electric blankets, stereos.

"Where's Abby?" Smith asked.

Marsh clenched his fists behind his back. "She's… She had to go to the doctor." Yes, that was it. Get the story squared away with the clients, then set the expectations with their families: no day care tomorrow, Abigail was ill, it was probably contagious, she'd been at the doctor all day. Really sorry for the inconvenience and no notice. Knew they'd understand. Really, really sorry.

Beside Smith, Joe started to rock and hit his hand

on his thigh. "Don't like the doctor. Don't like the doctor."

"She'll be fine," Marsh assured him, putting a big hand on Joe's shoulder. "It's just a virus. In a day or so everything will be back to normal."

"Don't like the doctor," Joe repeated, but his voice was quieter as long as Marsh was touching him. Abigail was going to need the doctor when Marsh got through with her, that much was certain. He'd make sure her legs were too sore to carry her off to the store, hell, go anywhere.

"She'll get some medicine and be fine."

Smith turned his head and looked up at Marsh. "I don't like it when Abby isn't here."

"I don't like you," Rosemary chimed in. "I think you're mean."

"Now, now," Marsh muttered. "That's not very nice, Rosie. I think we'll have to tell your families you can't come here tomorrow, since Abigail won't be feeling very well. We don't want you to catch her virus, do we?"

"Mean," said Rosemary, and Smith nodded, then kept nodding. Well, Smith could nod his head right off his neck, for all Marsh cared. He wouldn't stop the perseveration this time.

"Shut up and watch the movie. All of you. Or I'll turn it off, and you can just sit in your chairs until it's time to go. You don't want that, do you?"

Joe began to rock again. Idiots, all of them. Why Abigail thought they were worth bothering with, Marsh would never understand. When all of their faces were turned back to the neurotic fish-father searching for his lost fish-son on the television, Marsh walked into the next room to get his temper under control and plan what he needed to say to the families to keep them away tomorrow. He couldn't legally operate without a second certified attendant, but more important, he didn't want to.

He'd see to it that Abigail learned this lesson. Learned it well. Learned it pronto. She'd never leave him in the lurch like this again.

And she'd never get another chance to sneak off with someone while Marsh wasn't looking.

Ever.

While he took the bag of groceries back to the truck, Cade assessed what he knew about the woman seated at the picnic table.

Thirty-one years old, based on her driver's license. She was too thin in that nervous way of women who were perpetually on their guard, either out of fear that if they gained weight their lovers would abandon them, or anxiety for other reasons. He was betting on the latter. His cop instincts were telling him something much bigger than a shallow boyfriend was at work here. You didn't steal a truck because you were anxious about gaining a little weight from too many chocolates or not enough exercise. It was possible her thinness was from drugs, but her teeth weren't those of a meth-freak, rotting and ground down. Until he knew for certain, he'd be cautious and expect the worst.

Her face and hands were tanned, but at the gaping shirt neck where a button was missing, he could see pale flesh beneath. Above her wrists the flesh was pale, as well. So she got out in the sun but not in short sleeves. Her straight hair was light brown, edging past her shoulders but scraped back in a plain ponytail, with blonder streaks threading through it. He'd have bet money the streaks were from the sun and not a bottle.

Her shirt and jeans were worn. Maybe she'd been doing chores when she decided to take his truck on a joyride, or maybe she couldn't afford new things.

The groceries looked like lunch for someone. Herself? Did women buy chili for themselves? Potato chips, sure, as an indulgence or, as a few of his girlfriends had taught him, greasy burnt offerings for the PMS monster. But why shop at a convenience store, where prices were guaranteed to be high? Simple: because she didn't have a car, and the store was closest to where she lived. She'd driven before, though—you couldn't just steal a manual transmission vehicle without knowing how to drive a stick. She'd never have made it out of the parking lot, much less to a campground in the middle of nowhere an hour from town.

Her husband was dead. That lined up with the bare left hand, and perhaps the worn clothing, but not that nagging hum in the back of his head that told him this woman was terrified of more than just his anger at her theft of his property.

This woman was running away from something. When she looked up at him as he loomed over her, he saw the flicker of alarm in her gray eyes. Her straight, level light brown eyebrows were drawn together over her nose in a worried expression. She feared him, feared his reaction to her crime. As well she should—but Cade knew this woman was no hardened criminal, just a woman on the run. Now, to get her to give up her secrets, because he was sure there was a doozy lurking just beneath the surface, like a catfish in a murky lake.

"Why stop here?" Cade questioned, leaning too close. Intimidation often worked to jolt confessions out of honest people. Habitual liars were a different matter. They'd learned to sidle along the truth for maximum believability, but he didn't think this woman was a liar. A little judicious pressure would get him what he sought. "Middle of nowhere. How does a chick like you drive my beater truck to a campground? How'd you even know this place was here, much less drive straight to it?"

"I've…I've been here before. Fishing. Years ago."

"You're on a fishing trip, are you? Saw my truck, thought it would be just the thing for a little jaunt? Who are you meeting here? When do they arrive?"

"No, I— That's not how it is. I'm not meeting—" She flushed darkly and stopped. "You're trying to make me talk. Just call the police and be done with it. You have all the proof you need. My fingerprints are all over the cab of your truck. I won't even try to deny it."

"That's right, I'm trying to make you talk. I don't think it's unreasonable of me to want to understand this, do you? If the police get involved, I may never learn the whole story."

She narrowed her eyes at him speculatively, her soft mouth tightening. "Are you…are you saying that if I tell you everything, you might not…might not call the police?"

Was that hope in her voice? Cade felt only mild guilt at using law enforcement interrogation techniques on this woman, who every passing minute seemed less and less a criminal and more and more a runaway girlfriend.

"Whadd'ya know, I think maybe I am. Why don't you see if you can convince me not to truss you up, toss you in the back of my truck and haul you to the nearest sheriff's department? I'm not an unreasonable man. Maybe I won't bother with the cops. Maybe you'll get a pass. But your story's got to be good, and I've got to believe it."

Abigail sat there, considering, for nearly a minute. Then she looked up at him. "I stole your truck because I needed to get away from some bad things in my personal life. I know it was wrong. I would rather not go into them, but I can at least promise you they're not illegal things. I'm really not a criminal. I'm just…stupid, I guess."

Cade folded his arms. "Not good enough, Abigail. I don't buy the stupid part." He looked up at the sun. "But we've got all afternoon. You say this is a good fishing spot? Maybe I'll just see about that. What's biting, do you think? Some bream?"

She nodded, her winged brows drawing together

above her nose, revealing her confusion. “Maybe bream. That’s a tributary of the Styx River, and there’ll be bluegill or sunfish. Catfish, too, if you like those. Lake fish, mostly, here where the current is slow.”

Cade put a foot up on the bench and leaned his elbow on his knee. His hand dangled, not carelessly, but not aggressively. Her eyes went to it briefly, checking it as he suspected she would. Then her eyes returned to wander to the side of his face, where the acid had ravaged his skin, marking him as a monster, a beast, a savage. “Styx, huh? I just can’t get over how many backwoods Florida places have these scholarly names. I’m not much for catfish, unless they’re farm-raised. Taste too much like mud, otherwise.”

“They say you are what you eat—I suppose that goes for fish, too.” She lifted her chin to gesture at the unscarred side of his face. “You’re still bleeding a little.”

“Go on about stealing the truck, Abigail.”

“Someone should look at the injury. It’s swollen like a goose egg. You’re not feeling dizzy, are you?”

“You’re avoiding answering my questions. While you think about what you want to tell me, I’m just gonna do a little fishing. Don’t try to leave the table. Mort will stop you.” He strode to the truck, conscious that she turned her head and body to watch him. It wasn’t exactly kind to leave her sitting in the hot sun while he sat in the relative cool of the shaded riverbank, but it might be the thing that pried her story out of her.

Cade didn't really plan to fish, but he'd make a good show of it. And if a bream or perch or bluegill turned up, so much the better. He just might be in a mood for some fresh fish. There was charcoal in the back of the truck, and a handy metal grill rested on a concrete fire circle not far from the picnic table. He checked the pistol's safety and returned the Beretta to his waistband. Opening the truck's hatch, he reached inside for a camp stool and his fishing tackle.

As he walked past the table with his gear, Abigail spoke. "Since your dog will watch me and there's nowhere for me to go, could you please take these off?" She lifted her wrists away from her back to remind him of the cable ties he'd cuffed her with. "They're really uncomfortable." Her movements strained the front of her worn chambray shirt and hinted at the womanly shape of her beneath. Her throat was flushed with heat and dewy with perspiration, the cords of her neck trim and taut.

Cade looked at her thoughtfully and said, "No." He turned his back and found a spot on the riverbank where Abigail was in easy view and he could cast into the slow-flowing stream. He set up the stool and sat at an angle. Mort looked at him alertly, but Cade gave the hand signal to continue on guard, and the shepherd turned his brown eyes back to Abigail.

Abigail shifted, trying to make herself comfortable on the hard bench seat of the picnic table. The movement made Cade wonder what she looked like in motion, walking, bending, busy at whatever it was she did for a living. He forced his gaze toward the river for a few minutes, working at clearing his head. Normally his emotions didn't get this involved with the people he was investigating, or worse yet, taking into custody. He had to get his priorities back in order. Her problems weren't his. Intellectually he knew that, but he continued to feel a strong need to dig out the truth. It wasn't a rational need. He told himself he was off duty, on vacation, but it didn't make even a dent in his stubborn will.

She was just a woman with a problem. He'd seen hundreds of them, helped some, condemned others. He didn't have to fix the world. Hell, she probably didn't even want him in her business in the first place, but by stealing his truck she'd dragged him right into her mess.

What would she look like if she smiled? Would the smile reach her eyes, transform her from sadly pretty to beautiful? Or would she get a goofy grin on her face that made her more charming than pretty? What would it be like to be the man Abigail McMurray smiled at? He missed being the sort of man women looked at with interest, even pleasure. The scar on his face saw to that.

Cade shook his head again, continuing to gaze at the river so Abigail would not see him scowling. When he scowled, he was truly a monster. He was unaccountably unwilling for her to view him that way. He might be ugly—he couldn't help that—but he didn't have to be frightening.

She stole your truck, Latimer. Keep that in mind. He tried to summon his cop brain uppermost, but it was having trouble, fighting with the white knight living deep within. The two sides of himself weren't always incompatible, but in this case he wasn't merely a disinterested party. He was personally involved, and growing more so by the minute. The cop brain had made him one of the best at the undercover game. It was the knight that made him keep believing in the basic goodness and worth of most people. Some people were worth saving, and his instincts told him Abigail might be one of them.

He fought down the urge to whack his own forehead with his open palm. He was acting like an idiot, thinking with his hormones instead of his brain. Abigail was pretty, sure. She was ragged and worn with care and fright. Likely he'd never have a chance with her, and he shouldn't want one. She probably wasn't the sort of woman who'd date a deputy for any reason, even if he weren't ugly as sin these days. He hadn't had the best of luck in the past with women, at least the sort of women who might want a long-term relationship. It took only one or two late nights on duty, a missed date at a swanky restaurant or a story about a dangerous takedown and a gunshot blessedly gone wide, for a woman to decide she was better off without the worry and fear her man might not come home some night. There were moments when he himself had wondered if scratching the adrenaline itch was worth it, if he might not find similar satisfaction in some other job where his life wasn't on the line half the time. Maybe then a woman would find him a worthy recipient of her time and affection. Those kinds of women weren't out stealing trucks, however. They were making vastly different life choices.

He knew all that.

It didn't make a difference.

Cade reeled in the lure and tossed it again. If only getting crooks to take bait was as easy as getting a fish to bite. Some of them were too smart, like this one. He stole a glance over his shoulder.

Abigail was still seated like a good girl, her head drooping, staring at the picnic table's wood grain. The sun blazed down on her head, turning the paler streaks in her brown hair to blazing gold. Even confined in a ponytail, it was the sort of hair that would look gorgeous loose around her shoulders, alive with gleaming highlights as it fell forward along her cheeks.

Chapter 3

Abby sat at the table, hands behind her back, sweating in the sauna heat of the humid sky. The table was out in the sun, and the sweet black shade of the nearby moss-hung oaks taunted her.

What had just happened here? She would have sworn the man had started off in a murderous fury, having every intention of packing her off to the police. Somewhere in his interrogation of her the tone had subtly shifted from one of anger to one of curiosity.

She eyed him where he perched on the incongruously small stool and leaned his back against one of the tall cypress knees that jutted from the river's edge. His fishing line trailed lazily in the slow-flowing water, and every few minutes he reeled it in and flicked it back upstream to float past again.

He sat with the scarred side of his face toward her. Now she had the leisure to study it, and reflect on some of her limited nursing training, the few years she'd had before taking a professional course designed to focus on adult day care in support of the business. It looked like a chemical burn of some sort, raised and raw-looking, ropy and rough in places, shiny and slick in others. The outer end of his left eyebrow was missing, giving him a somewhat quizzical appearance. He was fortunate that the worst of the chemicals had missed his eye. Even from a distance she could see his thick sandy lashes, which gave his startling blue eyes a deceptively sleepy look.

His T-shirt fit him closely, limning muscles in his arms and chest and showcasing his flat belly between the open lapels of his fishing vest. With the single exception of the scar, he was a man she would have turned to watch on a street. Lean and strong, hair that was more gold than brown, tall. He had a way of moving that spoke of ease and friendliness, until his eyes caught those of an observer and the wariness surfaced. His voice, once the anger had drained away, was quiet and firm with only a slight trace of a Southern accent in the vowels.

She had liked his laugh.

Abby frowned at this thought. Overthinking this man's general attractiveness was beyond pointless. Shortly he would tire of waiting for her to talk. He would shut her in the back of his truck and haul her off to the county sheriff. He had every right to do it.

She wondered if the lawmen would give her a break if she showed them her bruises and filed charges against Marsh. It wasn't the first time she'd fantasized about reporting Marsh's various crimes. She was pretty sure she could make an assault charge stick, and maybe even domestic abuse. But it would mean facing him down in public, and he was so far inside her guard that he knew every last secret, every weakness. He had pried up the edges of all her insecurities and peered beneath to where her doubts and fears lurked, and he had magnified them.

The telephone rang at all hours. It was a comfort knowing he thought about her, even at six in the morning or eleven at night.

"How was the day? Got any good stories for me, Abigail?"

"Oh...nothing fun. Just the usual grind. And messes. Sam had a bad seizure, so I had to call the ambulance, which upset everyone else. Rosemary cried and broke her soup bowl. Tomato soup everywhere. The new girl from the agency is still getting the hang of things, so most of the work is on me."

"Ah, Abigail, honey. I'm so sorry. Tomorrow will be better, I'm sure. In fact, I'll guarantee it for you."

"Thanks, Marsh. I know you can't do anything from there, but it's just so good to hear a friendly voice. Someone who understands."

"Have you got any of that merlot I bought you left?"

"A little." Smiling to herself now, picturing his charming grin and the way the cork had resisted him when he opened that first bottle and they'd toasted Gary's picture on the mantelpiece the night of the funeral. Two shared bottles and a crying jag later, she'd fallen asleep on his shoulder with his arm around her and the light cotton throw from the back of the sofa drawn across them both.

Or a wake-up call, when she was drowsy and unguarded, warm with sleep and alone in a bed meant for two people.

"Hey, there...how's my gray-eyed sister-in-law this fine morning?"

"It's raining here."

"I didn't catch you last night—I called a couple times but you didn't answer. Were you out?"

"Yeah...what time is it?"

"Still early. You've got time to get a little more shut-eye, but I wanted to say hello before I have to start my commute. Were you out with Judy?"

"Yeah. She made me go dancing with her and her hubby. Said I needed a little smoky air and loud music."

"Abigail...it's too soon for that."

"I know. I came home early."

"I wish I was there with you."

"Me, too."

As the weeks after the funeral dragged on, she began changing her schedule to be home when she thought Marsh might call. She told friends she was fine, just tired.

Abby wrenched her mind back again. She had to focus, and try to relax. Her left shoulder was cramping, and she rotated it slowly as far as she was able with her wrists behind her. She kept one eye on the dog, hoping that none of her movements would be interpreted as aggression and trigger a reaction. Dogs had never frightened her, but she had a healthy respect for this one's teeth and intelligence and exceptional training.

Even more than respecting the dog, she respected his owner. That brought a question to mind. What did a man like him need with this sort of dog? What line of work was he in? Abby traced along this path like a bloodhound on a scent. He carried a gun, he knew how to secure a criminal—for criminal she was, like it or not—and he had a well-trained police dog at his command.

The question popped out before she could stop it. "Are *you* a cop?"

She thought he stiffened, but he did not turn and she couldn't be certain. "Why do you ask?"

"It would explain a few things."

"As I keep telling you, you're the one who needs to do the explaining. Have you thought about that a little more?" Lazily he reeled in the line, flicked it back out into the river, the reel whirring and the lure landing with a faint plop. Abby watched the rings ripple out and dwindle, erased by the flow of the tea-brown water.

"There's just…really, nothing to explain. I've told

you the truth. I'm running from some personal things and lost my head."

"You keep saying that, but I'm like those TV junkies who sit home staring at the Hollywood gossip shows. I want the dirt."

Despite herself a rueful laugh forced its way past her lips. "What I wouldn't give to be back at home staring at the TV." Even reminding Rosemary to share the television remote would be better than the stomach-roiling anxiety she was feeling now. It was hard to decide which was worse: the fear she'd be arrested and jailed for what she'd done, or the certain nightmare when Marsh caught up with her.

"I guess it would be better if you hadn't started down this road, huh, Abigail?"

"No kidding." She fell silent. Sweat trickled down her spine, making her itch as it went. She wondered if she was flexible enough to wriggle backward through the circle of her arms and bring her wrists in front of her. The man would probably stop her if she became too active. A droning sweat bee began to show interest in the moist skin of her neck, and there was nothing she could do about it except toss her head and hope her ponytail knocked the insect away.

"Something wrong?" Was that humor in his voice?

"Nothing a good toxic cloud of pesticide wouldn't fix."

Now it was a definite chuckle. "You're doing it to yourself, you know. Dish a little dirt, Abigail."

"I don't even know your name."

"What, you didn't go through my glove compartment and steal my registration?"

Abby scrubbed her face against her shoulder. The sweat was getting into her eyes, stinging with salt. "No," she mumbled. "I think your dog needs a drink of water."

At this comment, the man did turn. He looked with concern at the shepherd, and then nodded. "Wouldn't hurt. I was getting him a drink when you so rudely interrupted us in that parking lot by stealing my truck." He propped his fishing pole against a nearby scrub oak and returned to the truck, where he took a bottle of water from the back, and a blue plastic bowl, and proceeded to pour the bottled water in the bowl for the dog. Abby found herself swallowing reflexively, and with a gleam in his bright blue eyes the man spoke.

"Cade Latimer. And this is Mort."

"Pleased to meet you, Mr. Latimer." She was afraid that the words would come out sarcastically, but instead she was speaking the truth, to her own astonishment. Under any other circumstances she'd have enjoyed talking to this man. "He's a beautiful dog." She watched as Latimer cued the dog off guard and permitted him to drink his fill.

"Thanks. You look thirsty, too." He tipped his head back, bottle to his lips, and drank down what little he hadn't poured into the bowl. His muscular throat gleamed with a light film of sweat. "But maybe your stomach's still unsettled from the rough ride. Or the poor company. Your skin is pasty-looking."

Now that he was closer to her again, Abby could

see that the cut was still seeping, though slowly. He had smeared blood over the side of his face each time he wiped at the cut. It looked sore, and the little bit of nursing training she had made her fingers itch to tend the wound. "I'm not thirsty just now. Mr. Latimer, that cut really does need attention. I can see to that for you. It needs cleaning and some antibiotic cream. It might even need stitches."

He slanted a bright blue glance at her. "How do I know you won't take advantage of the situation and incapacitate me?"

Now Abby did laugh, the corner of her mouth curling up in a rueful smile. "I'm a thief, not a murderer. I did the damage, I'll clean up after it. I may not want to tell you all the gory details of my life, but I'm an honorable woman."

His smile, when it came, transformed him. "Damned if I don't believe you, Abigail. All right. Sit tight while I dig out the first aid kit, then I'll clip the cable ties so you can use your hands."

Abby watched Cade Latimer stretch over the tailgate and emerge with a small blue canvas kit with a red cross silk-screened on it. He brought it to the table and opened it.

"Some more of that bottled water would be good," Abby suggested.

"I thought you weren't thirsty."

"For cleaning the cut."

Cade nodded and returned with two more bottles of water. He twisted open both and set them near her. He stood very close to her and reached out to cup her chin and turn her face toward him. Abby met his gaze, startled anew by how very blue his eyes were. The work-roughened skin of his palm rasped her jaw-line and she swallowed, trying not to gulp.

"Understand me, Abigail McMurray. I'm going to let you loose so you can clean up this cut, but make one false move and I won't hesitate to stop you. It may be as simple as twisting an arm behind your back, or it might be Mort's teeth in your leg."

Or a bullet from your gun. She couldn't look away. The blue of his eyes was intense. A rim of darker blue edged the iris as if to keep the liquid color contained, and different shades of blue rayed from the pupil like spokes in a wheel. His eyes were so arresting she began to lose track of the conversation.

"Show me you understand."

"I don't understand what you want, Marsh."

"What's to understand? Didn't you do as much for Gary? C'mon. I know he was a boob man. He always was, from the time we were kids." Marsh's hands trembled as he grasped her shoulders, and Abby could tell his hands wanted to slide down, over the breasts he'd just complimented.

"I just want to see your breasts," he said. "Maybe touch them a little. Gary always said you had beautiful breasts. A little more than a handful, and sweet."

"Gary never talked to you about my breasts!" She didn't know what shocked her more—that Marsh wanted her to show him her naked breasts, or the idea that Gary had talked to Marsh about something so personal. "Our sex life is—was—private."

"He was my brother. He told me a lot of things that would surprise you."

"What else did he tell you?" Abby gasped, clutching at the front of her shirt as if the buttons might fly off by the force of Marsh's hungry gaze alone.

"He told me you're the sweetest bit of tail a man could wish for. He told me you're generous, and a little shy, and kind of prudish until you've had a little wine."

Prudish? Abby stared at Marsh, her mouth dropping open. Tail?

When he reached out and tucked her tumbled hair behind her ears, she didn't stop him. He leaned his forehead against hers and spoke sweetly, reminding her how much help he was around the place. He told her how much he missed Gary. When his fingertip touched the hollow of her throat and traced her collarbone, she didn't stop him. He told her grief had made her slimmer and more beautiful than ever. He talked about the projects he had in mind, how simple it would be to build a ramp out the back door to the patio for their wheelchair clients.

When he unbuttoned her shirt and smoothed the lapels back against the fabric, she didn't stop him.

And when, a little later, he straddled her, holding her down on the living room floor with his knees planted at her elbows in a promise of pain if she fought, and his hands pressing her breasts together while his hips pistoned his humid, naked penis between them, she couldn't *stop him.*

* * *

Marsh's silver Honda sedan started immediately when he turned the key. He adjusted the seat backward an inch. Abigail hadn't slid it back where it belonged last time she'd driven the car. Her list of sins was long, and getting longer as the day dragged into evening. Marsh backed out of the driveway, now that the last of the clients and their families were gone.

They wouldn't be back in the morning, either. He'd bought himself a day with the story of Abigail's contagious virus—a stomach virus, he'd explained to the families, lots of vomiting, the doctor would want her to rest and hydrate, give her body a chance to recover, certainly they were too professional to expose the clients to such a virulent ailment.

She'd need every moment of that recovery time when he was finished with her, Marsh thought furiously, spinning the Honda's steering wheel and guiding the sedan swiftly around the corner. It was only a few blocks to the convenience store. He could have walked there in the time it would take to drive and park again, but he had a sinking feeling he'd be chasing Abigail all over town half the night.

At the convenience store, he parked by the front door and waited, engine idling quietly, watching a few customers come and go. He didn't see Abigail inside, and the clerk at the register was a woman, not the idiot he'd spoken to earlier. Even better; he preferred to talk to women, anyway. When the last customer drove away, Marsh went inside.

He scanned the aisles quickly on his way to the refrigerator wall at the back, where he selected a soda and took it up to the register. Abigail wasn't crouching behind a display or sitting in one of the booths in the café area near the coffee stand and fountain drinks.

"Hey," said the clerk, smiling.

"Hey, yourself," Marsh replied with a big grin. She was a cute little number, a bit long in the tooth, but she took care of herself. No dark roots in the blond hair, though it was teased too high for his personal preference. Not too much makeup, except where her mascara clumped. Her top fit her body nicely without looking trashy. "Hope it's been a good one for you. You must be about to head home to your hubby and a good dinner."

She laughed and turned his soda around to show the barcode to the reader. "Not me, no. Hubby's long gone to hell or Arizona, I don't care which, not that I could tell the difference. Got a while left on shift, too."

Marsh fished slowly in his wallet, buying time while he thought about how to get the information he wanted from her. "A shame, great-looking gal like you."

"Well, hey, thanks." Her cheeks went pink, just a little, and Marsh smiled even wider.

"But speaking of great-looking gals, I was wondering if my own gal's been here. She's late getting home. I figured I'd swing by her work and give her a ride home, but they said she left a while ago. Sometimes she stops off here on her way home. Seen her? I hate to sound like a worrywart, but you know how it is."

The clerk shot her hip to the right and gave him another smile. "Least someone cares about her, right? What's she look like?"

"She's got long brown hair. She likes to wear it in a ponytail. Probably in jeans and a blue shirt, if she just got off work. Big gray eyes. Bet she looks tired, too."

The woman thought for a moment, took the five he held out and pursed her lips. "I don't think I've seen her."

"Maybe it was before your shift, then. Is the other guy still here? Maybe I could talk to him, too." Get a real good look at the jerk who'd had his hands all over Abigail. Unbuttoning her shirt. Letting down her hair. Touching things that didn't belong to him.

He hadn't said it just right, or maybe he didn't have his face blank enough. Either way, Marsh knew the moment he'd lost the connection. She straightened up and gave him a long, cool stare before counting out his change. She put it on the counter between them instead of putting it into his hand. She closed the cash drawer, and then took a step back. "He's not here," she said slowly. "Tell you what, why don't you leave your phone number, and I'll mention you stopped in. He can call you, maybe."

Marsh pasted a smile on his face again. "That's okay. She's probably just taking the scenic route. She likes the park. I'll try her there. Thanks for your help." *Thanks for nothing.*

"Sure you don't want to leave your number?" She pushed a pad of paper and a pen toward him.

So you can give it to the cops? Think I'm stupid?

Marsh shook his head and took his change and his soda. "Thanks, anyway. I'm sure she's just stopped at a friend's or something like that. I'm sure I'm worrying for nothing." He tried another smile, but it felt false on his face. He lifted the soda bottle in a cheery toast and kept his stride even, pace calm. Not a worried man, no. No reason to be worried.

The Honda started right up, as always. But Marsh looked at the glass front of the convenience store, where the clerk stood looking out at him, a pen and a pad of paper in hand.

"You'd better not be writing down my license plate number, bitch," he muttered under his breath, fighting the urge to screech the Honda out of the parking lot and into the street with the accelerator pressed to the floor. His heart gave a thud at the idea of the cops showing up at his house, asking about a woman who hadn't come home from work. A check on Abigail's welfare. For the first time the chance of Abigail reporting him to the cops seemed possible. Always before now he'd had her within arm's reach, where he could talk her around, explain to her how things worked, how crazy she made him. Crazy with love and desperate to keep her. He'd given up his life in Jacksonville to move to this pissant town, all because Abigail was here.

God, he loved her. Now she was his, the way she should have been from the start, before Gary somehow got between them. Marsh had seen her first, but it was Gary who'd managed to hook her, and Marsh had never figured out how that had happened. Somewhere between one bottle of beer at a neighborhood barbecue and the next, Abigail was laughing at Gary's stupid jokes and sitting next to him on the edge of her cousin's swimming pool. Marsh could still see her long tanned legs dangling in the water, the skirt of her sundress above her knees to keep it from getting wet. Then she and Gary started dating, going for long walks and dinners, having heart-to-heart talks that didn't include Marsh.

Marsh would find her; he had to. He hadn't worked this hard only to have her run away.

Thinking about the barbecue reminded him of the most logical place to look: Judy and Drew's house. They were easily a mile away, but Abigail had had all afternoon to walk there. If she was anywhere, she would be at her best friend's house.

Marsh slowed to a stop at the next corner, got his bearings and headed north, thinking all the while about the first time Abigail had taken him to Judy and Drew's for a barbecue, not all that long after they'd put Gary in the ground. He replayed the evening in his mind.

"Turn left?" Marsh had asked.

"Yes. Judy and Drew live in that blue house—right here."

"Where is it you know Judy from, again?" Marsh guided the Honda to the curb. It was quiet and sweet in the cabin of the car, with Abigail in the passenger seat. Sweet, so sweet. He liked when their elbows brushed, liked the way her light perfume fragranced each breath he took.

"She used to help me and Gary out sometimes, when we first opened the day care."

"Oh, yeah. What's Drew do?"

"He's a mechanic. Got his own shop."

Marsh and Abigail had been out to dinner a few times in the past couple of months, but this was the first time any of her friends would meet him since Gary's funeral. They stood by the car a moment. Abigail must have noticed him biting his lower lip, because she spoke softly as she came around the back of the car.

"What's up, Marsh?"

"I was just wondering if we turned off the iron. Maybe we should go back and check." He really wasn't in a party mood; he would rather be back at Gary's—Abigail's—house, having a quiet dinner in the kitchen, and maybe some television after. They'd sit on the sofa, only a foot or so apart. Where he could touch her, if he wanted.

"It shuts itself off after a few minutes. Gary was so forgetful, it was easier to buy one that remembered for him."

He nodded, reaching into the backseat for the fruit salad they'd brought for the potluck. Abigail touched his arm. "They liked Gary. They'll like you."

"I'm not Gary."

Abigail was clearly touched by his insecurity. Her smile was gentle and understanding. "Just stick close to me, then."

The party was on Drew and Judy's big patio in the backyard. Marsh was friendly to others, but attentive to Abigail, bringing her drinks and surprising her with a filled plate from the buffet table as she sat talking with one of Judy's neighbors. He stood behind her and reached for an occasional nibble.

"You know, they'll let you have your own plate, Marsh."

"Yours tastes better." Marsh laughed. The neighbor smiled at their banter. They were a couple, weren't they? It was apparent to others already.

Yes, he thought now. *That's where Abigail will be. Having coffee, getting sympathy from that bitch Judy, telling lies about me to explain why she isn't home tending to her business.*

He parked and got out of the car. It was time for Abigail to come home, where she belonged. His fists clenched at his sides and he shook them out, bouncing a little on the balls of his feet, loosening up, before he strode up the walkway to the little blue house. He couldn't arrive at the door angry. Drew was probably there.

Halfway to the door, Marsh turned around, went back to the car and drove around the corner before turning in a neighbor's driveway and driving slowly back, to park two houses down. He turned off the engine and the lights, and simply watched. Drew might be there, and he'd certainly understand Marsh's desire to have Abigail back at home where she belonged, but maybe Marsh would have a chance to see for himself just how traitorous Abigail had become.

Because what if…just maybe…Drew was the man Abigail had run off with?

Marsh sat in the early twilight, strong fingers drumming on the steering wheel, watching Drew and Judy's house. Thinking.

Planning.

"Abigail? Do you understand me?" Cade asked her a second time for agreement, looking into her cloudy gray eyes. Though she was meeting his gaze, she was far away in her thoughts, and they weren't happy ones, judging from the faint vertical line between her silky brows, and the tightness of her lips. Strands of her hair had escaped her ponytail and were sticking to the sides of her face and her neck. Cade knew a sudden urge to lift them away and put them back where they belonged, or to loose her hair entirely, watch it catch the bright light.

At last she nodded. "I won't try anything stupid. Promise."

"Good." He released her, moved behind her and used the short, thick blade of his pocketknife to cut the cable ties that served as impromptu handcuffs. The skin of her wrists was reddened where she had strained against the bonds, but unbroken, and not bruised. It was velvety soft where he touched it, slightly moist with sweat. He watched her shoulders slump in relief at the release of tension. She massaged her wrists and shoulders briefly before standing to examine the contents of the first aid kit.

"Sit down," she told him, adding "please" when he raised an eyebrow at her. He sat with his back away from her, so she'd have to reach around him to get to the gun, jammed tight in the back of his waistband. He gestured to Mort to wait not far away. The dog retreated to a blob of dark shade under a nearby scrub oak, and turned to face them.

"He's got the right idea." Abigail nodded toward the dog, opening a package of gauze pads and wetting two. "It's really hot out here. Shade would be nice. I'm going to wash the area of the cut. Speak up if what I'm doing hurts."

Cade felt her slim fingers probing at the wound, assessing the shape and size of the goose egg. Then came the welcome cool of the wet cotton, soaking first, and then gently swabbing away blood from his hair and skin. He sat alert, though it was more for show than need. She seemed absorbed in her task, dabbing, remoistening the pads and setting them aside as they became red with his blood. She was close enough that he could smell her skin, acrid with leftover fear and adrenaline, perspiration, an undertone of soap. She moved his head from one position to the next like someone who was comfortable touching others. An image of Abigail mending the cuts and scrapes of a child snagged in the screen of his mind. The abruptness of the thought and his vague, negative reaction to it startled him.

I hope I'm not keeping her away from her kids. But then,, if there are kids at home, maybe they're the reason she left. Sometimes they get to be too much. I don't think I ever want kids. He knew she was widowed, but how many people were in her family? The urge to know the answer was too strong, so he began to lead her to an answer.

"You seem like a pro at this first aid thing."

She replied promptly, though her tone was a little distracted. "Just part of a day's work. I get first aid and CPR training every year."

"Kids, huh? How many?"

"No, none."

He was pleased and relieved by her answer. "Nurse?"

"Adult day care. Hold still.... I'm going to probe around the edges of this lump. I can't tell you how sorry I am you got injured."

Adult day care. He thought about that for a while. It didn't jibe, the idea of Abigail as a skilled health care professional and the fact she was a car thief. People who took on that kind of responsibility didn't just walk away from their lives without cause. Nothing about her jibed, not yet.

"Lots of accidents like this in adult day care?"

Her mouth quirked in a rueful smile that made his fingers itch to touch the curling corner and the dimple just beside it. Under the mask of strain she was an attractive woman, if too thin. "If you mean do I take corners too fast when transporting my clients, and give them all head injuries...no. But things get knocked over and break, and then someone tries to help pick up the pieces and gets cut. Or someone will have a seizure. Sometimes the stress is too much for one of them and they think hitting their head on the wall again and again will help. Even obsessively gnawing hangnails until they bleed. Things like that."

Abigail put her palms on his cheeks and tilted his head far to one side. She didn't hesitate to touch his scarred face. *You get points for having balls, Abigail. Most people shy away from that on first sight. Almost none would be willing to touch me.* Her hands were gentle but firm, unintentionally caressing, and an image flitted through his mind of her bending to kiss him. Cade was thankful she couldn't read his inappropriate thoughts. The idea of dragging her ass—and it could be a great ass if she weren't so thin; he'd noticed the upside-down heart shape of it already—to the sheriff in Wildwood appealed less and less.

He was glad he didn't know the deputies in Wildwood, not the way he knew them here locally in his home jurisdiction of Ocala, or Gainesville, where he'd done undercover work, before the incident that marked him for life. He could just picture himself escorting Abigail into his home station and explaining he'd been stupid enough to leave his truck running and the door standing open like an engraved invitation, and this sweet-faced woman with the capable hands had waltzed off with it.

It would be joke fodder for months. Years. He'd hear about it at every stolen vehicle report, every poker night, fishing trip, birthday parties for their kids, weddings, funerals, K-9 training sessions. The ragging would never end. Even the administrative staff and the dispatchers would get in on the fun.

No. If he took her in, and that was looking like a more remote *if* all the time, it wouldn't be to any station where he was known, either currently or in the past.

She spoke again. “Does it hurt when I press, or are you just stoic?”

“It hurts a little, but I’ve had worse.”

“Really? Hmm.” She wetted yet another cotton ball and dabbed some more. “This may leave a scar. I’m sorry about that.”

The idea was ludicrous. Compared with the ugly raw meat that was the left side of his face, a half-inch nick in his scalp, easily concealed by hair, was nothing. He tried to hold in his laughter, and ended up shaking silently.

Abigail drew back and stared at Cade. “What’s so funny?”

“It might *scar?*” He thrust the left side of his face toward her and said, “Like I said, I’ve had worse.”

She blushed, darkly, and it made her gray eyes sparkle. He couldn’t tell whether she was holding back tears or laughter. One knee was up on the bench to balance her, and Cade knew a sudden urge to cup her hips, stroke the long line of her thigh. *What the hell, Latimer? Get a grip, and not on your suspect.*

“Oh. I…see what you mean.”

“Yeah.”

“Chemical burn? If you don’t mind me asking.”

“That old standby…acid.”

“Did something blow up in your face?”

Yeah...a meth bust went bad. They’d made me and I never knew it. That little twerp and his goon of a buddy... The little twerp was smarter than I thought. I got cocky, and he got lucky, and then I got scarred.

"You could say that." He hoped his tone would discourage more questions, but Abigail just went back to dabbing at the wound as if acid burns were something completely normal.

"It will bleed just a little more, I think. I'm going to put some of this ointment with anesthetic and antibiotics on it. It'll be hard to bandage unless we shave the area."

"No shaving. Does it need stitches?"

"I…don't think so, but I'm going to try a couple of these butterfly bandages on it and see if those help close the gap."

He felt a slight sting as she applied the cream, then it numbed the area of the cut. It was as Abigail was leaning to reach the kit again for the butterfly bandages that her much-washed chambray shirt, minus a button at bra level, gaped open. Where the plackets separated he saw the purple and yellow of bruises, both fresh and fading, on the upper curves of her breasts, where they swelled from the cups of a practical white cotton bra.

Bruises with a definite outline of the too-firm grip of a hand. She hadn't done that to herself.

Cop reflex took over. He gripped her upper arms and brought her upright again where he could review the evidence. She gasped and paled in pain.

"Sit down," he said roughly, rising. He hadn't grabbed her that hard, which only meant she had more bruises elsewhere, as instinct and experience had told him she must. He slackened his grip, but only slightly.

What happened next twisted his gut.

"Please. Please don't. Please. Please. I'll do whatever you want, just please. Don't." The woman was *begging,* scrabbling backward, trying her damnedest to get away, and her voice was filled with the most pathetic dread Cade had ever heard. Cade released her upper arms since it was clear he was causing her pain, and let his hands slip down to her wrists, where he locked his fingers in a grip she would not be able to break easily, even though she had more leverage. She flailed and thrashed, continuing to beg for release, until he caught both wrists in one hand and got close enough to thread the fingers of his free hand into her ponytail and immobilize her. She froze, gazing up with terrified, tear-filled eyes and half-open mouth, breathing as though she'd sprinted a mile.

"Stop. Abigail. Calm down. I don't want anything from you but the truth. That's all."

Her breath came in sobbing, hitching gasps, but she remained still. Holding her gaze, Cade dropped her ponytail and carefully, slowly, turned back the front of her shirt before he looked at the uncovered area he'd glimpsed.

Oh, yes, finger bruises. Someone liked to squeeze her small, pretty breasts to the point of pain and beyond. He bet himself he'd find matching bruises in rings around her upper arms, too. God knew where else. Anywhere they could be easily hidden, no doubt. He knew how abusers worked. Their private, sadistic indulgences were just that, and there would be hell to pay when their victims couldn't conceal the evidence any longer.

Or in Abigail's case, *wouldn't.* This was why she'd stolen his truck. She was running, running like hell.

She bent her head and her ponytail slithered forward over her chest, shielding herself from his gaze.

"Let me see, Abigail. I won't hurt you, but I need to know bruises are the worst of it."

"That…that *crummy* button!" The words came out in the most embarrassed, horrified tone Cade had ever heard a woman use.

He couldn't tell whether the trembling that shook her entire body was laughter, tears, fear, pain or all of the above. She swayed on her feet like an exhausted toddler, and he realized she might fall if she remained standing. He sank back onto the picnic table bench and drew her down with him. She drooped like a flower with a crushed stem, and it was the most natural thing in the world to put an arm around her. In all his thug-tracking days he'd never comforted a criminal like this. How many of them had wept and gazed at him with pitiful, wet eyes? How easily had he withstood those bids for sympathy and lenience? How many of them ended up in the back of the patrol car on the way to jail, where they belonged?

But how quickly, in just moments, had Abigail McMurray and her gigantic problem become the thing he most needed to fix in the world. He felt her stiffness melting away like snow in the Florida sun, and shortly she was leaning against his chest, her hands creeping up to hang on to his shoulders as if he were the only solid thing left on the planet. He took his gun out of his waistband and set it on the ground out of her reach. No sense in being stupid, even if his gut and his crotch were trying so damned hard to overrule his brain.

Now I have the truth.

He had what he thought he wanted, yes. But knowing what had pushed Abigail to take his truck wasn't enough. Now he wanted the man who had done the damage, wanted him fiercely, with a dark, chill fury that was more vendetta than justice. He shouldn't feel this way—his law enforcement training should have kept him from the brink. He hardly knew Abigail, and the fact she'd stolen his truck didn't make her domestic abuse issues his problem.

But somehow they were.

He felt her tears soaking his shirt, her sobs shaking her body, and stared over her head toward the tea-dark river where something had taken the lure on his fishing line and was merrily dragging his pole down the sandy bank into the water.

Aw, hell. You know it's bad when I choose a sobbing woman over the best reel I own. Goodbye, pole. Hello, trouble.

Chapter 4

That twice-damned button.

It had gotten her into this whole mess, rolling under Cade Latimer's pickup in the convenience store's parking lot. Now its lack had made things worse, revealing all the things she had struggled to keep hidden from this observant, determined, fierce man. In her urge to help right at least part of her wrongdoing by tending his head wound, she had unwittingly exposed herself, not to mention Marsh's crimes.

The shame she had felt in all the months before was nothing compared with the burning furnace of shame she felt now as her weakness was revealed.

Yet, in that scorching shame burned the relief that someone else knew at last. The tears flowed in earnest and she began to tremble.

She struggled not to give in to the comfort Cade Latimer was offering. It wasn't right. It wasn't *done*.... She couldn't just weep on a stranger's shoulder. Especially not a stranger whose truck she had stolen. She sank stiffly onto the bench when he tugged her to sit. She fought against his encircling arm—it was just another trap, another trick, another ploy to get her to tell more than she should. He only wanted the lurid details. He didn't want to have to understand, or judge, or help.

It would give him power over her. She could never permit that again.

"Where's your shadow?" Judy asked.

"Looking for a beer."

"Nice of you to bring him."

"Thanks for inviting me. Us. It's good to get out of the house. I haven't seen my friends enough lately."

She felt rather than heard Marsh approach out of her line of sight. He stood behind her, a companionable hand over her left shoulder, squeezing gently.

"Good to see you smiling," Marsh said.

The reminder of Gary made her smile falter. Marsh squeezed her shoulder again and spoke to Judy. "Abigail tells me your husband's a mechanic. He any good with imports?"

"Japanese, mostly—but he's right over there with the grill. You could just ask." Judy turned her attention back to Abby. "We should do a girls' night out. What are you doing next week?"

Abby opened her mouth to reply, but Marsh's hand

squeezed her shoulder again. "We're working on that wheelchair ramp to the back patio," he said.

"But that won't take every night next week," Judy said, smiling.

Abby smiled back. "We could maybe—"

"Things are tight," Marsh interrupted, and this time Abby realized the pressure of his hand was meant to quiet her, to let Marsh take the lead in the conversation. Startled, she lapsed into silence and was rewarded with a gentle rub over her shoulder blade. "We probably should head out. Seven o'clock comes early."

Abby ducked her head and nodded. She really hadn't meant to let Judy know how things were with Gary gone. Marsh set down his beer and she knew he meant for them to leave now. With her evening suddenly soured, she wanted nothing more than to be at home with the covers pulled over her head and maybe the blessed oblivion of a sleeping pill. She gave Judy a quick, embarrassed hug, nodding when Judy said quietly, "Call me. I miss you."

She had simply given the power into Marsh's hands without a second thought.

Abby fought against the bliss of comfort for another minute, but the softening of Latimer's hold was confusing. If he meant to control her, he'd have taken a firmer grip on her. The reservoir of hurt was simply too deep to stem now that the dam had been breached. It was as if the supply of tears was bottomless, salty and hot. She would never be cried out, even after months of mourning Gary and hours of late-night weeping into pillows to stifle her noise so Marsh wouldn't hear. But these tears weren't for Gary. Instead, she was mourning the loss of herself.

Her fingers clenched in his shirt. One by one her hands crept over his shoulders and caught there as if she were clinging to the side of a building, trying desperately not to fall.

Fifteen months with Marsh hadn't erased every scrap of trust, though they'd taken their toll. Every action she took had to be examined and reexamined, for fear it would trigger an unpleasant reaction from Marsh. Now she drowned in the torrent of tears, and Latimer said nothing. Did nothing, except allow her to thoroughly wet his shirt, and keep warm palms cupped at her back. She could feel their heat even past the humid sweatiness of her skin in the heat of the late afternoon. No matter how she gave in to her sobs, some part of her kept guard, alert to any hint of tension in Latimer's body, the telegraphy of imminent violence.

Long minutes later, head throbbing, nose thoroughly stuffed, eyes burning, Abby pulled a scrap of pride from somewhere deep and used it to push back from Latimer. She scrubbed at her face with the sleeves of her shirt, snuffling hard. He made a single quick move and scooped something from the ground as he left the bench—his gun.

When he walked to his truck, Abby sat staring at him. He'd gone from holding a gun on her to turning his back. He no longer considered her a threat. *Of course not, why would he? He's the one with a dog and a gun and the keys.* Her stomach lurched. What would he do with her now? Would his new knowledge change anything? She was still a car thief, no matter how she looked at it.

He came back with a roll of paper towels and put them in front of her. She tore one from the roll and blew her nose. "Thank you." Her voice was thick. Tears were still too near. She knew if she thought even a little about what had happened she would dissolve again.

Latimer set a bottle of water in front of her. "You'll be thirsty after all that bawling."

Abby's glance flicked upward.

He was *smiling.*

She searched his face for mockery, cruelty, for the blankness she had come to associate with Marsh's concealment of anger, and found none. Instead, there was amusement, and a wry kindness she hadn't expected to see. "You're laughing at me."

"No." He made a short gesture and the dog came to sit at his left. "I don't laugh at women running from domestic violence. Though I have to admit I've never seen it taken to the extreme of stealing a vehicle."

"I'm not—" Abby began the habitual denial, the all-too-familiar lie, and caught herself. Or, rather, was caught by the incisive blue of Latimer's eyes. She looked away, guiltily, and then looked back. *Why am I lying? I never used to lie. I never had a need to lie.* It was part of the way Marsh had broken her, changed her, made her over to fit him.

It was what she hated most about herself, even

more than the cowardice that made her second-guess every single word or gesture made where Marsh could hear or see. Even more than the way she cringed away from his physicality. More than the way he controlled every aspect of their lives together. She was relieved her parents were dead and she had no siblings to see what she'd become since Gary's death. She was a non-person, existing only within the context of Marsh's rigid parameters for approval and acceptance. In her grief, she had distanced herself even from her friends, and they had respected her wishes, letting her be. Her solitude was the perfect environment for Marsh.

"You can't tell me you walked into a door in the middle of the night. Doors don't leave finger marks on your breasts."

Abby looked toward the river, dimpled and purling, glinting in the sun's glare, eddies that spun downstream and faded, the expanding rings of a fish gulping an insect from the surface. She covered her mouth with her hand, drawing a shaky breath through her stuffy nose. Latimer didn't stop her when she got to her feet and moved into the shade of the cypresses at the river's edge.

It was cooler there, with a moistness more pleasant than the sticky humidity of her own sweat in the sunny clearing of the campsite. Her head pounded with the heat and her tear-stuffed sinuses. The breath of the river moved over her skin, luring her closer. She toed off her sneakers and edged her sockless feet into the wet, buff-colored sand at its edge. A foot or two from the shore, she saw a fishing pole beneath the water, its tip bent and caught by a cypress root a few feet out. It must be Latimer's—she didn't see his near the camp stool, and he hadn't brought it back to the picnic table. Abby moved forward two steps, the water rising to her ankles and wetting the slim legs of her jeans.

It felt like heaven, cool and soft and better than iced tea on a hot day. She thought about wading even deeper, diving in and submerging her whole, overheated, exhausted body. She would let the current take her slowly downstream. The tannic water would wash away the salt of tears and sweat, leaching the heat from her shame. She could float wherever the river took her, for miles and days, through the chain of lakes, maybe even on to the Gulf of Mexico. Instead, she rolled up the cuff of her sleeve and plunged her arm into the water to grasp the butt of the rod.

She drew the rod from the water, immediately finding resistance at the far end, where the line had been snarled among the stumps and knees of cypresses and ti-ti shrubs, so she pressed the button on the reel to release the tension, and backed out of the water.

Latimer, who had joined her on the shore, stood at the edge of the water and received the pole from her with a rueful smile. He used his pocketknife to clip the nylon line.

"Sorry, again," Abby said lamely.

"Stuff happens." Latimer shrugged and tilted the rod to empty the water from the reel's spool. "But bruises like yours—that's not the sort of stuff that should happen."

Tears welled and Abby jutted her chin out to stem the flow. "I really, really don't want to talk about it." She picked up her shoes, letting them dangle from two fingers hooked beneath their tongues. No sense trying to jam wet, sandy feet into them.

"I get that, believe me." Latimer followed her to the picnic table, where Abby opened the bottle of water and drank half of it. He closed the blade of the pocketknife and opened another, a screwdriver tip, and began removing the reel from the pole. "But I'm not letting go of the topic for long." His blue gaze flicked up and trapped her. "You can have a break while you build a fire in that grill over there. I want a steak for dinner, since I'm not going to get a chance at a bass or bluegill." His chin jerked toward the truck, where Mort the shepherd lay panting in the shade of the tailgate. "Sack of charcoal back there. Matches in the toolbox."

Abby stared at him, watching as a bead of sweat trickled slowly from his hairline to lose itself in the red, raised maze of his scar. He was disassembling the reel, using paper towels to dry its mechanisms. His hands were quick and deft, with long fingers. They were strong fingers, and gold hairs glittered at the knuckles and along the outer edge of his hands. She set what little she knew about him against the idea of those fingers curling into fists, and found she could not visualize Latimer doing something brutal out of sheer perversity. Unbidden, an image of Marsh's fists came to mind, his strong, stocky fingers and muddy hazel eyes always ready to teach her a lesson.

When she hadn't moved, Latimer looked up at her. "Abigail."

Jolted from her thoughts, she blinked rapidly, scrambling to respond. "What about your dog?"

"He won't bother you unless I give the word. Or you make a sudden move. So don't try something stupid like running away, and you won't have any trouble."

Abby moved slowly toward the truck. Mort was all attention, ears pricked forward, dark eyes unblinking, head turning as she moved. She kept her eyes on him, even as she stretched to reach the bag of charcoal and drag it out onto the tailgate. The matches were a different issue, however, since the toolbox was all the way to the front of the truck bed. She would have to climb in to get them.

She looked over her shoulder at Latimer, who stood at the picnic table with the reel in his hands, grinning. The small jerk of his head indicated she might as well get on with it, so she crept into the truck bed and opened the toolbox.

"That wasn't so bad, was it?" he asked, when she walked past him, still barefoot on the campsite sand.

Abby said nothing, shaking the charcoal into the cement fire ring, slipping a few twigs and dried, crackling live-oak leaves into the pile to catch the flame of the match and hold it long enough to light the briquettes. When a couple of the black squares began to glow at their edges, she got to her feet and went stolidly back to the table. At least the sun was getting low enough to put the table in the shadow of the scrub oaks.

Before an hour had passed, Latimer was cooking a steak on the iron mesh grill of the fire ring, using a fork and his pocketknife to turn and trim the meat. Mort received the tossed trimmings, catching them deftly and snuffling for more. Latimer gave Abby tomatoes to slice on a paper plate, and handed her a can opener and a can of green beans to heat on the grill. When she had finished slicing, he pointedly held his hand out for the return of the steak knife she'd been using.

She wondered if he planned to let her join him in the meal. She shook her head at herself. *Don't be stupid. This isn't a date, Abigail. It's house arrest.* Perhaps he wouldn't make her feel guilty if she fetched her sack of groceries, and opened the chips and chili. Now that she was calmer after the storm of tears, she was hungry. She sat on the picnic bench with the bottle of water, desultorily shooing flies and the occasional wasp from the tomatoes, watching Latimer grilling meat. The label on the green beans slowly charred and flaked away, and steam rose from the can's open mouth. He pushed the can to a cooler spot on the grill.

With Latimer, minding the grill was almost an art form, a choreographed dance. He half squatted, his haunches firm in their blue jeans. She could see the strength in his legs when he rose or crab-walked to stay out of the smoke. In the dance of the grill, there was the bend, the prod of the meat with a fork, the quick flip, the test of the thick part of the steak with the tip of a hunting knife he'd pulled from somewhere on his person. Abby had never even known it was there. Knives, gun. Attack-trained dog. Fishing pole. Camping gear. If she didn't know better, she'd have said Latimer was running away from something himself. The irony made her lips quirk.

He caught the faint smile on her face as he looked up from his squatting position, his leanly muscled body folded in on itself, ready for action. "Smells good, doesn't it?"

"Yeah."

"Get three plates ready. I'm feeling generous."

Abby obeyed without comment, taking paper plates and disposable cutlery from a plastic bin in the back of the truck. She had a couple of bottles of water in her hand when Latimer spoke up.

"Bring me a beer, too, please."

Abby swallowed down her suddenly queasy stomach. Did *everything* have to conjure up Marsh? She visualized her brother-in-law sullenly cracking a can of beer, but in the cooler were only green bottles of lager, and she felt her clenching muscles relax, stupidly relieved to discover it wasn't Marsh's preferred brew. And Latimer had said *please,* a word that had vanished early from Marsh's vocabulary once he had her firmly in his grasp.

"Split the tomatoes and green beans three ways, Abigail."

"Three?"

"You don't think I'm the kind of man who'd deprive my buddy there of this fine meal, do you?" His head tilt indicated Mort, still quiet, tongue lolling, under the tailgate. Abby didn't think the shepherd had taken his eyes off her for the past hour, and was not fooled, despite the doggy smile on his face. "Get a plate over here." Latimer had the fork and knife ready, and lifted the slab of meat onto the plate she held out, with two hands under it to support the weight of the hefty T-bone. He rose, followed her to the table and deftly excised the bone and the fatty edge from the steak, putting them on a second plate with a bit of tomato and green beans. She watched his hands while he carved the meat into two generous portions. There was grace in his handling of the hunting knife.

"I…uh, if you don't mind, I'd like to get the orange juice, and the potato chips, out of…" She looked back toward the pickup.

His eyes shuttered briefly, and Abby saw his calculations, no doubt running through what was in the front seat, potential weapons, perhaps. Then he nodded. She walked to the cab, still keeping an eye on the dog, and reached inside for the juice and chips, bringing them back to the table. As she returned, Mort rose from his place beneath the truck and paced alongside her. Her heart thumped, but the dog merely went to the end of the table nearest to Latimer and sat down again, alert and waiting.

"Sit, Abigail. Eat."

"It's…Abby. Abigail…" She trailed off, settling with the juice and pulling open the bag of chips, pushing them to the center of the table where they might be shared.

"Kinda makes you feel like you might be in some trouble, eh?" His eyes held more than a glint of humor.

"Yeah," she agreed, looking down at the meat on her plate. It was huge, but she was starving, and it smelled delicious. They sat across from each other, Abby and the man whose truck she had stolen, and shared a meal in the slow, blue twilight.

The mosquitoes came out at dusk, just as Cade finished his last bites of steak and beans and chased them with a couple of potato chips and a swig of beer. Mort lay at his feet, working with diligent relish at the T-bone between his paws. Abby hadn't managed all her steak, but she pushed the plate away from herself, one slim hand lying on her belly, and a slightly sleepy look on her face. It was the most relaxed he'd seen her.

Now was the time to get the rest of her story out of her.

"You gonna eat that?" Cade asked, indicating the remaining steak on her plate.

"It was delicious, but I couldn't possibly. Thank you so much. I know I don't deserve your courtesy."

Cade spoke over her. He didn't want to hear her voice turn soft and anxiously pleading now that their casual meal was over. He wasn't her abuser; he didn't want to hear her talking to him as if he were. He'd enjoyed the small talk about camp cooking and the best wood for smoking meat, and whether or not barbecue sauce counted as a food group. "There's this guy I knew, back when I was working a joint task force—drugs—in Ocala." For a moment, he remembered those months, working with the DEA and the local police forces in Ocala. It was his success with the task force that had put him in the limelight and shifted him to undercover work in Gainesville, still with the task force. Undercover work brought a fresh thrill to a job that had begun to seem, if not mundane, at least less of a challenge. Finding and chasing down drug dealers was a matter of patience, diligence and documentation of proof. Undercover work added the spice of risk, the possibility of being discovered and the danger that would bring. The fish were much, much bigger. His sense of fulfillment in a job well done had increased with each successful penetration of an illicit organization.

But then he'd been scarred, and the task force leaders said, "Sorry. No place for a man with a face like that. Wish it had turned out differently." Just like that, his life was over. Understanding the task force's reasons, even agreeing with them, didn't change the way he felt. It was as if he'd wrecked his car into a ditch and would never drive it again.

Once Cade was out of the hospital and back on desk duty, the Marion County Sheriff's Department had offered him an option: take K-9 training to replace a retiring deputy.

Cade jumped. Anything was better than the desk and going home at night to a six-pack of beer and the television.

Working with Mort was more than the consolation

prize it had seemed at first. He loved the dog. They made a great team, and Cade didn't have to spend his days with a partner disinclined to work with a man who looked like something out of a Dick Tracy cartoon strip. Cade's work was fulfilling in a different way, but the corner of his soul that craved something more went unsatisfied. He no longer felt as if he was creating, solving, building. He was just taking out the trash, day after day, with a happy four-legged partner. Mort's zest for every task made the critical difference for Cade, enabling him to stay with a job he—mostly—still loved.

Abby's gray eyes, darkening with the approach of night, flicked to his and pulled him out of the mire of his thoughts. Her thin face drew tight. He could almost hear the click in her brain as she registered *cop,* followed by her immediate return to wariness. He drew the plate toward him, using his hunting knife to cut the strip into four large bites, which he fed to Mort one by one while she watched.

Cade saw her throat move as she swallowed. The air wasn't cooling down with the approach of night. It was still disgustingly humid, but at least the last low rays of the sun lacked their former scorching glare.

"You started to tell me something, Mr. Latimer," she said softly.

"Might as well call me Cade."

There was a long pause, then, "Okay, Cade." As good, as obedient a woman as a man could wish for, even though he plainly heard the undercurrent of renewed suspicion and fear in her voice. His stomach tightened a little. Someone had done a thorough job on her, and he was going to find out why—and who—if it took all night.

"His name was Roy Lewis."

She flinched, but it wasn't at the name. It was at the mosquito that had found the tender cord of her neck. Her slapping hand left a smear of blood, but her lips flexed in satisfaction at having killed the biting insect.

"Come on around this side. The smoke will keep them away." Cade rose to put their plates on the low-burning coals and added a stick or two of broken scrub oak wood, as well as some fallen brown magnolia leaves. The leaves gave an acrid stink to the smoke. Abby coughed, but moved to his side of the table, sitting to face him on the bench. Her feet were still bare, and she drew them up in front of her, wrapping her arms around her knees.

"So, Roy," Cade continued, settling on the bench again, leaning his back against the table, "he wasn't a bad guy—in fact, he was kinda funny, in that big-dumb-ox way. He got in with the wrong crowd, though. It happens."

She just watched him, listening with her chin on her knees, her hands clenched tight on the arms ringing her legs. She looked prettier by firelight, without the glare of the sun to point out the lines of tension in her face and body. Her thick lashes masked her eyes, but she never took her gaze from him. Cade felt a trace of the old excitement, the frisson playing a role brought. He could make this work.

"We'd been working on this bust for a couple of

months. That night, we made our move. And good ol' Roy, wrong place, wrong time. He thought he was picking up his brother-in-law at work because the man's car had broken down, and instead he was picking up a couple keys of coke along with his brother-in-law. Picked up a tail from the Ocala police and the DEA, too." Cade put a few more sticks on the fire, lighting her thin, pretty face in the gathering dark. The glow highlighted her straight nose and ordinary but eminently kissable mouth. She cleared her throat as smoke puffed past her, but at least the problem of the mosquitoes was temporarily solved.

Cade wet his throat with another swig of beer. "We got to chasing those boys, and eventually Roy wised up and pulled over. But his brother-in-law ditched, sprinted away like a track star, leaving those two keys in the car where Roy was waiting. My partner went after the runner, and Roy and me had us a good long talk." Cade remembered the last time he'd seen Roy Lewis, edging free from that bust because Roy'd sworn on his life and his mother's and everyone else's he knew that he was turning things around. Technically Cade had enough to take Roy to jail, but he'd known the man was trying to get clean and maybe needed just one break, and Cade had given it to him... with a string or two.

Cade let the silence stretch. He looked away, watching the fire. Eventually Abby bit, as most suspects did, unable to tolerate the silence. "What did you talk about?"

"We talked about those two keys of coke in his

car. And his pregnant girlfriend at home. How his record was pretty much clean except for some crap he'd done when he was a few years younger and a whole lot more stupid."

More silence, and Cade knew Abby was wondering what Cade had done about the drugs. Was he a dirty cop? What would she, Abby, do with this knowledge?

In the end, she whispered pitifully, "I don't have anything except a little cash."

Cade had her where he wanted her, though it roiled his guts to have manipulated her so blatantly. "You've got a story, just like Roy had a story. That's what I want, Abby."

She turned slowly to look away from him to the campfire. She waved a little smoke out of her face. Her brows drew together above the bridge of her nose. "You…want me to tell you why I stole your truck."

"Yep." He finished off the beer and walked to the truck for a second bottle. "You want a beer?"

"No, thank you."

"Might make it easier."

"Can I ask you a question?"

"Sure."

"What happened to Roy?"

"What do you think happened to Roy?" He walked back slowly, twisting the cap of the beer off. He tilted the bottle toward her as he sat down, but she shook her head, chin still on her knees.

"That amount of drugs in his car…it's hard to believe he could be lucky enough to walk away."

"Tell me your story, Abigail, and if I like it, I'll tell you what happened to Roy." He knew he was practically giving away the farm, but if she was as smart as he thought she was, she'd figure it out and take the bait anyway. "Why don't you start with his name, get that out of the way."

Her mouth loosened, shook, as her lashes fluttered and firelight flickered on the fresh tears he saw there. Cade stretched out his legs, propping one boot on the edge of the fire ring, and sipped slowly at the beer. Condensation beaded the bottle's sides and softened the paper label. He'd need to buy more ice somewhere tomorrow, top off the cooler again. Pick up more fresh stuff, another steak. Find a place to buy a shower, maybe do a little laundry. Truck stop? Hotel for a night?

There was tonight to get through, too. He didn't yet know how it might play out. Abby didn't show signs of trying to talk him into anything particular, not yet. For now he would settle for prying the details out of her, give him the information he needed to plan, to make a decision between, say, jail or the bus station in Ocala or Gainesville.

It was a good five minutes before she said, "Marsh." She cleared her throat and stopped.

Cade could hear her swallow, and see the flick of her fingers at her eyes, banishing tears. She wasn't even going to try thc typical female felon's trick of crying for sympathy while telling her story? Good for her. The action pointed to an unbowed core of strength and self-respect he wanted to encourage.

"His name is Marsh. He's Gary's brother."

Cade hid his grim smile behind the mouth of the beer bottle and his fist at its neck. *Marsh McMurray. Marshall, probably. A man with a name like that can be found.* It would be easy. A telephone call to the sheriff's department in Abby's county, a little courtesy to Deputy Latimer from Marion County, and Marshall McMurray would have a whole passel of trouble in his lap.

Cade thought for a moment about the sequence of events that had led to this moment. If he were still working undercover, he probably wouldn't be on vacation this particular week, depending on what was going on with whatever case he was working. He wouldn't have been at the quickie mart in Wildwood. He and Abby would never have crossed paths. He'd never have met her or felt the impulse to insert himself into her life. Fate, and its convoluted workings, was a hell of a thing.

Marsh moved the Honda twice during the three hours he sat on Drew and Judy's street watching their house. He didn't want to attract too much attention. Each time he moved the car, he drove around the nearby streets for a few minutes before returning and parking in a different spot.

Drew came outside only once, to move a sprinkler to a new place on the thick lawn, and observe its pattern of spray for a few minutes. Judy stood on the front steps, leaning against the door frame with her arms folded beneath her breasts, and watched him. A yappy little dog panted at her bare feet.

There was no sign of Abigail. No curtain twitched at a window, a light didn't go on or off while Drew and Judy were outside.

At 10:00 p.m. the lights went out in the house. Early to bed, early to rise.

Marsh cursed softly, started the Honda and drove into the darkness of Wildwood. Street after street, lights were going out as the sidewalks rolled up in this dinky town. Abigail wasn't on any of them. She wasn't sitting on a bench in the town's sole park. He again passed the convenience store, where the same blonde clerk would close by eleven—nothing in Wildwood stayed open all night except the roadhouse by the interstate. He drove slowly a few streets over, into the business district, and parked far out in the grocery store lot, where he could watch the doors unobserved as the workers inside worked the closing, in case Abigail was waiting there.

It was worrying, not knowing where she was.

Marsh thought about going home to check the answering machine. Maybe she had called. When the lights in the grocery began to flick off bank by bank, he pulled out into the street again.

The house looked no different from when he'd left hours ago, clay still ground into the carpet, empty popcorn bags half spilling from the kitchen trash can, the living room in disarray. Marsh checked every room, but he'd known the moment he opened the door that Abigail wasn't there. The house had a different feel when she was in it. His radar always seemed to know where she was, what she was doing, and he was discomfited now by her utter absence.

Marsh went to her bedroom door and opened it slowly. Her fragrance, light and fresh—something like clean cotton, the scent of baby shampoo and a citrus undertone—lingered in the room like a ghost. The bed was made, the corners of the bedclothes sharp and crisp, the edges hanging even. He liked that Abigail was tidy.

He flicked on the light and there was Gary, grinning at him from the wood-framed photograph on the dresser. He remembered that photo from the funeral, where it had stood on a table at the front of the room near the casket, a single spray of bloodred gladiolus in the vase next to the frame. Gary looked mockingly happy in the photo—or maybe it had been Marsh's own tainted happiness reflected back at him. Marsh wasn't happy his brother was dead, but it meant the field to Abigail was clear, and it had given Marsh the easy way inside her guard. If Gary had simply not been Abigail's choice… Marsh fought down the regret. It didn't matter now. It wasn't something he could fix.

But still, everything roiled inside Marsh. Too many emotions fought for supremacy. Anger. Jealousy. Anxiety. Desperation. Love. Fear. Worry. Fury.

He lunged forward and knocked Gary onto his face on Abigail's dresser, satisfied by the ominous crack from the glass. He didn't want his brother smiling at him as he began yanking open drawers and cabinets, looking for a clue to where she might have gone.

At midnight he sat next to the telephone, where the answering machine was as dark as his spirit. His stomach was hot with acid. He knew he should have something to eat, even as late as it was, but Abigail wasn't here to cook, and he was sick of dealing with the kitchen and the clients. He'd found nothing of use in Abigail's room, just box after box of mementos, Gary everywhere. A wedding album. Vacation pictures. Letters, cards. There was even a small bundle of cards Marsh had sent Abigail in the first weeks after Gary's death, cheery greetings, short notes, all filled with the helpful brotherly sentiments of a man supporting his sister-in-law through her grief.

Even now, after the months Marsh had been living with her and begun to mold her to his ways, he was sure Abigail had no true understanding of the depth of his passion for her.

He had loved her before she married Gary, but he'd driven back his need with a ruthless will once she'd made her choice and said her vows to his brother. But fate had given Marsh a second chance, and he wasn't going to let her—his very *life*—slip out of his hands again. She was his.

It was just that simple.

He would do what it took to keep her. She'd learn, given time, where she belonged. Together they would erase the past, erase Gary, and Marsh would fill that space. He could hardly wait for the night when she would come to him, penitent and bare, and he would punish her only a little for delaying his ultimate possession of her for so many months. Punishment would make her utter surrender delicious. Marsh liked the taste of Abigail's tears.

He couldn't think of anyplace else to look for her. He sat, fists clenched, staring straight ahead.

At last he picked up the telephone and dialed.

"Central Sumter Regional Hospital," said a woman who answered on the first ring.

"Yeah…hi, I'm…uh, not sure who I need to speak to, but my…my wife is missing, and it's late and I'm really concerned that…" *My wife.* It would happen. She was that in all but name already, wasn't she? Even if he'd not yet slept with her in the biblical sense, they shared a house, a life, physical intimacy of a sort. He scowled a little. It would help if there weren't so many pictures of Gary around, looking down at him from the walls. Maybe he should take Abigail away—maybe a hotel, without Gary's eyes watching every move he made, would help him consummate their relationship at last. Show Abigail what she did to him, how much he wanted her. Loved her. *Needed* her.

"What's your wife's name?"

"Abigail. Abigail McMurray. She's got long brown hair, gray eyes. She should've been home hours ago."

"Hold on, sir, while I transfer you to the proper department. Someone will help you. Try not to worry."

There was a silence of perhaps thirty seconds. His heart thumped hard in his chest. Was she there? Had something happened to her, or was the sneaky bitch there to report him for the bruises, the ones he gave her for not holding still enough while he finished taking what pleasure he could—the pleasure she owed him—at her breasts.

"Sir?" It was a different voice, another woman. "Mr. McMurray?"

"Yes?" He tried to keep the pathetic eagerness out of his voice.

"We show no one by that name has been admitted to Regional today."

The knot in his gut eased. "Thank you. Thank you very much."

"You're wel—"

Marsh hung up on her. He didn't need her now, and he didn't have the patience for stupid courtesies.

He needed a drink. Something to help him think more clearly, unwind the tension in his strong, stocky body.

Marsh went to the kitchen and used a key to open the cupboard where they kept the liquor. Everything had to be locked away, or the clients would get hold of it, ruin it, cause trouble. When he had Abigail back, it would be more than time to make a change. Get the hell out of this crappy little town. Jacksonville had so much more to offer the two of them. He could start off at his old job again—he was sure he'd be welcomed back—and Abigail could keep house.

The bottle of rye was lower by more than a couple of fingers when he put his glass down on the counter and rasped his palm over his stubbled cheeks and chin.

Abigail wasn't with friends. She wasn't at the stores. She wasn't in the hospital.

That only left the cops, didn't it?

Bitch.

Chapter 5

Ten minutes into her story, when Cade tilted the beer bottle toward her again, this time Abby took it, swallowing down the slightly fizzy, hoppy lager in large gulps. The beer was getting warm, and there wasn't enough in the bottle to do more than take the edge off, but in her agitated, hyperaware state she could feel it hitting her bloodstream in just a couple of minutes. She tried not to think of putting her mouth where his had just been—there was something unquestionably intimate in the action, as if she had committed to trusting him. She didn't want to examine her actions or motives too closely just now; everything was too unsettled, and she knew well the danger of making decisions under duress.

"Sounds like things started out just fine, friendly

and all. Helpful when you needed it most." Cade got up again and walked to the truck. Her eyes followed him in the gloom, watching his lean figure. The fire lit him from behind, revealing the fit of his jeans—not too loose, but not too tight, straight-leg jeans that moved with him instead of in spite of him. The orange light also brought out the blued steel of his gun, riding in his waistband. She heard him open the cooler, and the clink of bottles. He came slowly back to the table, his gaze meeting hers, and she realized Cade had let Roy Lewis go. Cade was playing her like a violin, and even though she resented him for it, even if she was falling for his cop line, it felt so good—so boil-lancingly, painfully good—to tell it at last.

Cade sat next to her, closer than he had before. He twisted off the caps and handed her one of the beers. He took a couple of long swigs, looking into the fire. "Go on. Marsh was helpful, pleasant. He was Gary's brother, and you needed help with your day care business. But you couldn't keep steady help, even with the agency looking for staff. Why d'you think that was, Abby?"

"We've got to let her go, Abigail. I caught her looking through Rosemary's wallet."

"Oh, no, surely she didn't, Marsh. She's so good with them, so kind and always gentle—"

"Lots of people talk a good line. Janine got inside our guard. We're just lucky we found out now, before she did real damage to someone, or to our business reputation. I should have looked into her background

more carefully. I'm sorry, Abigail. It won't happen again."

So Janine had gone. Abby fired the woman herself. Marsh gave her the words to say. "We're going to have to let you go, Janine. We wish you all the best, but we're looking for a more experienced caregiver."

A few weeks later, the woman who had taken Janine's place resigned on her own, citing personal reasons.

The third try was not the charm—the assistant they hired didn't come to work after the first week, and Abby had to call her house and leave a message that she would mail the first and only paycheck to the address she had on file.

They'd all been females, hadn't they? Abby wondered for a moment what might have happened had she wanted to hire a male, but Marsh had helped her screen the applicants and she'd been guided by his advice when it came to hiring.

The answer startled her with its inescapable logic, when it came. How had she not seen it months ago? How could she have been so blinded, so distracted, that she wouldn't notice a trend like that in her own business? "Marsh. Marsh must have…done something. Run them all off. Lied to them, lied to me. I don't know."

"Why do you think he'd do that?" He turned to look at her, and she was surprised to discover she could still see the blue of his eyes, even in the darkness, lit by the dimming glow of the fire. "Tell me that, Abby."

"Because…because he didn't want anyone finding out about him. About *us*."

"Is there an *us,* Abby?"

She wanted Cade to stop ending every question with her name. It made her squirm like a bug on a pin, it never let her relax. She had no respite from him, not even for a moment. *Is there an* us, *Abby?*

Yes.

But no.

Hell no.

But yes, in a horrible way, there was an *us*. She and Marsh were linked, through his brutality and her own fear and inaction. Two deformed halves of a twisted, terrible whole. He had broken her to fit him, and she had done nothing to stop him. The shame rose afresh.

"Shut up," she whispered. "Shut up, shut up, shut up!" The words rose to a shriek at the end. "Just take me to jail. That's what you want. Take me to jail for stealing your truck. Get it over with! Go ahead and arrest me, because I'm done telling you my dirty secrets. I'm done talking. I know you're a cop. Arrest me."

Cade's hand shot out and caught in her ponytail, forcing her to look at him. "I don't need you to talk anymore. I know this story. I've heard it a hundred times. Marsh wormed his way into your life. You needed him, and he was there. He told you how difficult it was for him, and how much you should appreciate him, didn't he, Abby? He told you how hard he worked to make time for you and the day care, told you how needy you were. And maybe he needed a little money to help you out, or maybe you even put him on the bank account. Little by little, he took it all." Cade shook her. "Everything. Your money. Your house. Hell, has to have been your car, too, or you wouldn't have wanted that heap I'm driving. All of it. Am I right, Abby?"

The silence was full of the song of crickets and cicadas, the soft noises of the river only feet away, something small rustling in the oak leaves that dotted the sand of the campsite. Mort, on the other side of the fire out of the drifting smoke, got to his feet and went to investigate.

Cade put his face closer to hers, and his next words were soft, almost loving. "Somewhere in there, he took you, too. Your pride. Your self-worth. Your independence. You, Abby. *You.* Come on. Just admit it to yourself."

There were always more tears. Always. Even in her fury, there was misery. She felt them rising in her eyes, burning like never before, a hot and stinging tide. And still she stared at Cade, hating him for his knowledge, hating him for making her say it.

"When did he start hitting you? Was it before or after he screwed you the first time, Abby?"

"I'm—going to—throw up—"

"Oh, no, you're not. You're not wasting my good steak and beer. Come on, Abby. Say it. He hit you first when…?" He wouldn't let go of her, and she couldn't look away. His eyes compelled the truth, and oh, God, she wanted to tell him, wanted to say it, wanted to scream it until her throat burst, but she couldn't.

"Before or after?" he pressed. "Just tell me. It's so much easier if you just tell me." Now his voice was soft, wheedling, promising comfort if she'd only give in, tell him what he wanted to hear.

He was no different from Marsh.

"After! After, all right, after, he found a bill that was… It wasn't late, it had only been in the basket two days. It was after, after! After!" She screamed at him, her fist flying off her legs to pound uselessly against his shoulder. Cade leaned forward and pressed his forehead against hers, his eyes closing, shutting away their penetrating, all-knowing blue, releasing her from that unbearable scrutiny. His hand cupped the back of her head, and when her scream of rage and humiliation turned into desperate, wrenching sobs, he pulled her across his lap and into his arms.

"It's over," he whispered. "Over. I've got you."

"You *bastard*." But she burrowed hard into the strong curve of his neck and shoulder, where he smelled of sweat and disinfectant, and faintly of blood from his head wound, and maleness, and she wept in his arms for the second time that day. Her tears were jagged, made of broken glass, born in the darkest part of her, that shameful place deep within where she had hidden her inadequacy from the world.

His big frame shook with what had to be amusement. "I've been called worse, Abigail McMurray. By better criminals than you."

Cade knew he shouldn't have pushed her so hard, but now the scab was off, and he wasn't sorry. He had his answers. His curiosity was satisfied for the moment. What he wasn't prepared for was the depth of his fury toward Abby's abuser. Now that he thought about it, he hadn't really wanted to know Marsh had screwed her. The idea brought to mind ugly dark thoughts, thoughts he didn't want to have with Abby in his lap. This was always the weird part of his cop brain, how he could watch dispassionately the terrible things people did to one another, and still go on with his life, untouched.

Mostly.

Some memories lingered unpleasantly, and now Cade found himself wondering what Marshall McMurray looked like. Like the Gary in the driver's license Abby carried? Her weight across his thighs made him think of other women he'd known, held, slept with. It awoke an unmistakable response, too, his maleness hardening. He hoped she was too wrapped up in her emotional upheaval to notice, but her ass was parked right where it would do the most good. The two things in combination—the thought of Marsh's violence, and Abby's heart-shaped ass—warred for his attention.

Cade sat still, willing his erection to subside, moving his palms slowly over Abby's back, feeling the dampness of her chambray shirt. A mosquito droned near his left ear. When he waved it away, Abby stirred, pushing back from his chest and his embrace.

"God. That's twice today." She scrubbed hard at her face with her hands, scooting from his lap and reaching for the paper towels. "You probably think I cry at the drop of a hat."

He let her go and crossed one leg over the other. She wasn't likely to notice the bulge in the firelight, but why look like a caveman needlessly? It would only alienate her, and he was discovering he didn't want to do that.

"So what happens now?" she asked. "You've heard my story. And now it's night."

"What do you want to happen?"

Abby looked at him suspiciously. "You mean I have choices? Like what? You're holding all the cards. You haven't told me what happened to Roy Lewis."

Cade reached for the beer bottle. "Roy learned his lesson that night, I think. I let him go. His story was good."

She snuffled hard and blew her nose once more. Damn, she was tough, those gray eyes not letting him off the hook yet, even though she had no leverage. "What about my story?"

"Not nearly as detailed as his, but I guess you had reason for doing what you did."

"What's that mean? Are you letting me go?"

"I took the cuffs off you hours ago, Abby."

"You've got a truck and a gun and a mean dog and a badge somewhere. I'd have been stupid to try to get away. How far do you think I'd get?"

"Yeah, that's right. And why the hell would you want to go back, anyway?"

"There are six people besides Marsh who depend

on me going back." She snuffled again, her voice wavering.

"I'd bet money he's been on the phone canceling with every single one of them. I know you feel guilty, but to Marsh they've never been more than a way of controlling you."

She stared at him, huddled on the bench not far from him. He could still feel the heat of her leg close to his, smell the yeasty beer on her breath when she spoke. "He might hurt them. Take his anger at me out on them."

Cade shook his head. "Your day care folks aren't Marsh's kind of target. They don't interest him. *You* interest him. He knows exactly how to push your buttons, get you to do what he wants. It's how abusers work. With you gone, he won't bother with them unless he thinks he can use them to get you back."

"I didn't even call any of their families—"

"Will you listen to yourself? You committed a felony to get away from him, and now all I get from you is that you think you'd better go back. What part of this doesn't make sense to *you?* Because it's clear as day to me. Tell you what, Abigail McMurray. I'm bushed. It's been a hell of a day, and this headache isn't gone yet." He gestured to the lump on the side of his head. "We're gonna go over there to my truck, roll out the bedroll inside it, and we're going to sleep. We'll talk about all this crap in the morning."

"S-sleep? Here?" There was a long pause, a very long pause, before she said, "We?" in a shaky voice.

He rose, walked across the sandy campsite to the

truck and shoved some of the gear to the sides of the bed before unhooking the bungee cord holding the bedroll. "It's a campground. They don't mind if people sleep here. Maybe you've heard of the idea."

"I… Look, it's only an hour or so back to Wildwood. You could just—"

"I could, but I'm not gonna. In the morning, Abby." The pad unrolled with a soft thump. He reached into a duffel bag and found a flashlight, which he put into her unresisting hand. "I'll give you five minutes to pee, and then I'm coming after you."

It took her maybe three minutes at the campground's pit toilets before he saw the flashlight bobbing back. She stood next to the tailgate, shining the light in at him, examining his face, her own hidden by shadow behind the glare of the flashlight. "No funny stuff? I mean, I know I stole your truck. But that's no reason for…um."

"What the hell? No funny stuff. On my honor." He held up his hand in the Boy Scout's salute. The flashlight beam played over him, settling at last on his face as she studied him. He tried not to squint in the light. He already looked like hell, scarred and bloody. No need to make it worse by looking suspicious on top of that.

"This is…surreal."

"Welcome to my day. Climb in. Right side's yours. We're closing the hatch to keep the bugs out. I opened the side windows and the top vent because they have screens. It'll still be too damn hot, but we won't have the bloodsuckers."

She handed the flashlight in to him. He watched her as she crept inside on hands and knees, her shirt gaping open, her old, fitted jeans sexier than any short skirt she could have worn. *Hell. What're you doing, Latimer? Just drive her home, be done with this situation. She's made her bed with that bastard, let her lie in it. You can't save her from herself if she's determined to screw up her life.* But he couldn't. He'd do his damnedest to save her, even if it was only for a few more hours. He could be the rock that kept her from the hard place.

Abby sat, legs out stiffly, hands clenched in her lap. Cade leaned forward, pulled up the tailgate and brought down the hatch with a slam and a twist of the handle.

"What about your dog?"

"He prefers being outside. Three's a crowd in the back of a truck. Gonna be hot enough in here without Mort. Plus he'll keep an ear open, let me know if anything turns up."

Abby blew out a long breath and wiped sweat from her face with her sleeve. "I can't believe this is happening. You sure you don't want to just drop me off with the nearest sheriff?"

"I'm sure. Shut up and go to sleep." He lay down and shifted to get comfortable, shoving a clean pair of jeans at her. "Pillow. Sorry, it's what we got. They're not bad if you roll 'em up tight and put them under your neck." He turned off the flashlight before setting it next to him in easy reach. "Good night."

There was a long, still pause in which the insect

noise outside and the sound of the river seemed to fill the camper shell, then Abby lay down, curled as far from him as possible, her back firmly toward him. She smelled of the acrid campfire smoke, sweat and old fear. And Cade wanted her, more than he could ever remember wanting a woman before. He laced his hands under his head and stared out the side window, where he could see the tiny green and gold glows of fireflies signaling to prospective mates in the darkness of the scrub woods.

After a while, he spoke again, knowing she wasn't yet asleep. "There's just one thing I don't understand. Why didn't you leave before now, Abby? Why did you wait so long? What stopped you?" The answers were never simple in domestic abuse scenarios. There were sometimes children, or the woman had no means of support, or her self-esteem had been so damaged that she never even considered leaving. In Abby's case, he suspected it was the people at her day care, as vulnerable as children. Marsh had undoubtedly been a master at slipping the thin end of the wedge into her awareness, making her dependent on him before he began his campaign of making her over to suit himself.

Abby didn't answer. Instead, she sat up again and drew her legs up the way she had at the picnic table. Cade realized he'd blown any chance at all of ever getting to know her better. Like her abuser, he'd made it clear he considered the abuse her own fault. Even if that wasn't what he thought or meant, it was sure as hell what it sounded like. He clenched his fist in the darkness and shook his head at himself, but he didn't apologize. Maybe she would at least give it thought, if she hadn't already.

Chapter 6

Abby wasn't sure how long it was before she finally felt she could lie down again. She sat in the darkness, her mind churning. The events of the day played over and over in her head. Every slightest noise from outside caught her ear—the jingle of Mort's tags on his collar. The change in pitch of the cicadas' buzzing. A faint splash from the river, perhaps a fish jumping, or some animal coming to drink.

The truck cooled gradually, but the night remained too hot for restful sleep. She was still sweaty, and she wanted a shower and an enormous glass of iced tea. She stretched out carefully, trying not to disturb Cade, who slept quietly, hardly snoring at all, one hand on his belly, the other lying lax at his side between the two of them. She wondered where he had put his gun. Surely it wasn't still in the back of his waistband—he couldn't possibly sleep like that—but she hadn't seen him deal with it in the darkness. He'd probably hidden it while she'd been at the toilets.

Gary had been a noisy sleeper, but Abby had thought, *I always know where he is. He's right here beside me.*

Marsh—well. At least she didn't have firsthand knowledge of how he slept. He stayed in his own room, except when he woke in the night to use the bathroom or to stand in her doorway and stare at her in the darkness. She didn't know whether he snored or not, and she was grateful not to know. When they were awake, he struck her, did other disgusting things to her, but so far he hadn't forced her into the intimacy of sleeping in the same bed.

Somehow, the thought of that was worse than everything else he had done. It would have destroyed the last sweetness remaining from her life with Gary, had Marsh invaded the bed they'd shared. Silent tears rolled down the outside of her face, dribbling into her ears and making her itch. She bit her lip to make herself stop. What was done was done—no sense weeping again. In the morning, she'd find a way to convince Cade to take her back to Wildwood.

After a while, she saw the stars disappear one by one. The night was clouding up. The song of the cicadas changed, in concert with the dropping barometric pressure and the lateness of the hour. Abby hoped even insects had to sleep sometime, and would stop their ceaseless noise. She closed her eyes at last, dizzy and all but spinning with exhaustion. Her fingers twitched sleepily, and she felt them brush against Cade's arm, fine hairs tickling. She drew back, but it was uncomfortable to hold herself at such an awkward angle, and each time she relaxed, their skin touched.

In the end she stopped fighting her own body and the slope of the truck bed. Her elbow pivoted, her forearm turned and the back of her hand lay against his strong wrist.

She told herself it was so she'd know if he moved; it was for safety's sake. She counted his pulse, and after fifty, she forgot to count, she simply drifted. The darkness seemed to throb in time with his heartbeat behind her eyelids.

After a while, Abby admitted to herself she was touching Cade because she wanted to. The simple purity and comfort of a human connection, a touch that didn't involve menace or pain.

Yes, it had to be that, she told herself, and when sleep came like a slow-rising river in flood, she went with it. Her last thought was of the furnace-heat of Cade's long body, touching hers, and a vague, confused amazement that she was here at all, sleeping next to a stranger, and feeling safer than she had in many months, let alone finding comfort. It made no sense, but it was welcome nonetheless.

The hand was warm as it cupped the flare of her hip bone. Perceptibly warm, even in the blood-heat of the summer night. It made the rest of her feel cooler, and when the hand slid across her belly and curved to her waist, where she lay on her side in the bed of the pickup, she didn't resist an automatic movement to relax into the heat of his body, curled behind her. In the humidity, it was only moments before she felt the hollow of her spine grow damp with perspiration, but still the heat was welcome. To be close to another body, without fear, without trembling…it was both all she had wished and more than she had dared to hope for in the past year.

Cicadas still droned their monotonous song outside the stuffy shelter of the truck. Abby had always wondered how the insects knew when to change pitch and tone, for they did it all at once as if a conductor directed them from on high. Did they sense a change in temperature, or a movement in the air? How could so many insects, in so many different trees, be so in tune? Was it the same sense that told her, now that she was awake, that Cade was awake, too, and aware of her in the same way she was aware of him? She listened to Cade's breathing for a moment and knew in the darkness behind her, his blue, blue eyes were open, all pupil in the night, seeking her reaction.

His hand slid, as if in sleep, gently along her rib cage, and stopped just short of cupping her left breast. Abby wondered if he could feel the sudden slamming acceleration of her heartbeat, or the manic trembling that was turning her insides to liquid. Could he hear the tentative, silent, anxious thought-words about how she'd known this man only a few hours, and not because of good circumstances. He was a man with secrets, this scarred man with his dog like a weapon, his gun and his easy, casual strength. The trembling whispered to her of fear, of dread, but also of allure and excitement. Despite the surface appearance of Cade frightening her, there was the thing her instinct kept telling her: he was a good man. A considerate man. He'd shared his food with her. He'd given her privacy while she went to the pit toilet. He'd held her when emotion overwhelmed her and she'd spilled the story of Marsh's treatment. He'd made a soft nest here in the back of his truck. Above all, he hadn't turned her in for her crime, something she knew she richly deserved.

Mimicking Cade's drowsy attitude, Abby rolled slowly toward him until she lay on her back, her left shoulder pressed snugly against his chest. The movement brought her hand in contact with his body, and to her surprise she felt the slight moistness of bare skin and wiry body hair against the back of her hand. Her breathing hitched, and she opened her eyes at last. Cade's hand moved to her side and held her firmly.

"You're awake," he said quietly.

"Yes."

"Good."

How his mouth found hers in the utter darkness, Abby didn't know. Its descent was unerring, its touch on hers sure and firm. A vision of Marsh shot like a meteorite across her vision and was gone in less time than it took for Cade's tongue to stroke her lips apart. Kissing Marsh was never like this, never such a drowning pleasure, never a matter of give and take—only give. And give, and give, until it hurt and Marsh was ready to be satisfied with a few rough thrusts and his climax into her hand or between her breasts. In the darkness Cade's hands shaped her, molded her, guided her. Above all, they encouraged her shy exploration, moving her sweat-dampened palm to his ribs, where she could feel his heart thudding like a jackhammer, and then starting her on a downward trek along the indentation of his midline. He opened buttons on her shirt before tugging it free of her jeans. When his palm flattened on her belly, gooseflesh rose over her entire body, a reflex of dread. She waited for his hand to slide upward and squeeze her breast, hard and then harder, but his touch remained lightly teasing, as he freed her breast from the cup of her bra. Her nipple tautened and crested in response to his touch, and she heard herself release a gasping moan.

"Am I hurting you?"

"No. No. It's all right…."

Cade's hand slid over the waistband of her jeans and followed the stitching of the fly. Down, and farther down, until he cupped her mound and his long fingers slid between her legs and traced the stitching where the leg seams met. Even through the multiple thicknesses of fabric, she could feel the scorch of his hand. Bright spangles of light played behind her eyelids as she screwed her lids shut tight. Cade kissed her again, slower than before, deeper, dreamlike and languid. His hand pressed against her snugly, and Abby felt herself needing to squirm against that touch and seek a pleasure she hadn't known for too long.

Cade groaned as her hips moved, and he lifted

his mouth to rasp breathlessly in her ear. "I want to touch you there. Will you let me? Let me touch you, feel you on my hands?"

Abby could have wept with the beauty of his voice, ragged with desire for her, and the urgent poetry of his words. She nodded, not trusting her voice not to break, and moved her hand to the waistband button of her jeans, only to meet his fingers there, already pushing the metal rivet through the buttonhole. When he nuzzled her neck, she shuddered. His cheek and chin were rough with stubble. A hot, sweet throb went through her abdomen, and a moment later the zip slid down. Air met her skin and she lost her nerve.

"Wait. Cade, wait." Where she found the courage to ask him to stop, she couldn't imagine. Surely now he would be angry with her. "I'm sorry. I'm sorry. I shouldn't have— I'm sorry."

She could feel the tension in his muscles when he froze and held back. In that moment Abby realized there would not be anger. Nothing would happen without her permission. Nothing would knock her off-kilter, or surprise her, except perhaps her own overwhelming physical response. Cade was nothing more than a looming shadow in the darkness, a shadow that breathed and trembled. She knew he was looking down at her and wondered if he could see more than she could.

"It'll be all right, Abby."

She wanted to believe him. She thought perhaps she *could* believe him. When his hand moved gently, slowly, back to its task and slipped beneath the elastic of her panties, she didn't stop him, and she didn't speak. She had only to wait with held breath and shivering eagerness and that glittering edge of nervousness for the moment that would come, *must* come.

The moment *did* come, with gentleness and warmth, and a sweetness that was nothing short of total devastation. She knew exactly which of his slightly roughened fingertips slipped first into the crease at the apex of her thighs. She had studied those hands so often over the course of the day it almost seemed she could see the half-moon at the base of the neatly trimmed nail and the crisp sandy hairs on the last knuckle as they disappeared within her jeans and flesh. His other fingers flanked her labia and massaged deliciously while that middle finger pressed slowly inward to find the swollen pout of her clitoris.

"Yes," he breathed. "Yes. Like that. So wet, so warm."

Abby arched upward, gasping, when he found his goal. The jolt that ran through her at that single stroking touch caused every inch of her skin to flush with blood as if she'd been caught reading "The Song of Solomon" at church when she should have been listening to the preacher. Illicit, lushly arousing, and oh, so forbidden. Beyond erotic, leaping into wantonness and hedonistic self-indulgence. The powerful touch of a stranger, anonymous and deliriously debauched.

"Yes. Let me." Cade slid a knee between her own and nudged her legs apart. Abby felt the hairs on his thigh rasping against her bare skin and realized she did not know how or when he had removed her clothing. Fear rose again inside her a moment later when she felt his weight settling above her. Then there was that most intimate of touches, the head of his shaft nudging bluntly, blindly, at her entrance, and she sat up, fighting and flailing.

Her own gasp startled her and she groped around her in panic. Next to her in the back of the truck Cade lay still, breathing deeply in his sleep. Her heart raced and perspiration broke out over her body. Quick flutters of her hands informed her she was still fully dressed. She swallowed hard and pulled her hair away from her sweaty neck.

She'd dreamed the whole thing, except for Cade's hand, lying loosely over her upper thigh, where it had fallen from her hip when she bolted upright.

It was a struggle to control her breathing and refrain from panicked laughter. When they'd first lain down, she hadn't expected to get any rest at all, much less sleep, let alone have blatantly erotic dreams of Cade making love to her. Her body still broadcast its need. Her nipples stood out in the cups of her bra, and her lower body felt far too warm. Exactly as if she'd been awaiting the fulfillment of an orgasm after sweet foreplay, a feeling she hadn't experienced since Gary died.

Marsh pushed her into the angle of the kitchen counter. His breathing was harsh and erratic. She could feel his erection pressing against her hip, and was appalled. Had he always wanted her like this? Even before Gary died? She felt his mouth roaming over hers, and though he looked a little like Gary, and even smelled like him in the way that siblings could, she was not aroused.

But she felt obligated, and maybe this was all her fault. She'd been so grateful to him for helping pull the weight of the day care center. He'd even taken a leave of absence from his own job to help her out. And she...she'd gone on wearing the casual work clothes she'd worn when she and Gary were doing the grunt work of cleaning up after their clients had gone for the evening. Skimpy, much-washed T-shirts and soft, battered jeans that clung to her curves and had threadbare holes in places that perhaps were best kept hidden.

When he pulled her hand to the crotch of his trousers and mumbled, "Please touch me, Abby, just a little, I promise," it was somehow the least she could do. Should do. She owed him. A few strokes, gently cupping, until he pressed his face into her neck and sucked hard there as he came, dampening his boxers and the crisp khakis.

He'd marked her in his excitement. In the morning a dab of concealer hid the red place that bruised to purple and then greenish-yellow before fading.

It happened again a few days later. They were on their knees in the kitchen—why had it been the kitchen so often?—scrubbing at some of the paint that had been spilled when James's spastic hand disobeyed while they all did art together. They'd mopped up most of the tempera, but some had managed to stain the grout between the tiles and now she and Marsh were doing the detail work of bleaching and scrubbing. Marsh clutched at her from behind, grinding his pelvis into hers—both of them fully clothed. He had an erection, but only moments later she felt it softening. He shoved her away as if disgusted with them both.

He brought her flowers the next morning when he showed up to help for the day. His kiss on her cheek was sweetly apologetic, and his hazel eyes, almost Gary's eyes, were sorrowful. Everything was better after that—until a month later, when he struck her for the first time because he found a few recent bills in the to-be-paid tray on the desk. While she was on the floor, felled and stunned by the blow that had hit her at the junction of her neck and shoulder, he sucker punched her belly.

"Why can't you listen? It's important that you understand I'm the one who makes the money decisions. I'm the one with the business background, Abby. I can't help you if you fight me like this. You make me crazy when you don't pay the bills the day they come in the mail." She could hear the punches landing, low meaty thuds as if she were pounding a tough steak on the cutting board. "I'll write the checks from now on. I'll handle the mail." She curled around herself and waited for the hitting to stop. It would stop. It had to stop. Hitting her like this had to hurt his hands, surely.

In the darkness of the truck bed, her heart squeezed painfully. She shifted to her right and Cade's hand slid off her thigh. He stirred, turning to his other side, and was still. The rocking truck settled. Abby crab-walked to the tailgate and squeezed herself into a ball. While she waited for Cade's breathing to deepen again, her fingers explored the lump of luggage at her side. It felt like a duffel, with a wide-toothed plastic zipper just like the bag Cade had tucked her wallet in earlier in the day, after he'd taken it from her and rummaged in it for her personal information. Her fingers opened the zipper and felt carefully inside. Long years of carrying a handbag and groping within for various items made it easy for her to identify her wallet when she touched it. She brought it out and sat with it in her hands, thinking for a long time before she slowly turned the inside handle on the hatch and lifted it open.

It was time to go, wasn't it? It was only a few miles back to the main road, and maybe from there she could hitchhike into Gainesville. The night was dark, but she felt sure she could follow the forestry road without getting lost, even at night. The pale sand of the campsite gleamed in the low light, and so would the sun-bleached gray marl of the road.

All that remained was to slip out without alerting Mort. Abby climbed over the tailgate and set her foot on the truck bumper.

The first flicker of lightning woke Cade. He lay in the darkness, eyes wide and ears waiting for the thunder so that he'd know how far away the storm was. He'd also have to bring Mort into the back of the truck with them. Brave as the dog was in most circumstances, including gunfire over his head, thunder reduced him to a quivering jelly. If Cade commanded him to a task during a thunderstorm, the dog would perform it, but without joy and certainly with fear. Mort much preferred to stick close to his master when the thunder rolled.

"Are you awake, Abby?" Cade said softly, after the rumble died away. "I'm going to bring Mort into the truck with us. He'll feel safer."

When there was no answer, Cade moved a hand toward where Abby lay next to him.

Or, rather, should have lain.

The pad in the truck bed was empty except for him. He moved his hand in a broad arc, knowing he wouldn't find her. When the next flicker of lightning grayed the blackness, his quick eyes scanned the back of the truck. No Abby. Perhaps she had crept out to relieve her bladder, but a feeling of unease plagued him. The next flash showed him the open zipper of the duffel bag near the tailgate, and his concerns were confirmed: Abby had gone. He found himself somewhat confused by the depth of the disappointment he felt. Dinner had been so charmingly relaxed until he'd forced her confession with his story about Roy, and despite her trepidation at sleeping next to a stranger, she'd crept into the truck bed and eventually succumbed to her exhaustion, even relaxing enough to touch him in her sleep as they lay side by side. He'd thought that they'd taken some sort of step forward; to what, he didn't know, but he'd been sure she trusted him, after a fashion.

But she was gone.

He groped first for his Beretta. It was where it should be, in its pocket holster under the mat at his head. He brought it out and put it in his waistband, holster and all.

Cade scrambled to the tailgate and found the hatch very slightly ajar, and not latched. If she'd closed it all the way, she'd have wakened him. What he didn't understand was why he hadn't noticed when she left. How did this woman sail beneath his radar so successfully time after time? He lifted the hatch and saw Mort standing there, gazing up hopefully.

"Hey, boy. *Such* Abby! *Such!*" Cade grabbed at the pair of folded jeans she'd used as a pillow, and held it to Mort's nose. The dog gave him a mournful look as lightning flashed again, but dutifully snuffed the earth. It took only seconds for the rangy shepherd to find the scent and begin to track it out of the campsite and straight toward the forestry road rather than the pit toilets. Cursing, Cade called Mort back and climbed out of the truck, letting down the tailgate. Mort leaped up immediately, and while Cade ruffled his neck fur to reassure him, the rain began, a drenching downpour that would have soaked Mort even through his thick coat. Cade closed the tailgate and crouched beneath the hatch while he thought.

Abby had slipped away, and now it was storming. Cade wondered how far she'd gone and if she would be able to find shelter in this remote area. How long ago had she left, and why hadn't Mort alerted?

Coming to a decision, Cade patted his front pocket. Keys right where they should be. He thought about what Abby would do once she left the campsite. It was night, and a dark night at that. She'd stick to the road. There wasn't any other real choice, was there?

Cade reached into the bed of the truck and groped for the flashlight. Might as well pack up now, rather than leave anything behind. If he managed to find Abby, he'd figure out what to do with her then. Regardless, now that he was thoroughly awake, there was no reason to stay at the campsite.

The fire pit was rapidly becoming a sodden mess, hot ash puffing into the air with every raindrop, sizzling as it was quenched by the storm. He needn't worry about it causing a brush fire. Cade shined the light at the picnic table, where the empty beer bottles and Abby's jug of orange juice still stood. His fishing reel was upside down in pieces on sodden paper towels. That reel would never be the same, he thought, heading for the table and gathering up everything he found there. The fishing pole was leaning against a nearby tree. He broke it down into its three components and stashed everything in the back of the truck. He'd find someplace to chuck out the trash later. Mort panted into his face, anxious and distressed in the thunder and lightning. He rubbed the dog behind the ears.

Cade took one last look around, saw nothing else that needed to be collected and hopped into the back of the truck to change into dry clothes. Dressed and relatively dry, he waited a couple of minutes for the rain to slacken, commanded Mort to lie down, closed up the back of the truck and made a quick dash for the cab.

The faithful red truck started immediately. It might look like hell, but its innards were sound; Cade kept them that way. A tool or weapon was worthless if it wasn't ready to use at a moment's notice. He backed out of their campsite, then slowly circled the campground and aimed his headlights into each site, in case Abby was crouching beneath a picnic table or sheltering in the pit toilets, before he turned the truck out of the campground and began the slow, sodden drive back toward the main road.

The marl road was a mess already, though the rain had been falling for only fifteen minutes or so. Marl roads usually fared better than packed sand, but the rain was bucketing down, and where the road wasn't rutted, the marl was slick. He shifted the pickup into four-wheel drive for better traction, wishing he could go faster, but aware he might miss Abby, if she were hiding in the scrub off the sides of the road. Slower was better.

His fingers alternately drummed and clenched on the wheel. He had no idea how much of a lead she had on him. Glancing at the clock on the dashboard was no help, though it did tell him he was wide awake at one-fifteen in the morning.

A mile crept by, then a second. A third, and still no Abby. Cade gritted his teeth and slowed even more, windshield wipers in overdrive. He squinted and peered and glared and cussed.

And worried, more than he wanted to.

She should mean nothing to him, except a problem to solve. It wasn't his job. He was on vacation, and Abby didn't even live in his department's jurisdiction. Yet he couldn't leave it alone. He wanted to fix it all for her, see her shy smile become more real, more confident. He wanted to reveal the woman he had glimpsed beneath the sadness and hurt. She didn't flinch at his face. Maybe she could see past it, find something to value within him.

"Maudlin crap, Latimer," he muttered to himself. "You're romanticizing a car thief. Get yourself a hotel room and leave Abby to her problems. You've got your truck back, that's enough."

But he kept driving. Somewhere in the pouring rain and the black night, Abigail McMurray was soaked and scared and almost certainly heading for Wildwood, her responsibility to her day care clients, and Marshall McMurray and his fists.

Cade wasn't sure he could live with that thought gnawing like a rat in his brain.

Thunder roared, waking Marsh where he lay on Abigail's bed in a scatter of her clothing. A moment later there was another flash of lightning, and more thunder hard on its heels.

His bleary eyes turned toward the lighted digital clock on the nightstand.

One-twenty in the morning.

Marsh groaned, rubbing a hand over his face. He turned from his back to his side, and the buckle of his loosened belt pressed painfully into his belly. The nearly empty bottle of rye rolled toward him on the bed, clinking against his wristwatch. He touched it, recalling an hour of satisfying excess in an empty house, Abigail's laundry hamper emptied over her bed. Quality time with a pair of her silky panties in his good right hand, and the rye in his left.

He pushed to his feet and tucked himself back into his boxers. Zipped up. Had she come home? If she had, Marsh hadn't heard her, but he had been pretty far out of it, hadn't he? The buzz was a good one, better than he'd had in a long time. He'd cut out a lot of the hard stuff because Abigail didn't like having too much liquor in the house, not with the clients around, and while he understood and complied, he resented it. Beer made him slow and sleepy, but rye…rye was the good stuff, gave him the clarity and focus he needed.

Marsh reeled into the living room, the last swigs vanishing down his throat. He tossed the bottle toward the corner wastebasket and gave himself two thumbs-up when it swished in and clanked loudly against the other contents. "That's a three-pointer from downtown for Marshall McMurray," he announced to the room. "Nothing but net." He put a hand on the back of the sofa for balance while he looked around the room. No Abigail. He looked at the front door, where the key was still in the dead bolt—no thumb latches for the clients to open and skitter out onto the sidewalks by mistake, nosirree—and locked. She hadn't come in.

Another bolt of lightning lit the room with a brief glow, flashing behind the closed curtains. The thunder was virtually simultaneous. The storm was right on top of him. Rain pounded on the roof and gurgled noisily through the downspouts.

If Abigail was out there, she was getting soaked. She deserved it, for the hell she was putting him through right now.

But even through the warm, comforting buzz of the rye, Marsh felt a niggling doubt. He hadn't driven past the local sheriff's station earlier in the night, that little concrete bunker of a building tucked just one street off the main drag. What would he have seen, if he had? Nothing, so he hadn't risked his car being seen passing the station. If Abigail was there, she would be inside, out of sight, spilling her guts to some fat-bellied good ol' boy. While Marsh was clear on the proper use of corporal punishment, he was worldly enough to realize not everyone shared his views—not even men who should know better, like cops. Hell, who better to know women sometimes needed the back of a hand to help them learn where the limits were than cops? But the laws tied cops' hands these days—laws made by bleeding heart liberals, and women!—who thought women should be treated like precious, fragile snowflakes. Don't touch them this way, don't touch them that way, or you go to jail, buddy.

Whose word would the cops believe, if it came to that? Marsh, just trying to make a life for himself and his brother's widow, or that same widow, bleating like a sheep about how he was too rough, how he didn't honor her femininity and her individuality?

She didn't understand her duty. Gary hadn't taught her, but Marsh would. He loved her enough for that. Sometimes love had to be tough; and afterward, it was stronger. This was how they would make a bond that would last, a strong relationship with clear roles and boundaries.

Marsh went to the front door and turned the key. He opened the door to a world black with night and yet blurred white with rain, bouncing up from the pavement nearly to knee height, splashing like fountains. The streetlights pinkened the wall of water in cones half a block apart. He thought about Abigail struggling through the rain on a backstreet of Wildwood, maybe passing a cluster of junked cars or a ratty trailer park, her long hair streaming with water, her chambray shirt plastered to her sweet, high breasts.

"Come home," Marsh yelled into the crashing thunder and deluge. "You come home right this minute!"

There was no answer from the wall of water overflowing the gutters on the eaves, or the churning clouds above. Marsh's shoulders slumped as the good feelings from the rye bled from his system, leaving a queasy sickness in their wake. He leaned against the wall just outside the front door, water only inches from his face. "Don't you do this to me, Abigail," he muttered, scrubbing the heels of his hands over his eyes. He gritted his teeth at the storm. "I need you here with me, where you belong. You don't understand how much I love you. You're making me crazy."

The rain, splashing up from the concrete walkway, wetted the legs of his jeans. He looked down at his bare feet and turned slowly back to the house.

Where the hell was she? This was unlike her. She was always so responsible, even if she sometimes had to be reminded about important things like paying bills immediately or making sure there was always mouthwash in his bathroom. Marsh was torn between the fear that something bad—maybe *really* bad, maybe she was hurt, or dead, or *taken*—had happened to her, and the fear that she was exposing him to others, who might not understand or condone the things he knew were necessary.

He closed the door behind him, his wet feet slick on the tile of the entry. But this time he didn't lock it. If she was out there, trying to get home to him, she'd need to be able to get in the house. They would discuss her stupid, risky behavior in the morning.

Marsh slid down the wall and sat on the cool tiles. He'd just wait right here for her—the room was beginning to swim a little, anyway, and he felt like being still for a while. He'd wait right here.

Then, first thing in the morning, if Abigail hadn't come home, he'd go see that clerk at the convenience store. Look in his eyes, see what was truth and what was not. Maybe knock a little sense into him.

He nodded to himself and watched the living room whirl and teeter. It was a good plan.

Marsh's eyes closed and he sagged gently to the side, coming to rest with his cheek against the wood panels of the front door. He slept the sleep of the drunk and the just, not even twitching when a terrific blast of lightning struck somewhere nearby.

Chapter 7

Progress was good along the marl road at first. Its shadowy-pale ribbon was easy to follow, and while Abby kept alert ears for noises in the underbrush to each side of the road, she heard nothing but an occasional night bird calling, and the ceaseless screeching of the cicadas with a choir of crickets for harmony. She stayed on the high crown at the middle of the road, where wheels hadn't rutted or softened the grade. The footing was more sure and firm there. The moon was low in the sky already, but her eyes were well-adjusted, and its glow was enough to delineate the road from its edges. For a while her pace was rapid, as she sought to put distance between herself and the campsite. Then, feeling a little more certain she had managed to escape without Cade discovering her absence, she slowed enough to catch her breath.

Before long, Abby wished she'd thought to grab a bottle of water along with her wallet. The night was still warm, and she had a headache from the day's heat and her own emotional excesses. Water would have helped. She swallowed, but her mouth and throat were dry.

Stupid, she told herself. Once again she had jumped without looking, without a plan. But on she trekked. By morning she hoped to be somewhere far down the highway, on her way to Gainesville and a different life, no matter how rough the beginning might be. Maybe in a few weeks she could go back to Wildwood, after she had her feet under her, a job, a place to live. She would go back only long enough to gather up the critical things from the house, and she'd get Judy and Drew to go with her. After this debacle with Cade Latimer and his truck, she'd never again feel reluctant about revealing the truth of the relationship she had with Marsh. Marsh had played on her pride and her humiliation to keep her in thrall, but never again.

"I was stupid not to tell Judy the first time he hit me," she said aloud now. Her voice sounded strange in the darkness. Judy would have helped, Abby knew that now. Distance from the situation had lent the necessary perspective at last.

A ways off she heard a soughing, rushing noise, and before long a light, dancing breeze cooled her sweaty skin. She lifted her face to the sky and saw the fat bulges of thunderheads blotting out stars. Summer thunder was more common in the sauna conditions of afternoon, but not unknown at night. As she looked up, the clouds lit from within, heat lightning flickering inside. The breeze increased, gusting past her, and bringing with it the electric stink of ozone.

At first the breeze was like the wet warmth from a steaming shower, but it quickly pushed the heat away and brought the rich scent of wet earth and thirsty greenery quenched by storm rains. The heat lightning became bolts shooting from cloud to cloud, blinding Abby so that she had to halt, eyes closed, until the afterimage faded and she could see to walk safely again. Clouds thickened overhead, and at last the moonlight was gone, leaving only the weird storm light and the gray marl to show her the way.

With a massive crack of lightning and a rumble of thunder, the rain crashed down as if someone had upended a bathtub. The rain was warm at first, but it rapidly cooled the air and Abby's overheated body. Within a few moments her clothes were as waterlogged as if she had plunged into the nearby river. A shiver trembled through her, followed by another, and then a third. Her pace slowed even more as her shoes became soaked and squishy, with the wet material rubbing her sockless feet in multiple places. She'd have blisters before long.

Soon the water on the road was deep enough to seep into her shoes just above the soles. She stayed on the crown of the road in pointless hope that the flood was shallower there, but each step became a slog, heavy and splashing, and the shivers increased. She clenched her jaw to keep her teeth from chattering.

It was just a thunderstorm, she told herself. It would pass in a few minutes. Florida storms didn't last. They passed like speeding trains and were gone. Her jeans grew heavy on her hips, dragged down with the weight of water. The seams felt cold and rough against her skin as she walked.

Stupid, she told herself again. *You should have known from the feel of the night we were due for thunder.* She knew she'd have done it all over again, though, given the chance. She didn't need to involve anyone else in her mess. She'd done enough harm. She wrapped her arms around herself, tucking her hands in her armpits, where there was little warmth.

Abby didn't hear the truck over the noise of the storm. It wasn't until she saw headlights splattering across the dimpled, streaming surface of the road that she knew Cade had found her despite her having slipped away without waking him. By now she was shivering uncontrollably. She thought about ducking into the pinewoods and running; it would be easy to disappear forever. But instead she stopped, turning. It could be only Cade, anyway. She already knew the sound of his truck's engine, familiar, and strangely welcome—the agent of her deliverance from Marsh. She stumbled to the side of the road, where the water rushed from the low crown and poured away into the sandy scrub and swampy river land beyond.

As the truck neared her position, the headlights dimmed from high beam to low. It pulled alongside, and Abby heard the clunk of the engine when Cade shifted out of gear and set the hand brake. There was a short, sharp screech as the passenger door opened. The dome light came on, and Abby looked into the dry interior with a longing nearly as intense as that she'd experienced at the convenience store earlier in the day.

Had it been less than a day? She felt as if she had been struggling along for hours. Maybe forever. She was so tired. Maybe she'd been wrong to sneak away. Maybe she didn't have to be afraid.

The warm, dry cab drew her, but Cade's face—tired, eyebrows drawn together in irritation, raw red scar and all—was a more welcome sight still. His blue eyes seemed to glow, and though his mouth should have been tight with annoyance, instead a smile was growing there. He wasn't angry with her. There wasn't something ugly lurking beneath the surface. He was Cade Latimer, a good man—she was sure of that—and even though he was an officer of the law, she didn't have to be afraid. He had changed clothes since she saw him last. The fishing vest was gone, and he was no longer wearing his sooty jeans.

Cade had come after her, but not to punish her. By now, Marsh would have hold of her arm to drag her to wherever she was supposed to be. If there were anyone else around, his excruciating grip would be hidden by her long-sleeved shirt, and his angry words would have been whispered in her ear. She shuddered and pushed the thoughts of Marsh away. Right now, the only thing she wanted more than to climb into the warm, dry truck was to have Marsh erased from the face of the earth and for her life to be normal again. Maybe that "normal" could even include friendships and relationships with someone decent, like Cade Latimer. Though why he'd bother with her, she couldn't think. Why he'd come after her at all—the thought filled her with irrational, giddy hope.

"I'm impressed," said Cade, speaking loudly to be heard over the flapping wipers and the downpour on the truck's roof. "You managed to get out of the camper without me hearing you. And Mort let you. I'll be damned if I can figure out how you charmed him."

Abby stared at Cade, rain running down from her hair, over her face, into the collar of her shirt. There was no hiding her nipples, hardened by the chill she felt after the rain had so abruptly cooled the night and her body, except by wrapping her arms around herself. She didn't speak. Her teeth were chattering too hard and she was afraid she would bite her tongue. In the back of the truck she could dimly see Mort's nose pressed against the side window, and the pale fog of his breath on the glass. A good dog, one she would have liked to know better. In so many ways Mort was a subtle echo of herself, as finely tuned to Cade's every movement and word as she had been tuned to Marsh's. The difference was obvious, however—Mort, while watching attentively for his master's commands, wasn't seeking to avoid the next blow.

Cade sighed and flicked off the slapping windshield wipers. It was as if the truck's heartbeat had suddenly ceased, leaving the hum of the engine and the noise of falling water everywhere, everywhere, everywhere. Abby suddenly noticed the cicadas had ceased their noise. It was a relief not to have that continual tension and screech. The rush of water and crashing thunder had taken its place. "I know you're not a criminal, Abby. You'll catch your death of pneumonia or be struck by lightning. You're probably well on your way to hypothermia. Get in."

As if to reinforce his words, lightning flickered in the distance and a slow, deep rumble of thunder wandered toward them. She knew the center of the storm was far away, and besides, she'd been out in thunderstorms for years, rejoicing in their violence before she understood what violence truly was. Marsh was the lightning—when it was close, it struck before she could hear the warning. Was Cade any different? Was he, a man so comfortable in his physicality, his strength, his command, the thunder? Was there a storm waiting within? Or was he what she thought—*hoped*—she sensed: an honorable man, confused by her irrational fears, but drawn nonetheless?

"Come on, Abby."

"Where will you t-take me?" The words were painful, spoken between jaws locked to keep from chipping her own teeth as they chattered.

"I *ought* to take you to a hospital. But I think instead I'll take you to a hotel and get you warm and dry."

Abby stood, undecided, at the side of the road, its surface softening beneath her feet. Standing at the edge as she was, runnels of water moved swiftly past her feet like waves racing back into the ocean. Soon there would be a newly eroded rut or two just next to her sneakers. She felt herself focusing helplessly on the water, the dirt, the silt, and bowed her head. She was defeated. The thought of a hotel room, comfortingly anonymous, two white-sheeted beds, white towels, tacky mass-produced artwork and a hot shower—maybe even a tub bath—made her guts twist with longing. To be safely indoors, and out of reach of Marsh's hands, and warm, and dry…

Cade cursed to himself, quietly, but saw Abby flinch even at that low volume. He cursed a second time and got out of the truck. It took only a moment to reach the back, lift the hatch and yank out an old quilt. Only two moments more to reach Abby herself and throw the quilt around her, ignoring her shudders as he wrapped her snug and then lifted her into the cab and closed the door. But in just those few moments, the rain had soaked his upper body and water ran down his face from his hair as he hurried around the truck to slide behind the wheel.

Before he pulled the door all the way closed, he looked at his passenger. The dome light revealed Abby was somewhere between relief and shock. Her face was drawn and pale, her eyes huge and fixed on his. She was shivering violently. What a strange mixture of strength and vulnerability she was. And how he longed to fix what was wrong here.

It would be easy.

He had her personal information; for a lawman like himself, finding Marsh would be child's play, probably no more complicated than a knock on Abby's front door. Beating the bastard to a bloody pulp—*Like that? Feel that? Not what you thought, is it, asshole?*—might be the greatest validation he'd felt in months, since being forced to leave the undercover task force. Even the sense of accomplishment he felt when he finished his K-9 training and returned to active duty with Mort as his partner would seem small in comparison.

And it would be the surest way to lose Abby forever—in a blink, just like that. She might want to see Marsh punished, but it would mean she could never feel secure with Cade, not ever.

Cade blinked at himself. That shouldn't matter to him. Thinking in terms of "forever" with a woman like Abby—there was no point. He had to find a way to turn this into just another job, just another case he was working. He was an idiot if he didn't distance himself from this problem. He had a life of his own, a vacation he was missing out on, a good job he enjoyed, even if it didn't fill all the voids in his soul.

He pulled the door shut and turned the truck's heater on full. Abby gasped at the blast of air, but then she moved her feet to be in the hot draft. Cade leaned across the cab once more and fastened her seat belt across her body, since her arms were bundled in the quilt like a caterpillar in a cocoon. Rain from a tendril of her hair fell on his neck, a drop like a tear, and Cade knew a powerful urge to find something with which to dry her face. He could see himself in his mind's eye, his much-washed bandanna handkerchief in his hand, wiping away the wetness and following up the tenderness with a kiss. Or six. Kisses accompanied by the slow peeling away of the damp quilt, and then the wet clothing beneath.

Hell, what was he thinking? Here she was, safe in his truck for now, and here *he* was, fantasizing about getting her to a motel room and taking off every stitch. He would tuck her into bed, slip under the covers with her and wrap himself around her until the shivering stopped. Perhaps she would sleep then, curled close in his arms, or perhaps he would turn her to face him, and kiss that soft, timid mouth until it opened beneath his and whispered his name. He would roll onto his back, bringing her with him, and she would set the pace there in the private cave of clean-smelling sheets and tacky motel bedspread. He couldn't think of a more satisfying way to warm them both through and through than sex.

But Abby would probably turn away from the approach of a face like his, ferociously scarred. His was the very visage of viciousness, even though she hadn't done more than anyone else would, gazing at the scarring until it lost its capacity to shock.

Abby's teeth chattered in a new wave of chills. Cade shook his head, shoving away the fantasy. Convincing his body to settle down was not as simple. Only time and distraction would quiet the sudden raging erection constrained within his jeans. He buckled his own seat belt and put the truck into gear. God only knew how far it was to the main road, and from there a hotel or motel—anything dry and sheltered from the savagery outside. Lightning flashed frequently now. A new band of the storm was well and truly upon them, more furious than the first. Best to put this unpaved road behind them as soon as possible, before it washed out altogether.

Thank God he'd found her when he had.

Ten rough, jouncing minutes later he finally found the paved road. He stopped, looking at Abby. "Which way to town?"

Her teeth were still chattering, and he knew he had to get her really warm soon. She probably needed fluids, as well. Her head bobbed hard to the left. "The i-interstate is that way. Maybe something at the Micanopy exit-t, the one north of this one."

"How far?"

"T-ten miles?"

Cade stretched to the vents on her side of the cab and aimed them directly at her. "Are you warmer, at least, Abby?" The blast was making him sweat.

"A l-little."

"We've got to get you warm and dry, real soon now." He looked to the right. "What's that way?"

Abby shrugged, a motion that was hard to detect in the dark because of her shivering and the bundle of the quilt. "I can't r-remember. It's b-been too long."

He looked both ways, and at last turned left. At least the interstate would mean he was that much closer to a town or a hospital if it came to that. It might also mean, if Marsh had the cops looking for her by now, that she'd be found, but he decided to take that risk. She'd left voluntarily and she was a grown woman. They couldn't force her to return against her will. He didn't have to mention she'd stolen his truck.

It wasn't ten miles to the interstate, but the storm didn't let up. The wind clipped small branches and cones from the pines along the road, sending them to the pavement like missiles. The road was half an inch deep in water, sluicing over the surface and forcing him to be cautious or risk hydroplaning. The windshield wipers couldn't cope with the heavy rain unless he drove much slower than the posted speed. Abby continued to shiver, though Cade thought perhaps the shivers were less frequent.

At the interchange was only a gas station that sold bait, but it was locked and dark. Cade muttered under his breath and paused, trying to decide whether to head south or north. When he turned his head toward Abby, she leaned forward, meeting his eyes in the dim light from the dashboard.

"P-please, Cade. Not s-south. Not yet."

South meant home for Abby. Home, and Marsh. Cade gritted his teeth and turned north, rewarded by her soft exhale and the barest slump as she relaxed against the seat belt and the door frame.

The interstate was even wetter, if possible, than the back roads had been. More open to the elements. Oncoming headlights seemed exaggerated in the water streaming from the sky, and lightning added to the distraction. The truck's pace was frustratingly slow, but as they crept along, a highway sign appeared at last, advertising a motel. Cade let out breath between his teeth. "You'd better be open," he muttered to the sign.

Luck was with him. The next exit ramp led them down a slight slope and curved directly toward a small motel, none of the big chains, just a small old-fashioned vee of a place with two wings of cinder block rooms flanking a central office. Cade pulled up to the office and killed the engine. He pocketed the keys with a significant look at Abby, who smiled sheepishly. "Stay put, or I'll send Mort to find you. And don't think he won't bite you, even if he's decided he likes you. He does what I say."

"I know." She sat there in the light from the dome, rain-darkened hair clinging to her cheeks, her arms still inside the quilt, the fingers of one hand gripping the quilt's edge and keeping it snug against her neck. Impulsively he reached out and touched her shoulder through the quilt.

"I won't be long."

She closed her eyes, nodding.

Inside the motel's rinky-dink office, Cade leaned on the buzzer to summon someone. From the rooms behind the office, he could hear thuds and a groan. Several moments later a tousled-haired man stumbled into the office, belting a bathrobe.

"Kinda late to be out, bad night like this," he said with a yawn into Cade's face. "Need a room?" Then the man blinked, catching sight of Cade's scarring, and took the slightest step backward.

Cade wondered what the man must think, seeing

a monster in his office on such a wild night. "Yes, please. I apologize for the lateness, but the storm got to be too much. I decided to play it safe and pull off the road for a rest."

The man nodded and rasped his hand over his face, in the same place Cade's scars were, as if he were feeling for himself his own skin was still intact.

"Industrial accident." Cade gestured briefly to the scar and tried on a smile. "I know it's off-putting, but it's not contagious." How many times in the past few years had he said those exact same words, apologizing for other people's misperceptions and superstitious fear? It wasn't his fault, yet it was his problem. Every single time. It was rare for someone not to mention the scarring, even on brief acquaintance, and the frightened stares of children in grocery stores sometimes made Cade want to leave civilization altogether.

The man shook his head, clearly readjusting his thoughts and assessment of Cade. "I didn't mean to stare. It's just startling, middle of the night and all. I guess I've seen too many scary shows on the TV. I got two rooms left, one on the far end. Queen bed. Will that do ya?"

Cade knew he ought to ask for a double room. Two beds, not one. They were both exhausted; they should sleep. But the image of Abby held close in his arms crashed over him like an ocean wave, and he nodded. "The one with the queen bed is fine." He handed over his credit card, signed the slip. The man slid the key over the counter, and Cade tucked it into his shirt pocket, plunging out into the downpour.

Abby was still in the cab, but her shivers had returned while the truck's engine and heater were off. "It won't be long now," Cade promised. He cranked the engine to move the truck the several yards down the parking lot to the room, and Abby burst into tears.

"Oh, for the love of— What is it now?"

"Th-th—"

"What?" He backed the truck into the parking space at the very end.

"Thank you." Her words were a tortured whisper, and she stared at him with tear-wet eyes.

You wouldn't thank me if you could see what's in my head, Abigail McMurray. If you could see how much I want to keep you with me, how I want to peel away that wet cloth and taste your cold skin and—

"Stop. Just—stop. Let's get you inside. Stay put, let me get the door open and Mort inside and I'll come right back for you." He himself was beginning to shiver from his repeated wettings. How much more chilled must she be, even wrapped in the quilt? People had been known to die from hypothermia in the torrid depths of a Florida summer. He jumped out of the truck and went to the back for Mort, who leaped out, ears flattened in the storm, and stayed at his heel while he opened the motel room door and flicked on a light. Cade pointed to an empty spot on the carpeted floor beside the bed—*one bed, just the one bed, just that one, soft, warm bed*—and commanded, "Mort, *platz*." Mort curled up there, nose on paws, ears pricked and eyes on Cade.

He ducked back into the storm and opened the passenger door. Abby pushed with her feet and shuffled over the bench seat. Cade didn't wait for her to step out. He slid an arm beneath her knees and his other arm behind her back, and swept her out of the cab. Abby gasped in protest, but he ignored her and hurried with her into the room. He set her on her feet next to the television.

"I'm going to grab some stuff from the truck. Get out of those wet things and into a hot shower, Abby." He went out once more into the storm, and reached inside the back of the truck for a blanket for Mort to lie on, and the zippered kit containing his gun and other equipment. He grabbed his duffel, tucked it under his arm and secured the truck before hastening indoors, closing the door behind him and fastening every locking mechanism the door possessed.

Abby still stood in the middle of the room, bundled in the quilt. She stared blankly at him. Shudders racked her frame. The quilt was sagging from her shoulders, but she had not made any progress toward the shower. Cade put everything down on the tiny, cheap dresser with a sigh. "Abby, why aren't you in the shower? You've got to get warm, baby." Her head turned and she tried to speak, but her teeth were once again chattering so hard that Cade was afraid she would bite her tongue. He heard his own words and wanted to cringe, but the endearment had slipped out so naturally that he couldn't stop it. He went to her and took her gently by the shoulders.

"Here. Sit. Let's get your shoes off." He pressed her down to the edge of the bed. She sat, still shaking uncontrollably, and Cade knelt in front of her, lifting each foot and pulling off the sodden sneakers while her legs jerked. He saw the raw spots at her heels and insteps where the shoes had rubbed on her feet. Abby's eyes were fixed on his, great dark pools of uncertainty, following his every move, dropping to his mouth when he spoke, and occasionally flicking to his hands as if she must always be on watch for every least cue to his next move.

Oh, yes…Marsh had a lot to answer for.

Cade controlled the abrupt movements his hands wanted to make at the thought of what Marsh had done to Abby, how Marsh had changed this vital woman into a trembling, frightened child. He set the shoes aside, tongues pulled high to dry. He rose to his feet and drew Abby up with him. She didn't seem able to make it to the shower under her own power. He pushed the quilt off her shoulders and draped it over a chair so it might begin to dry out. Then he put his hands on her shoulders again and looked her in the eye.

"You've got to get warm, Abby. I'll help you. We'll shower together."

Abby tried to shake her head, and Cade continued. "In our clothes. We both need to get warm, and our clothes are soaked already. It won't matter." As he spoke he emptied his pockets of wallet and keys and damp handkerchief, and turned Abby gently so he could fish her wallet out of her back pocket for the second time that day. He toed off his own shoes and stepped close, putting an arm around her to help her into the motel room's bathroom. Holding her was like holding a wild animal, all wiry trembling and tight muscles and fear. She stumbled as they walked, so Cade pulled her closer and took more of her weight in the bend of his arm.

The bright light of the bathroom made Abby flinch again. Cade settled her next to the wall, where she could lean, and opened the small shower stall's door. A few quick twists of his hands started the water flowing. He waited for it to warm, then stepped into the shower himself and held out his hand to Abby. The hot water cascading over him felt wonderful, melting the chill, but also soaking his clothing the rest of the way and making his jeans sag on his hips. She stared at him with those huge eyes before she put her hand in his and let him guide her over the short sill. He closed the stall door behind her and moved her carefully into the stream of water.

Chapter 8

The spray of deliciously warm water hit Abby in the middle of her back. Cade's hands were at her hips, steadying her. She was glad of the support, even though she felt a pang of aggravation at herself for her own inadequacies. How stupid of her, really, to creep away in the night in the middle of a thunderstorm. She had known in her soul that he didn't intend to turn her in for her crime. Had known it, really, from the moment the whole sordid story burst from her and he'd shifted to her side of the picnic table to offer a shoulder and the strength of his arms around her. Maybe even before that, when he uncuffed her hands and allowed her to tend to his head wound.

She really didn't deserve such consideration. She'd been stupid, selfish and careless and had endangered him—unintentionally, it was true—and his dog. Hot tears filled her eyes, and she turned her face up into the stinging spray to hide them from Cade's perceptive, incredible blue gaze. She couldn't keep crying like this, he would think she was a fool.

Well…really, she was. A fool to have slid into the morass that was her relationship with Marsh. A fool not to have seen how each tiny step forward Marsh took was one more step that backed her toward the cliff, until only his grip on her kept her from falling over the edge, completely within his power. She'd encouraged his daily phone calls out of loneliness. She'd allowed him to forward his mail to her house when he took his leave of absence to help her with the day care. When it seemed more reasonable to move him into the guest room rather than pay for a hotel, she'd suggested it. She'd put him on the checking account. She'd even allowed him to tell her what to wear and how to style her hair. She herself had cut off her friends, fearing they would see the telltale marks on her and force her to face what frightened her most: living without a man in her life, even a man like Marsh, to keep the problems at bay. Problems she should have been able to address herself, or with hired help. It didn't require a life partner to feed lunch to six disabled adults. It didn't require someone else on the checking account for her to pay the bills. It didn't require a man to deal with the automobile repair shop.

When Cade had asked her, as they lay in the bed of the pickup, waiting for sleep, "Why didn't you leave before now, Abby? Why did you wait so long? What stopped you?" she hadn't responded. Yet some small part of her had glowed into hope.

Because it *could be* that simple. All she had to do, really, was make a few telephone calls. Go through a few official channels to shut down the day care as far as the state was concerned; the clients would find somewhere else eventually, and in the meantime they'd be out of Marsh's reach, though she didn't really think he'd take out his ire on them. Close the bank account. Put the house on the market and never go back.

Never.

Go.

Back.

Abby's heart raced so hard she thought it would burst. She shifted to look at Cade, who stood outside the stream of warm water, ensuring that she stayed in it.

She gazed at him in amazement. His eyes were closed in the spray that splattered from the walls of the small space. After Marsh, how could she trust her own judgment, even when everything inside her shouted that *this* man was good? What else did she have besides intuition, except her wallet and the clothes on her back? Even if Cade wasn't exactly selfless, he wasn't destructive. He was strong. He was scarred, but not bitter about the disfigurement that had to have made his life more difficult than it should have been.

Cade must have sensed her scrutiny. His eyes opened. His hands moved from her hips to her shoulders and gripped there, tightly—almost unbearably tightly—and then abruptly released her and floated the barest half inch above her body. She saw the effort it took to control himself—*saw* him control himself, in a way Marsh had never done.

"Cade," she whispered. She wondered if he could hear her over the pounding water, but in the end it didn't matter if he could or not. He read his name on her lips, and a moment later his head swooped. Again that iron control snatched him back and his lips hovered…waited.

Abby was the one who tilted her head the minuscule amount that allowed their lips to touch, and it was as if she had flung wide a locked gate. Cade's mouth came full onto hers, settling with the shocking skill of long familiarity, and her lips parted willingly, eagerly. The shivering had nearly stopped in the heat of the shower, but a new trembling began deep inside her, something born of that small coal of hope. There was a brief moment of wondering if he would touch her as he might touch something delicate and easily broken, but then his hands settled on her shoulders with the same surety of touch with which he had handled her as he handcuffed her, or touched Mort. Firm. Confident. But also gentle. It was welcome, despite the months of Marsh's angry touch.

His big body moved close and his hands slid around her. She felt him twitch when the shower struck his face, but he never released her mouth. He fed there, nibbling, sucking, stroking. Asking, not demanding. Coaxing, not coercing. Hungering, not devouring.

Abby's fingers clenched in the wet fabric of his T-shirt. Her bent arms were caught between them, maintaining distance. The water streamed over their faces and down their bodies. When Cade's hands moved firmly up her back, she felt the drag of wet cloth against wet skin. The intensity of her need to feel his hands on her—without cloth between—made her gasp and turn her face away from his. Cade lifted his head sharply and she knew she'd given him a signal that said stop. His hold slackened and he moved back half a slippery step on the puddled floor of the shower. His scar stood out in harsh relief, raised and stark against the flush of his unscathed skin. Her eyes went to it, sought its radiating edges, and then followed the path down to those blue, blue eyes, now dark with pupils communicating his desire.

But she didn't want him to stop—far from it. She wanted to finish the dream begun in the heat of the night, before the storm. She wanted to know if the touch of his hand would be as sweet and sure as she imagined it. Abby groped for the shower knob behind her, still gazing into Cade's eyes.

"Are you warm enough?" His voice was husky.

"Almost." Her hand shook, but with excitement and not fear or chills, as she tried to turn off the water. Cade reached past her to complete the task.

"You…uh, should get out of those wet clothes."

"I know." Her voice was a mere whisper when she added, "Will you help me?"

It was as blatant a request as she dared to make. Abby bit her lip, wondering what he must think of her now.

"Holy hell, Abigail..."

"I know we hardly know each other—I know I stole your truck. You have every reason to say no and I know I—" The rest of her panicky disclaimers faded when Cade's big hands went to the buttons on her shirt. He fisted the much-washed blue chambray, tugging it from the waistband of her jeans, separating the shirtfronts. Beneath was the practical cotton-lycra fabric of her brassiere. Cade was deft as he rid her of the soaked garment, slipping the straps down her arms before the bra joined her shirt on the shower floor, but then he noticed the dimming sunsets of bruises along her ribs and the sides of her breasts. She saw Cade's flat belly, clad in the clinging wet T-shirt, suck far under the staves of his ribs with his angry reaction.

"I have a lot of bruises," she said hastily, clutching at his hands. "They're healing. They mostly don't hurt anymore, but I know how they look—"

Cade bent, and pressed his mouth to the dark shadow of a bruise on the softly rising curve of her left breast. "Hush. Hush. I know." He pulled away from her and met her gaze while he peeled off his shirt. At his collarbones she saw more scars, angry dapples where the corrosive had spattered. Below the strong articulation of bone and tendons was his naked chest, sleek with water and lightly furred with glinting sandy hairs at his sternum.

"There's something I want to tell you. He… Marsh… We…never *did* it, not like that—other things, but not that. Ever." Fierce emotion and longing clutched at her heart and her lungs and she stumbled forward to bury her face against him. While she leaned there, breathing hard and feeling water trickle down her body from her soaking hair, his arms came around her again.

"Did you think I'd reject you?" Cade whispered. "Did you?"

Abby didn't—couldn't—speak. Instead, flushing darkly, she nodded, but reached for his belt and pushed the end through the buckle. Beneath the fly of his jeans was a prodigious bulge that, when she opened the zip, gave a muscular flex that reminded her of the muscles of his throat working as he swallowed half her bottle of juice earlier in the day. She bit her lip again and closed her eyes when she pushed his jeans over his hips and heard them slap wetly on the shower floor around his ankles.

"Hell." Cade's voice was harsh. "Tell me you mean to go through with this, Abigail. Tell me you want what's going to happen. Tell me I can take these wet clothes off you and carry you to that bed in there and—"

"Yes. Yes. Yes." On a tiny laugh, she added, "Please."

From the instant of her acquiescence it was only seconds before the rest of her clothes were heaped on the floor with his. When Cade opened the shower door, cool air rushed over her skin and pebbled her nipples. He breathed another oath and caught her up against himself, arms beneath her buttocks, lifting her so he could take first one nipple in his mouth and then the other. Abby inhaled shakily, her fingers clenching on his shoulders, her head tossing backward. He shifted her in his arms with a small bouncing hop and guided her legs around his narrow waist. She felt the hard length of him pressing against her and snuggled her pelvis close. Nothing mattered now, nothing except sensation, and the slippery wetness of their skin sliding together. Cade stumbled out of the shower with her, fumbling the bathroom door open. In the few steps it took to cross the room to the bed, Abby felt his hips moving against her tender flesh and cried out in pleasure. With a wriggle she sought to position herself so that he was at her entrance. If Cade didn't enter her soon, sate the terrible demands of the flesh between her legs, she was sure she would die.

He tumbled her onto the bed and turned away to scrabble through the duffel at the side of the bed. "Damn it. Damn it!" Mort raised his head to look at his master.

"Cade—Cade, what's the matter?"

"Rubbers—I mean, condoms—where the hell did they go?"

Abby heard the urgency in his voice, and felt a wash of happiness heat her skin. She sat back on her heels and watched his lean figure as he tossed one item after another to the floor.

"Take your time."

"Are you out of your mind, woman? I can't risk you changing your mind."

"I won't." Abby slithered off the bed and pressed herself against his back, wrapping her arms around his middle and taking his erection in her wet hands, learning the shape of him, the way bone articulated with bone and muscle gave way to the eager evidence of his desire. A few strokes of her palms hardened him even further. She could feel her own eagerness in the trembling of her insides and the throbbing moist nest at the top of her thighs. It had been so long since she had felt desirable, and even longer since she'd *wanted* this way. What most surprised her was the boldness she felt. She was startled by the lack of dread, and even the lack of guilt. She hadn't had sex since Gary died—the *things* she did with, or rather *for* Marsh didn't count. There was no emotion involved except fear.

"Don't...*do*...that...please, Abby. Just get in the bed. Get under the covers. I— Ahhh, your hands feel good. Let me alone long enough to find these damned rubbers. *Condoms*."

A bubble of laughter broke free of her. The laughter felt honest and wonderful, as if it had torn something dark and sharp away from her and banished it. There was Cade, buck naked in a cheap motel room, worrying about using the polite term for a prophylactic.

He turned on her with a triumphant growl, rending a foil packet in his fingers. "Don't laugh at me. Just because I seem a little—overeager—that's no reason to laugh." The smile on his face belied his words. Abby backed toward the bed, beginning to feel cold again. Though the shower had warmed her considerably, she'd still been chilled to the bone, and when Cade flung back the top covers and sent pillows scattering to the four winds, she was more than willing to scramble over the sheets. Cade joined her and yanked up the sheet and bedspread over them both. His hands were briefly busy at his crotch, and then he reached for her, tangling his hand in her hair. Her wet hair was still draining water freely down her neck and shoulders, transferring to his face and body as he tugged her close.

"I'm soaking wet," Abby said, looking down at his chest, where rivulets of water had begun to pool on his sternum. Lying down, he didn't seem so bulky and tall, but his muscularity was still more than apparent in the ease with which he manipulated her, shifting her to pull her leg across him and in the process bringing her entire body to lie atop his.

"Please-God-let-it-be-so," he breathed.

Abby laughed, out loud and happily. Cade stared at her with an expression akin to wonder. They lay beneath the covers, heedlessly soaking the sheets, until something more intense than humor began to take root. Cade's hands shifted from her body to cup her cheeks, his fingers pushing past her ears and into her wet hair. He looked for several long moments at her mouth, his eyes growing heavy-lidded. His thumbs brushed across her lower lip.

"I probably shouldn't tell you I've been thinking about this half the day. And almost all night. When I caught up with you on the road I wanted to warm you exactly this way. Bring you into my bed, hold you. Touch you. More than touch you." There was a catch in Cade's voice that surprised her with its sweet roughness, its naked honesty.

Abby couldn't quite tell him about the dream that had wakened her, the dream of Cade making love to her. Instead she turned her lips against his palm and pressed a shaky kiss there. Now that they were out of the steamy intimacy of the shower stall, naked in bed together, virtually at the point of intercourse, she found herself strangely shy. It made no difference that she could feel the hard length of him raised between her thighs, the occasional throb reiterating his arousal. How should she go about asking a stranger to please come inside her body? With Gary she had never needed to ask; he knew her so well. She turned her eyes to Cade's and met and held his gaze. Please let him read her shyness and take the decision out of her hands.

Cade saw uncertainty enter Abby's expression and realized he was rushing her, that his baldly stated admission was probably off-putting.

It was too soon for him to be making love to her. Bruised and battered as she was, she could only be capitulating out of fear or seeking to placate him.

But by God, he wanted her more than he'd ever wanted a woman. Wanted to feel her body warming to his touch, see her arch in the pleasure he knew he could give her. Knew, too, that the scar on his face didn't disgust or alarm her. He remembered the gentleness of her fingers as she cleaned his scalp wound and lightly traced the barest edge of his burn. Remembered the thrum of electricity that skittered over his skin and heralded a different kind of awareness of her—no longer only a criminal in his mind, but a woman.

Last of all he replayed the long minutes she had spent in his arms, awkwardly held by him as she sobbed out her terrible story. Those minutes had entirely changed his view of her, and himself, as well.

"Abby, I—" He was about to tell her he'd changed his mind, though he thought the unsatisfied desire might halfway kill him, when her head turned and she kissed his palm. She looked back at him, lips warmly parted but eyes meeting his with hesitation, and Cade was stunned by the realization that she simply didn't know how to continue the dance they'd begun in the shower. He brought her lips to his and felt the tension begin to melt out of her.

Take it slow. It was desperately difficult to hold on to that thought with Abby sprawled above him and his erection lying snug along her crease. The small writhing movements she made as he kissed her obliterated good intentions and made him crave the sweet release of burying himself in her body. He could feel her arousal in the slipperiness of her flesh against his as she moved. It would be so easy and so utterly satisfying to reverse their positions, catch the backs of her thighs in his hands and *take* her.

The urge was so strong that he had to let go of her with one hand and clench it in the sheets to control himself. A moment later he released the sheet because her mouth had opened and she was gasping something against his lips, something he urgently wanted to hear but couldn't make out. His hand came to rest against her hip and suddenly there was no turning back, not when he could cup the sweet flare of her iliac crest in his palm and from there slip his hand lower, and lower still, until he was pushing her back against him and his thumb slid between their bodies.

Abby *did* arch in pleasure at his touch. Her upper body lifted away from his and Cade watched with desire-slitted eyes as she caught her lower lip between her teeth. The shattered groan she gave when his thumb stroked the slick bud of flesh it found was nearly enough to make him come on the spot.

"How about you ride?" he managed to choke out.

"What?" Abby looked down at him, confused, her back still arched, breasts jutting forward.

"You set the pace, baby," Cade heard himself say, giving voice to the fantasy that had so aroused him only an hour ago in the truck. "It's all up to you.... It's all for you."

"I—I feel so clumsy, Cade. I'm not good at this. It's been so long—"

"I can help." *Sure you can. You can wait. You're a grown man.* He stroked a hand down her body, brushing her breast and lingering to stroke the puckered peak. He wanted to pinch the nipple, watch her head fall back in the passion he thought he could evoke, but the bruises deterred him. *Easy. Be tender.* "Lift up, just a little."

Abby, trembling, did as he suggested. Cade watched her closely as his fingers slid between her legs and stroked her. Her eyes closed when he pressed a finger into the sweet, dark center of her desire. Her flesh was snug around his finger, snug but slick. She would feel better than good around him—she would be a haven of heat, a silky grip. He stroked the inner walls once, twice, and heard her moan softly.

There could be no more waiting, not for him. His stroking hand shifted to guide her pelvis back and up. And then he was in and Abby was settling slowly onto him, her eyes dark and distant, as if her focus was turned inward and she could see what was happening where their bodies joined.

The thought made him arch upward and he learned how deep she was—deep enough to take him, all of him, yet she was lusciously snug. He let go of her hips and clenched his fists in the sheets again. Thank God the rubber helped, reducing sensation just enough that he thought perhaps he might be able to hold out more than a few thrusts before convulsing in his climax. He wanted more than anything not to leave Abby unsatisfied. He had already pictured her orgasm in his mind, her skin flushed, eyes closed, head hanging down and hair tossing while he parted her the way a stone in a stream parted the current around itself.

Abby slumped forward when he pushed inside her, catching her balance with her palms over his pectoral muscles. He heard her panting harshly, and then she gave a sudden gasping moan that dwindled into the half-sung sweetness of a sigh. A moment later she began to move and Cade was lost. His hands moved to her hips and helped drive the slow, rocking grind of her body against his own. It was better for both of them when he snugged her body tight against his own. His restriction of her movements meant she pressed harder, striving for more and more friction. With a cry she was there—he felt the clench of her around him—and her climax was just as he had pictured it, the flush of blood over her skin and the boneless rag-doll tumble of her against his chest.

"Baby," he heard himself saying again as he let himself follow her into the maelstrom, where the slowing rhythm of her hips and his deep strokes were all he needed, all he could feel. "*Baby.* Abby."

So much what he'd pictured, right down to the slightly stunned look on her face when she lifted her head from his chest and pressed a slow, deep, open-mouthed kiss on his lips. Cade, mindful that the condom was probably filled to near-bursting, shifted his hips away from her and helped her slide gently to the side. He pulled her close once more, pillowing her head on the bulge of muscle between his shoulder and upper arm. Her breathing was still quickened, and with her heavy head resting on his shoulder he could feel his own pulse hammering hard down his arm. She lay with her eyes closed, leaving Cade free to gaze down her body at her curves, the way her breast trembled with each fierce beat of her heart.

What he hadn't pictured was the way the rush of blood made the bruises stand out on her tender skin. The thought of someone touching her in anger was like a brand burning his brain. He kicked a little to bring the tumbled covers into reach and pulled them over their still-damp bodies, cooling rapidly now that passion had left them beached, tired and sated.

Minutes later, Abby gave a giant twitch like a toddler settling into sleep. It half wakened her enough to turn her head toward Cade, and ask him if he needed more room in the bed.

"I've got what I need," he told her softly. "Sleep." He was aware of the wetness of the sheets they lay between, and as he ran a hand down her flank, felt the coolness of her skin. He moved them both so that she lay cupped in the bend of his body, his knees drawn up to warm her as much as possible. She murmured again, but he felt the sudden laxity of her muscles and knew she had fallen asleep. He lifted his head enough to see his watch on the nightstand.

Four in the morning. The time he always wakened and rehashed old debts, wounds and aggravations. The time he remembered the hypophosphorous acid at the meth lab flying his way too quickly for him to do more than fling up an elbow, how the liquid seared away skin and scored muscle. The period in the hospital afterward when he knew he'd have a face of sorts, but more important, undamaged vision. The time he remembered reporting for duty and being told he couldn't do undercover work anymore, he was too distinctive. The time he thought about walking away from law enforcement entirely, walking away from his life. The time he saw the faces of old girlfriends, trying to hide their revulsion at the raw meat that had once been a face, pleasant and balanced if not exactly handsome.

Four in the morning. He should have been exhausted enough to sleep. Sex should have been the sweet end to a long but perversely rewarding day, yet all Cade could feel was a sense of dread. He didn't want to think about what had to happen next. Abby seemed to fit him like the matching ragged end of a broken bone, but what did that even mean? Where was there a path forward for two people like them?

Four in the morning. He stroked Abby carefully and got no reaction. She was deeply asleep at last, despite the last of the thunder outside and the noise of the rain on the roof, and the heavy splatter of water overflowing the motel eaves. He eased himself out of the bed and went into the bathroom to clean himself up and take a piss. It might be easier to think clearly if he could see his own eyes in the mirror, mine their blue depths for what little sense was left. Get that grip on reality he needed so badly, because at the moment all he wanted to think about was ways to convince Abby to leave behind everything in that rattletrap little town of Wildwood and come away with him.

Maybe even forever.

His big hand pushed the bathroom door closed, and then he leaned his forehead against the door, which smelled more of paint than wood. *That's stupid talk, Latimer. The woman has serious trouble written all over her.*

Trouble, yes—but Cade would have bet his life—even Mort's—that the worst thing Abby had done in her life was steal his truck out of desperation. That kind of trouble he understood. She'd gotten herself the hell out of a rough situation. Maybe it wasn't the best solution, but it was a step. How many women had he seen who hadn't made it this far before someone broke them for good? And how many had he seen who got this far, and then went back?

He pushed away from the door and met his own blue gaze in the mirror. Good eyes, yes—they'd always been his best feature, the one that conned the ladies and the crooks alike. Sincerity writ large and clear, impossible to look away from, impossible to doubt.

Cade turned to the shower, where their soaked clothing was still in a heap, draining in a slow trickle. With a small smile at the memory of that delicious encounter, he bent to wring them out and hang them where they might stand a chance of drying sometime in the next week. Then he took a few minutes for himself before he padded silently back to the bed and the uncommon luxury of nestling behind a sleeping woman who woke only long enough to speak his name.

It went through him like a spear, that soft murmur.

He'd just have to convince Abby to stay with him, where she would be safe.

He and his blue eyes. He had nothing else.

The storm had left Wildwood clean and cool, the sky blue as a little girl's hair ribbon. By noon it would be hot and humid again, building toward more afternoon thunderstorms. Marsh didn't care about the weather. All he cared about was getting the sign on the door, the one reminding families the day care was closed for the day. He was up and out well before the first client could've been dropped off—not that he expected any of them, since he'd warned their keepers the night before.

He was headed to the convenience store. He had a job to do. Abigail hadn't come home last night, and it was time he took things into his own hands.

The clerk on duty was exactly the sort of hipster pest Marsh hated most. Pierced and tattooed, growing a smudge he called a beard on his chin, hair looking unwashed and uncombed.

Disrespectful, that's what it was.

Marsh clenched his hands on the steering wheel and tried to convince himself Abigail wouldn't have slept with a little weasel like the one standing behind the cash register handing a pack of smokes to a customer. The kid was nothing like Gary or himself, too young, fresh-faced and fresh-mouthed, certainly, but that might make the kid ripe for the picking if Abigail turned on the charm.

He could feel his face reddening. His pulse stepped up a little, revving to that point he sometimes felt when Abigail made a mistake that needed correcting, or when he found himself wanting her, aroused and yet unable to follow through on the most basic of male duties because too much was at stake. He could practically see her leaning on the convenience store counter, gray eyes full of smiles.

Smiles for someone other than Marsh. It had been

a long time since Abigail smiled at him. For him. With him.

Marsh unbuckled his seat belt and stepped out of the Honda. He stood next to it, head down, breathing deeply, until he felt he could go into the store and not instantly reach to throttle the hipster behind the register.

Maybe coffee would help. The rye had done a number on his head, left him feeling fuzzy, less acute than it had done formerly. It had been a long time since he'd last polished off a bottle. Aspirin had taken the edge off, but coffee might finish the job. Of course, sleeping on the floor in the front hallway hadn't been the best idea he'd had lately, but he'd been waiting for her to come home. One more thing to lay at Abigail's feet. He lifted his head, took a deep, calming breath and pushed open the glass door.

"Morning," said Marsh, as he headed for the back of the store where the coffee urns waited.

"Good-looking day out there! Did you hear that monster of a thunderstorm last night?" The hipster was grinning like a fool. Marsh didn't doubt the kid had been out in it, dancing in the lightning. Too bad it hadn't struck him. "Just let me know if I can help you find anything. Got a great twofer on candy bars up here at the counter."

"Coffee to start." Marsh put a cup beneath the spigot of the urn marked Dark Rich Roast and twisted the lever. Brown liquid gurgled into the foam cup, but it didn't look dark or rich to Marsh. He capped it with a couple of tubs of too-sweet creamer and stirred slowly, giving himself a chance to think.

"Hey, I hear ya. Can't think without my caffeine, either."

Marsh's hand tightened on the cup. The coffee level rose dangerously, threatening to slop over the rim. *Shut up. Shut up before I make you shut up.* He let go and reached for a lid before he made a mess. Carrying his cup to the register required every ounce of control he possessed. He had to be sure he didn't walk as if he was angry, that his expression was schooled and bland.

"Yeah, heck of a storm last night. Which brings me to an important question for you." Marsh put the coffee on the counter, and the hipster punched it into the cash register. Marsh reached for the fabled twofer, twin candy bars he didn't want—his gut was still letting him have it about all the rye—and put them on the counter, as well.

"For me?" The clerk grinned again and pointed to Marsh's total, glowing green on the register's display.

"Yeah. I have this girlfriend, and I haven't been able to get hold of her since…oh, I guess it was about this time yesterday. She was coming here, I think, to pick up some stuff before she went to work. Maybe you saw her. After that storm, I'm kind of worried about her." There, thought Marsh, that had to be the right note to strike with this kid. He looked at that scruffy little beardlet, clinging to the underside of the kid's chin like mildew, and felt rage boiling anew at the thought that Abby had perhaps done something with the kid. Something she shouldn't. Something she hadn't done with Marsh.

Now the hipster looked right at Marsh, honest concern written in his clear brown eyes. "Wow, man, that doesn't sound good. What's your girlfriend look like?"

What Marsh wanted to say was "She's beautiful, but she was in love with my brother when she should have been in love with me. Now she's mine, and I'm going to find her and bring her home where she belongs. And you'd better not lie to me, you little jerk. I'll know it if you do."

What Marsh said was "Oh, about five-five, slender, light brown hair with blond streaks in it, gray eyes. Pretty."

"Yeah, she was here, buying chili and potato chips and juice, other stuff. I remember her. She comes in every now and then. Nice lady."

Marsh clenched his fists and put them below the counter, where the kid couldn't see. "Did you see her leave?"

The kid nodded, and pointed to Marsh's total again. Marsh grimaced and dug for his wallet. "Yeah, she drove off."

"She…drove." It was a napalm news flash.

"Yeah. Big old red pickup truck." The beardlet rippled a little as the kid nodded.

Marsh carefully counted out three dollar bills. "Was she alone?" He thought the studied indifference was just right. He didn't care, no. He was just asking.

Just…asking. Just curious. Just a welfare check on someone he cared about.

"No, there was that guy. I figured he'd be driving again, since he drove in, but it was her behind the wheel, kinda in a hurry."

Marsh fumbled the coins the hipster put in his hand. They went everywhere, rolling across the floor, spinning, ringing loudly, the only sound he could hear except for his own brain sizzling.

Abigail was not alone. She was with another man, in a truck.

Marsh couldn't think. The store around him seemed to pulse like an obscenely inflated balloon.

"Whoa, you lost a quarter—over there." The hipster pointed.

"Which way did they go?" Marsh followed the quarter, trying to hide his clenching fists and reddening face from the fool behind the register. The words felt as if he had dragged them up from the depths of the earth, in a place where lava seethed and bubbled and melted everything it touched.

"Right there, by the potato chip rack—"

Marsh whipped up from where he had bent to pick up the quarter. "The truck. Which. Way. Did the truck. Go?"

"Oh." Marsh saw the beard again, in all its under-chin glory, stubbly and thin and patchy, as the kid tilted his head back, gesturing. "East. Toward the interstate, I guess."

The world began to dim around Marsh. He recognized the red rage he sometimes felt, the need to strike something, to set it right with violence. He went out the door, ignoring the kid's stupid, pointless bleating.

"Hey, man, don't you want your stuff? Your coffee?"

The interstate. A big old red pickup truck.

Marsh got behind the wheel of his silver Honda and headed east.

Chapter 9

It was all noise. Noise, and light. Noise, light and confusion. Abby turned onto her back and flung her forearm over her eyes to shut out the hot yellow glare from the motel window.

Motel window.

She sat bolt upright in the unfamiliar bed and then scrabbled for the sheets when she realized she was naked.

He was naked, too. Very naked, and doing something with a rustling plastic bag. That was the noise, that and the clink of metal against metal. She turned her head to look for its source and saw Mort with his head in a dish, crunching kibble with every appearance of relish.

Abby's stomach gave a long, loud growl in sympathy.

Cade, naked, glorious Cade, turned to look at her and a grin split his asymmetrical face. "I'm working on it, Abby. How does dry cereal and bad black motel-room coffee sound?"

"Heavenly." She smiled back, but then her bladder demanded her attention. "Er—excuse me while I… Could you maybe turn your back?"

Cade's grin turned into a lascivious smile that was nothing short of a proposition. He sauntered unabashedly to the bed, placed a hand on each side of her hips while she clutched the sheets to her chest and told her, "Nope." Then he kissed her.

He kissed her slowly; he kissed her thoroughly; he kissed her as if he had nothing he would rather do for the rest of his life. He touched nothing but her mouth, and when he had finished Abby could only stare into his eyes, feeling her lips throb and fighting the urge to lick his taste from them, catch and savor every last molecule. Cade's eyes really were *that blue.* They bore a certain sleepy, self-satisfied look—almost smugness—that nevertheless pleased her, for she knew she was the cause of it.

She was also, apparently, the cause of the erection that was lifting well past half-mast at his hips. He followed her gaze and one corner of his mouth quirked upward.

"Don't mind that. It'll settle down after a while."

"Er. If you say so. Cade, I need to use the restroom."

He levered himself away. "Far be it from me to interfere with a woman's bladder."

When he turned back to the cereal, Abby fled for the bathroom, closing the door on his murmured, "Nice ass," with her face flaming. She emerged ten minutes later, having resigned herself to wriggling into her chilly panties and the chambray shirt—both damp. The jeans were still dripping slowly from their hems and waistband, and reluctantly she hung them back over the shower rod to continue drying.

Cade was in the bed, sheets pulled up to his waist, she saw with relief. He had a cup of coffee in each hand and an open box of granola lay near his knee. Abby approached the bed shyly and perched on the edge, reaching to accept the coffee he held out to her. She decided to brazen out his knowing smile.

"You'll catch cold, outside the covers like that. I'm betting your clothes are still damp."

"You'd be right." She took a tentative sip of the coffee, and then a deeper gulp. It wasn't so hot that it burned, but it felt good as it went down her throat. It had been more than twenty-four hours since the last cup, surely. She looked around for a clock but could find only the watch on Cade's wrist. She craned her neck to look and gasped. "Is it really two in the afternoon?"

"Guess we needed the rest." Cade dug into the box of granola, and Abby's stomach announced its needs again.

"Two p.m. I don't think I've ever slept so late in my life."

"I don't think you've ever had the kind of day you had yesterday, either. Eat some cereal. I'm sorry I don't have something more, but it's easy camping food. I don't want you fainting with hunger—we have things to do."

"Like what?" Abby scooped a handful of nutty oat clusters from the box and began to munch.

"Like walk the dog, find some real coffee and maybe some protein, and pay for another night here since we slept past checkout time."

Abby felt herself flushing again. "Cade, I—"

He interrupted her with a lifted hand, and she was riveted by those blue eyes once more. "If you're going to talk about how much you regret what we did last night—this morning, rather—don't. Because I don't have a single ounce of regret, Abby. In fact—" he gestured to his covered lap "—I'd be more than willing to repeat that activity. Just say the word."

"I don't regret it, either, but, Cade—" She faltered, unable to form her flickering thoughts into coherent sentences. Yesterday had been a day out of time, a day so fresh and raw it could never be repeated. Now it was a new day, and as Cade said, there were things to do, but they weren't the things he had listed. First she had to apologize yet again for what she'd done, and persuade him not to press charges if she would reimburse him for expenses and time lost.

She didn't want to think about where or how she could get the money. She could write a check and perhaps hide the check register for a few days, but eventually there would be trouble. She could not imagine explaining yesterday to Marsh, much less what she had done with Cade only a few hours ago.

Unless you really do make that break, Abby.

Perhaps the problem was more that she *could* imagine the explanation. She was paralyzed by the prospect of the confrontation, Marsh's terrifying and certainly physical reaction. She felt sick to her stomach, despite her hunger, at the thought of the beating. Mixed with the fear was the blinding exhilaration of the idea that she could just keep running, walk away from everything the way she'd thought in the shower last night. The whole mad balance was tipped by the elephant of guilt at leaving the people in her care behind. Hot tears threatened and she turned her face aside, but not before a drop welled and spilled.

"Hey. *Hey.*" There was a click as he set his cup aside, and then the rustling of the sheets. He took her coffee away, setting the cup next to his before pulling her easily into his arms. "Don't do that. You don't have to do that, not here, not with me."

"I can't help it." She turned her face into his throat to hide. "I'm just..."

"Afraid, I know."

Cade was a *man,* and her recent experience of men left a blackened crater where comfort should have been. But here he was, a near stranger, busily proving her wrong. He smelled so good. With her nose pressed to the hollow of his throat, his skin smelled soapy and warm, with a musk of sex and sweat. How a man could smell safe she didn't know, but Cade did. As her nose and cheek brushed blindly over his skin like a kitten seeking a nipple, she felt goose bumps rise, and his hold tightened. That muscular grip should have frightened her, but instead it made her turn her face up so her mouth was waiting when his descended. Probably Cade would see this as buying his forbearance with sex, but she couldn't resist. She wanted the comfort and the sweet oblivion that came with making love.

Cinched with his spare belt and generously cuffed at the hems, a clean pair of his jeans didn't look too bad on Abby's curves. Cade liked the way his shirt—a plaid flannel—positioned its buttoned pocket flaps at the peaks of her breasts. He could visualize the soft mounds beneath the fabric, the rose-taupe nipples.

And the bruises.

He scowled and turned away so she wouldn't see his face except obliquely. Abby was tucking the tail of the shirt into the jeans and blousing it, watching her reflection in the dull finish of the cheap mirror screwed to the wall above the dresser.

Mort waited patiently at the door, tongue out in his doggy smile, tail half-lifted. Afternoon light glowed at the edges of the curtains and sent a prism over the carpet from the peephole in the door. While Abby sat on the bed and laced her feet into her still-damp sneakers, Cade quickly checked his small duffel and made sure his gun was secured. He would lock it into the back of the truck with Mort while he and Abby ate.

"What are you hungry for, babe?" He turned, the duffel in his hands. Again the endearment slipped out before he thought to censor it.

Her slow smile, half-sleepy and satiated, nearly made him put the duffel back on the dresser and tumble her back onto the mattress. “Food.”

“You think you could manage something more specific?” He cleared his throat and swallowed hard. He felt himself harden, but a quick mental memory replay of booking an ugly dope dealer into the county jail calmed things down.

She pointed to the pile of damp, wrinkled cash on the dresser. “Whatever that’ll buy. I owe you, Cade. I owe you a *lot*. Much more than I have.”

He felt the *aw, shucks, ma’am* rising to his lips, and smiled instead. “I think we can eat real good for that. Ready?”

Abby got to her feet. “Starving.”

“I’ll drive, though.”

Cade was rewarded by her laugh, rich and genuine without a hint of nervousness or fear.

Micanopy’s live-oak-shaded streets were sleepy and hot in the late afternoon, and to the west, thunderheads were building. Kids on bikes zipped across the road in front of the truck, causing Mort to woof briefly from the back. Cade knew the town from previous enforcement visits, and followed turn after turn till he arrived at an out-of-the-way building perched on a weathered gray dock at the edge of a sea of sawgrass. In wet years, a lake flooded the area, but this late in the summer the lake had shrunk far out into its bed, leaving cracked greenish muck behind. A few cars were parked on the oyster-shell lot. Cade chose a spot in the shade, where the sinking sun would continue to miss the truck, saw to Mort's comfort with a little kibble and some water, and came around to where Abby waited, hands thrust into the pockets of the baggy jeans.

Country music spilled from the building as he tucked her hand into the bend of his elbow and led her up the sloping wharf. He could smell the sun-warmed creosote of the fat pilings, and listened to the creak and pop of the silvered boards beneath their feet.

"Best catfish in Florida," he said. "Or alligator tail, if you'd rather."

Inside, the smell of hot grease, grilled meat and fish nearly sent him to his knees, and from Abby's little moan, he knew she felt the same. His stomach growled in response. The hostess, a cheery girl in shorts and a T-shirt with the restaurant's logo on it, met them with menus and a smile.

"Deputy Latimer!" she said. "Long time no see." Her smile faltered the smallest bit as her eyes drifted over the scar, which he hadn't had last time he was in the place.

"Howdy, ma'am." He smiled at the hostess and touched a nonexistent hat brim. "It has been a while, hasn't it? Table for two? Maybe that one, by the window?"

Abby's hand had tightened in his elbow. He didn't look down at her—he could feel her gaze, narrowed and speculative, on him. Yeah, he'd cuffed her and held a gun on her, but he'd hidden most of the details of his rank and job in order to control what she knew about him, while he pried her story out of her. *Everybody's got their secrets in this game.*

He saw Abby into her booth seat with a gentlemanly flourish, then sat opposite her where he could keep an eye on his truck under the moss-hung oaks, and Mort's muzzle poking out the back hatch. The hostess's smile was still uncertain, as she adjusted to his changed status and unattractive, even frightening, appearance.

"Something to drink?"

"Two beers, whatever's on tap," Cade replied. Then he thought about what Abby might think of him, commandeering her preferences as though he had a right to do so, and said, "Unless you'd rather have something else?"

"Beer is fine," Abby dismissed. She opened her menu as the hostess turned away.

Cade looked at her studious disregard of him, and sighed. "Let's just get it over with."

"I think I had a right to know you're actually a deputy. Isn't that...part of my basic rights as a prisoner?"

"As if you have any right to dictate terms." He grinned to soften his words.

"I think you forfeited your right to judge me once you decided not to take me to jail. And now the...the sex has complicated the matter."

The two beers arrived, delivered by a college-aged kid with wiry hair and glasses, who followed up by tucking the tray under his arm and getting out his order pad and a pen. "Ready to order?" His eyes skittered over Cade's scar and moved to Abby's face.

Nice of the kid not to stare, though Cade understood he wanted to.

"I would like the fried catfish platter." Abby closed her menu and slid it to the edge of the table.

"I'll have the twelve-ounce steak, medium rare, and a baked potato with all the fixings."

"Got it." With a grin, the kid was gone.

Cade stuck his hand out across the table. Abby took it, bemused. "Let's just start this dance over. Cade Latimer, at your service. I'm a K-9 deputy with the Marion County Sheriff's Department. And for the record…the sex was great."

Abby flushed bright red to the roots of her hair. "Don't try to change the subject."

He shifted their handshake to a more gentle grasp, lacing his fingers with hers. "I meant what I said, but I see your point. And you?"

"Abby McMurray. Adult day care center operator, and car thief."

"Former car thief."

"Sure, okay." She pulled her fingers from his and drank a deep swallow of her beer. "You know, I'm still wondering why you didn't just haul me off to jail."

"I was curious, and you were—" A grin crooked at the side of his mouth. "You were sexy, and you just didn't seem like the type to go joyriding in someone else's beater truck. I had to know."

The waiter returned with a basket of soda crackers and a dish of butter pats perched on ice, and was gone again. Three minutes later he was back with small dishes of coleslaw, bright with flecks of red cabbage and carrot, and glossy with dressing. Cade and Abby fell on the salad like ravening wolves. The waiter hardly had a chance to reach the kitchen again before the dishes were empty.

Abby pushed away her bowl slowly. He watched her count forks and leave the sticky slaw fork in the bowl. Her mouth tightened the slightest bit, and he knew he was in for an interrogation. Funny, which of her mannerisms he'd homed in on, and how quickly.

"I want to ask you a question, but I don't want you to take it the wrong way."

"Shoot, Abigail."

Her mouth twisted in wry amusement. She'd corrected him enough, but he liked the reaction he got when he used her full name. She knew very well what he was doing. "I told you my story—"

"You mean I dragged it out of you kicking and screaming—"

"—and now I want yours. I want to know how you got that scar."

Cade could feel himself blanch, and then flush. This wasn't what he'd expected her to ask at all. "I know it bugs you—"

"Bugs me? What?"

"It turns women off."

She bit her lip, flushing as darkly as he, and looked shyly aside with an expression that made every cell in his shaft take notice. "I…think we, uh…proved that's not the case. More than once." When her gray eyes at last climbed back to his after lingering at his mouth, he flattened his palms on the tabletop and drew a deep breath.

"Holy hell, Abigail, if we weren't both half fainting from starvation, and if this weren't a public place—"

She gave a tiny, breathless laugh. "And that's another thing. We should talk about your plans."

He pitched his voice low and intimate, for her ears alone. "You and me, just as soon as we have dinner, right back in that motel bed. We'll sweat off all these calories. That's my plan. I think it's genius." He reached for the hand she had curved around her beer glass, and she let him take it, even returned his grip.

"I mean…I have to go back home sometime. This has been nice—" She broke off when his grip tightened, and smiled. "Better than nice. But the reality is—"

"Why?"

"Why…what?"

"Why go back? At all? Ever? What's there you gotta have?"

She was still staring at him, mouth open, when the kid brought their dinners and grinned at their linked hands on the table. She blinked hard, and Cade guessed she was fighting back tears. He relented. "Eat your catfish. And I'll tell you about my scar."

Marsh sat in the silver Honda at the stop sign where the street split and went two ways: onto the interstate headed south, or under the interstate to climb on it headed north.

He realized he had no idea which way Abigail

had gone. He didn't doubt she'd gotten on the interstate, though. What quicker way to leave Marsh than the nearest high-speed roadway? What he still didn't comprehend was why, and with whom, she'd gone. He'd been over and over the short list of Abigail's friends, which had grown even shorter since Marsh had moved in and helped her see those friends weren't good for her. He simply couldn't picture her with any of the men—there were only two, both married, and Marsh had already proved to himself Abigail wasn't with Drew. The other man was in his sixties.

But the hipster had said Abigail was the one driving.

Marsh drummed his fingers on the wheel. Which way? North was Ocala, not too far away. South was Tampa.

He thought hard. If he were Abigail, which way?

The loud honking of a horn from behind him startled him. His head flicked up and he stared into the mirror. Behind him was a small blue sedan.

Marsh got out of his car. He needed something on which to expend his rage, and an impatient, rude driver was just the thing. As he slammed the Honda's door, the car behind suddenly jerked left across the double yellow line and headed toward the intersection. The person in the passenger seat turned to stare at Marsh as the sedan passed; a stiff middle finger from the passenger, and one from the driver, greeted him.

Marsh yanked open his door again, jumped into the car and took off after the sedan.

It went north.

So did Marsh and his fury.

Ten minutes later, he had to concede that for a small sedan, it had more engine power than his Honda, and he gave up the chase. He hadn't once been able to get closer than about fifty feet to the blue sedan, and after several drivers honked and thwarted his aggressive tailgating, Marsh realized that he was focusing on the wrong thing. He needed to find Abigail, not chase down a couple of redneck jerks from Wildwood. No doubt he'd find that sedan in town another day, and when he did, he'd figure out how best to point out to them the error of their ways.

Ocala was only another fifteen minutes or so up the interstate. He began to see signs advertising fast-food restaurants, hotels, shopping.

Marsh nodded to himself; north felt like the right direction. He imagined he could feel the pull of Abigail, drawing him to her. He twisted the vents for the air conditioner so they blew full on him, cooling his hot face. When the sign for the Ocala mall turned up, Marsh took the exit. Abigail sometimes shopped one of the department stores there for new clothes, though it had been a while since she'd gone.

The mall didn't feel right, once he was there. Marsh made a quick pass through the department store, then zipped up and down the main shopping concourse, but he couldn't feel Abigail. He didn't think she was there, or if she'd been there, she was long gone now.

Still, to be sure, he took the silver Honda up one

aisle and down the next of the vast mall parking lot. He stopped once or twice when he found red pickups he thought the hipster might have described as "old," but none held evidence of her—not that she'd leave much, he thought. She hadn't had anything but her wallet on her when she went out for groceries.

It was a needle in a haystack. But he couldn't stay at home and wait. He knew she wasn't coming back on her own. He'd have to find her and bring her back. Teach her about duty and responsibility and the debt she owed to Marsh for all his help since Gary's death. This time he wasn't going to stop at kisses and squeezing her breasts between his hands, burying his hot, hard flesh there. He was going to take her as a man took a woman he loved, take her and claim her and make her understand she belonged to him body and soul. When Marsh was finished with Abigail, she would have no more questions, reservations or excuses. She would be utterly and irrevocably his, and as soon as the bruises were faded he would take her to the courthouse and they'd have a civil ceremony. He would stake his claim not only physically and spiritually but legally, as well. She wouldn't even have to change her name. She was meant for him. He should have taken steps much sooner, but he'd thought she'd come around on her own.

He'd been wrong.

He hated to be wrong.

Even more than that, he hated admitting it. It left him feeling as if he wasn't in complete control of a situation. Somewhere she'd met someone who had no qualms about taking her away from Marsh, and she'd gone.

A sweaty hour later he was convinced Abigail was not at the mall. She might have been there yesterday—because of their day care clients, Marsh had lost the better part of a day. She'd planned her escape well, but he knew he'd find her. He headed back toward the interstate, passing through horse country. How she loved the neat white fences and the spacious pastures dotted with live oak trees and dark, cool shade for the racehorses raised locally.

Wouldn't that be the life? Marsh let himself dream a little, watching a mare and a half-grown colt streak through a pasture to his right. Raise some Thoroughbreds, be a part of the racing elite at the local tracks, work their way up to Hialeah. He could see Abigail in a slim, cool sundress and a matching picture hat with a big, swooping brim to shade her tanned shoulders. Marsh, of course, would take a rye on the rocks from her hand—she'd serve him before she served their guests, because she loved and honored him. He'd even let her have a julep, as long as it was just the one. He didn't like the idea of Abigail drunk. Drunken women were unattractive.

Before he merged with the interstate again, Marsh pulled the Honda to the side of the road and sat with his hands on the wheel and his eyes closed, trying to visualize Abigail. Which way, now that he wasn't chasing a couple of smart alecks? Which way?

After he breathed for a while and calmed himself, he thought he could still feel the pull of her.

North it was, after all. He put the car into gear and headed for the on-ramp. North, past Ocala. He decided she wouldn't have stopped at the closest big town. No, she'd be farther away than that. Somewhere she thought Marsh wouldn't think to look.

"I'm coming for you, Abigail," he half sang. "Just sit tight. I'm coming. And when I get there we're going to have a lot of talking to do. A whole lot of talking."

The miles ticked by. Exit after exit zipped past, and none of them felt right. Before long Marsh noticed he was both hungry and thirsty. The rye was just about cooked out of his system. He wanted breakfast—a very late lunch, by now—and he needed to put a little fuel in the Honda's gas tank.

"Fuel up both our tanks," he said, patting the steering wheel. "Can't think right on an empty stomach." He started watching for signs again.

Micanopy.

He'd been there once a few years ago. From what he remembered, it was a small place, not any bigger than Wildwood, but it was probably big enough to have a diner of some kind and a gas station.

Marsh took the exit, nodding to himself. It felt right.

It sure did.

Because right there just off the exit was a rinky-dink motel, one of those junky places made of thickly painted cinder block, the classic cheap Florida construction material.

In the motel parking lot was a red pickup truck with a camper shell. It looked old.

Marsh pulled in and parked right in front of the office. He had some questions for the motel clerk, now, didn't he? Yes, indeed.

Chapter 10

Why go back? At all? Ever? What's there you gotta have?

Abby was trying to listen to Cade's story of a sting operation gone bad, of the meth lab somewhere out in farm country. It was interesting to learn the DEA flew over the countryside with infrared equipment that could detect the heat signatures of a meth lab cooking up a batch and pass that information along to local enforcement agencies.

She was trying to listen to him. She kept bringing her attention back to his quiet voice, the way he alternated steak and potato with story.

Trying to listen.

But part of her brain kept shouting the thing that he'd said before he began the complicated tale of chemical reactions, criminal personalities, the motivating factor of money and going undercover as part of the joint task force. *Why go back? At all? Ever?*

Why go back?

Because she thought she had to. Because there were people depending on her. A house. A life. Memories. Years of commitment and sweat she couldn't bring herself to throw away.

Yet only hours ago—or was it an entire day? she was losing track—Cade had told her Marsh wouldn't hurt the clients, that they mattered to him only as a means of controlling her. The clients' families wouldn't tolerate abuse of their loved ones. Marsh had to realize that. Cade was right.

Why go back at all?

Because Marsh had everything, everything that had ever belonged to her and Gary, except what was in her wallet right now.

Everything. It galled her to think she would let him walk away and never challenge him. Surely she was stronger than that. Surely she could go back home, change the locks. Call the police. Show them her bruises—

"It's highly corrosive, hypophosphorous acid," Cade was saying, his fingertips straying up to his eyebrow, cupping the side of his face where the skin still looked raw and puckered.

"You were lucky not to be blinded," Abby said, forcing her attention back to the present. She stared into Cade's blue eyes and thought how dreadful it would be for their beauty to be diminished in any way.

"No kidding." More steak, more potato. A swallow of beer. Abby looked at his throat working and suppressed a ragged indrawn breath of mingled horror at his story, and arousal at the sight of his tanned, bare neck.

What's there you gotta have?

Nothing.

If she were brutally honest with herself, there was nothing in the house she *had* to have. There were things she wanted, of course there were. Mementos. Financial records. The computer. Business files. Photos of her life with Gary. Her small jewelry collection.

But what if, instead of the reality of Marsh's manipulations, there'd been a disaster, like a hurricane or a fire? Those were all *things,* and things could be replaced. Even things like birth certificates. It would be a hassle, it might be expensive, the loss would even be painful, like grief—but it would be possible.

She could walk away.

She could.

She looked up at Cade, who was explaining how he'd gotten himself out of the lab before the volatile chemicals sent the whole place up in flames, even though he could barely see, and made it to the road, where a passing motorist had stopped for him and driven him to the hospital.

"I swear that guy broke a land speed record."

"Where was your team, your backup?"

"I was undercover, remember? Being undercover means you don't always have someone else standing by to help out."

"So it wasn't a drug bust."

"Not right then. I was there to figure out both ends of the supply chain—where the guys got their raw materials, and where the meth went after the cook. But they made me—somehow, they made me, and one of them chucked a dish of that crap at my face."

"They meant to kill you."

"Yeah." More beer. "Instead, I look like a villain out of a superhero movie, and I was still alive to give evidence."

"They went to jail?"

"You bet." The satisfaction in Cade's voice spread to his fierce smile. "For a long, long time."

"But you didn't go back to working undercover, did you? By then you'd have looked pretty distinctive." Abby personally thought Cade looked pretty distinctive anyway, even if she ignored the furious presence of the scar. He was physically imposing, fit and strong, and she had fallen hard for his blue eyes. She thought that if a cop had stopped her for speeding and had blue eyes like Cade's, she would have remembered those forever, and would recognize them if she saw them elsewhere. But maybe she was just a sappy woman infatuated with the first man who'd shown her tenderness in months.

"I did for a while. Long enough for them to decide I was too easily remembered and cut me loose."

Why go back at all?

"So somewhere in there you decided on a career change?"

"My department was great with me coming back

on regular patrol duty." He shrugged. "But after only a month, I knew it wasn't going to be enough for me, not after I'd been a part of busting some of the really big drug rings in the state." He turned his beer glass around and around on the table. Abby waited, watching his hands. She liked the way his fingers moved, slow and careful, sure.

After a while he spoke again. "One of the older K-9 guys wanted to retire. When the man goes, pretty much the dog has to go, too, because of the bond. It's really rare for a dog to be shifted to a new deputy. So when the county offered me that K-9 slot and training, I took it, even though it meant going back to patrol duty and looking for lost kids or old people who've gotten confused and wandered off. Dogs don't care if you don't look like other people. Dogs only care about how you smell, how you act." He looked up at her, and there they were again, those blue eyes. Except now there was a shadow in them, evidence of his struggle to put his life back together. Again she waited, nodding slowly, not looking away. She looked at his scar. He meant for her to, she thought. He had it turned toward her. She took a good long look. It took getting used to, but Abby was used to looking past people's surfaces to the person inside—sometimes locked far, far within, the way some of her clients were.

He drank the last swallows of beer and pushed the glass toward the edge of the table, where the staff would notice. "I thought a lot about quitting altogether. But what kind of job can you get when you look like I do? Night watchman at some high-rise in

Jacksonville? Full-time zombie at a traveling carnival? Telephone sales?"

"Oh, Cade—"

He shook his head, looking away from her at last. "I've adjusted, don't worry. Doesn't mean I like the way I look. It doesn't make things easy, you know? But I don't want to punch the living daylights out of people who comment about it anymore—" He stopped, realizing what he'd said, and stared at Abby. "That didn't come out right."

"You're not talking about irrational behavior," she said quietly. "You're not Marsh."

"I'm damn well not. Though I wouldn't bet on his chances of remaining a pretty boy if I ever get hold of him."

Abby flushed. She couldn't allow Cade to take that kind of risk for her. She was thrilled by his white-knight words, but this was her own battle. He was just pointing out to her something she should have known for herself, but couldn't see through her grief over Gary, and later, her own vulnerability and self-loathing. "Tell me about how you and Mort got to be a team."

Cade grinned, glancing out the window to where they both could see Mort's silhouette in the back of the red pickup. "The training school isn't far from Wildwood, actually. Just the next town over, right outside Bushnell. The people who run it bought a former Thoroughbred horse farm."

"Bushnell! Not even ten minutes down the road from my house."

"Mort and I were just coming back from a refresher course when we stopped at the store in Wildwood. I'm sure you know the place." Cade's wink was long and slow. Abby felt her face burning, but a smile also crept across her lips.

"Go on with your story."

"Mort was my first training candidate dog. We pretty much grew up together in the training. Officers don't always bond with the first dog they work with, but Mort and me, yeah. The instructors gave me a few chances with some other candidate dogs, but it just didn't take." Cade grinned and looked out the window beside them in the general direction of his pickup. "Mort and I climbed a ton of fences, crawled through bushes and culverts, chased down the bad guys in their protective suits. Working with Mort was… It wasn't the same as a really big bust, but there's something to be said for having your best friend around all the time."

"Knowing he's always got your back, and you always have his." Abby nodded, pleased to hear the animation and engagement in his voice. "So now you and Mort find lost kids and old people."

"Thugs and drugs sometimes, too, but yeah. People pay attention to a dog like Mort when they might not listen to a cop giving them directions."

"I know about that firsthand," she said ruefully. "He's pretty intimidating. Those are some big teeth, and a fierce growl."

Cade nodded. "The refresher course reminded me how much I liked the training. Police dogs are athletes. Working with Mort pushes me to…I don't know, be at my best, I guess. Mort always gives one hundred percent. This time Mort and I got to be the demo team for some new K-9 trainees. I think we really made a difference, showed them what it's like in the real world."

"It sounds rewarding. Fulfilling."

Cade looked at her oddly and Abby wondered why what she'd said could bring that quizzical expression to his face. She blinked and let the subject drop, afraid she'd put her foot in it somehow. She looked down at the table in confusion. Cade's steak was nearly finished, but she herself was still picking at her catfish. The hush puppy rolled around on her plate, too dense and greasy to be appetizing now that it had cooled. She glanced out the window, looking toward the pickup and Mort, and saw a silver Honda sedan coming into the parking lot too fast, whirling to a stop virtually nose-to-bumper with another car near the wharf.

Every nerve in her body fired at once.

It was Marsh's car. She knew it. Somehow he'd tracked her here—somehow he'd found the motel, maybe talked to the clerk. He'd scoured Micanopy, found the place the locals went for dinner, and he was here.

"Oh, no, no no no," she moaned. Her fork clattered into her plate and she bolted out of the booth so forcefully that she knocked against the table, jolting their plates and glasses. "Where's the back door?" she hissed. "Is it through the kitchen?"

"What?" Cade reached out, caught her wrist. "What the hell, Abby?"

Everyone in the restaurant was staring.

"He's here," she moaned. "That's his car. I have to go. I have to get out of here!" She tried to jerk free of Cade's grip, and instead he came up from the seat with her as she pulled.

"Don't be a fool." He looked out the window to see what had upset her, never letting go. In fact, he was reeling her in, hand over hand, until he could get his arm around her waist. He kept the pitch of his voice calm and even. "First, that's not Marsh. How could it be? He has no idea where you went. Second, everybody and their dog drives a damn silver Honda. I'm in law enforcement, I should know. It's like the car of invisibility, millions of them on the roads." His head bent to hers. He put his mouth close to her ear. "And third, if that *is* Marsh, believe me, *nothing* would give me more pleasure than to meet him." The cold menace in Cade's voice sent a shiver up her spine.

She wanted to see Cade beat Marsh to a bloody pulp, she realized, panting.

Cade's arm scooped her back toward the booth, bringing her along with him as he moved. "Come back and sit down. First of all we'll watch to see the driver get out." He urged her into the booth—on his side, where the vinyl was warm from his body—and came in beside her, effectively trapping her.

"It's him. It's him. It's—"

"It's *not,* Abigail." He caught her chin and turned her panicked face from the window. "What the hell did Marsh *do* to you?" His blue gaze searched her face. "What haven't you told me?"

"Let me out. Let me go. You can't keep me here. I can't stay. Don't you understand? *I can't stay here with him out there.*"

"What I understand," Cade said softly, all but whispering, "is that you're terrified out of your wits by the mere sight of one of the most common vehicles in the country, and you're not rational right now. Get hold of yourself, Abigail McMurray."

If he'd ever doubted the reality of what prolonged stress could do to a person, he'd had it proved in spades by the simple expedient of a silver Honda sedan in a backwoods parking lot. Cade let Abby turn back to the window to stare fixedly at the Honda, though her hand was up to hide her face from outside view. They didn't have to wait long for the driver to open his door and step out.

It was a kid, as Cade had known it would be from the Honda's flashy entry into the oyster-shell lot. The kid bounced to the car he had blocked in, an arm shot out of the car's window and there was an elaborate exchange of grips and fist-bumps.

Abby slumped in the booth, trembling with reaction. "I'm such an idiot."

"Yeah," Cade agreed. "Drink some water."

"Is it bad that I want a giant shot of bourbon instead?"

"If that's what you want, babe, I'll get it for you."

"I can't believe I freaked out like that. The whole restaurant must've seen me."

"They did." He couldn't hide his small but growing smile.

"I'm such an idiot."

"Don't keep beating yourself up about it."

"*Such* an idiot!"

"Yeah." Cade was grinning.

"You don't have to agree so quickly, you know."

"How about that bourbon now?"

Abby rubbed a hand over her face. She slumped a little in the booth, leaning against Cade's shoulder. It didn't matter how hot the summer was, or the warmth of the late-day sun coming in through their window. He liked the warmth of her next to him, and the impression of trust he perceived from her body. She wasn't frightened by him.

I'm not the problem here, for a change, he thought. It wasn't his face, or his job, the things that usually erected a wall between Cade and women. It was Marsh who was the problem, and Cade could be the solution, or at least part of it.

"I…don't want to get drunk," Abby said, slowly. "I mean…well, it might help, but it's only temporary. Right?" She looked up at him. "What I want is for this all to be over."

He could drown in those earnest gray eyes. They were deep and beautiful, full of honesty and unspoken truths. The women he'd dated before now, even the ones he thought he might be in love with, seemed shallow in retrospect. Were they only surfaces reflecting his own ego? Cade had chosen them for their beauty or the way they made loving seem fun, but not something to be taken seriously. With Abby, he'd somehow fallen straight through the surface to the real woman beneath, and found an ache he knew he could heal, and the desire to know her better. More than better; he wanted to probe to her very soul and protect what he found there.

Crazy thoughts, he told himself.

He didn't speak for a long moment, untangling her words while he set aside the discomfort of these unfamiliar feelings. She had to mean the situation with Marsh, not the situation with him, but he couldn't ask for clarification. He couldn't let himself be fooled by their overwhelmingly intimate situation over the past thirty hours or so. Just because he'd slept with her—twice—didn't give him the right to wedge himself into her life or tell her what to do. The best he could hope for was giving a little advice based on his years of experience in exactly her domestic situation. He could have bulldozed his way into her homelife, shoved Marsh out and shoved himself into the void left behind, but that wouldn't make him better than Marsh, just less prone to settle disagreements with fists.

Cade wanted to be better than Marsh.

"It's your choice, babe. Bourbon or no bourbon, what's happening in your life is your choice." He shrugged as her brows drew down in confusion. "You can do what you want. If you want to go back to Marsh, you can do that."

Abby blanched, her mouth opening to defend herself, but Cade held up a hand.

"Hear me out. I'm not going to tell you I want to see you go back to Wildwood and that situation, because I think if you do that, the only way it'll end is with you in the hospital and him in jail, or one of you dead, probably you."

The muscles in her throat worked hard. "He's not a killer—"

"That's what they all say. They make excuses for the piles of garbage who ought to be men. But you're better than that, Abby. You deserve better, and I—I want to help you get there. Not just because I'm a deputy and I'm trained to deal with situations like this. Not just because the sex was great and I'm grateful."

I'm grateful. He cringed inwardly at his own words. He was indeed grateful, but it was more than that. So much more. Dangerously more. He had to guard against the urge to luxuriate in her nearness. It couldn't last, and he knew it. Meanwhile, he'd take what he could get, and continue to be grateful.

"You want to help me?"

"You don't see that? You really don't see that? What the hell else have I been doing for the past day and a half, if not that?"

Abby's eyes welled with tears, but they didn't spill. "But I stole your truck. I ruined your trip, your vacation. I—"

"Tell me what you want. In words. You have options, no matter what you may think. I've heard it all—women think they're too weak, or not smart enough, don't have the money to make it, they love the bastard, what about the kids, the house is in his name, whatever. But you have choices. Make them."

Cade ached to touch her, ached to take it all out of her hands, make the choices for her because he knew what was best, what would be right and good. But he kept his hands on the table, where Abby could see them, because despite everything they'd been through together, she was still checking the emotional weather by watching his hands.

She might never get over that, and Cade hated Marsh sight unseen for that one thing alone.

"I don't want to be afraid anymore," Abby whispered. "What if Marsh calls the police, reports me missing? My poor day care clients—"

"He won't call." Cade's voice carried a tone of finality, of utter certainty. Marsh would call the cops only when he went too far one day, and a fist-crunch took her life, and he had to cover his tracks. "If he's doing anything at all, he's looking for you himself."

Abby stiffened, and her gaze went involuntarily to the Honda sedan in the parking lot.

"He sure as hell won't find you here, Abigail." He gestured to the rustic restaurant around them.

"The motel, though… It's right off the interstate."

"You're not driving a vehicle he can track, and I didn't tell the desk clerk I was bunking with the sexiest car thief in Florida. Nobody knows where you went except me and Mort."

Abby blushed a bright, furious red. "Cade!"

He bent for a swift, light kiss on her startled lips,

then drew back and looked at her seriously. "I've got the answer for every objection you can make. The choice is simple. It's sticking to it that's going to be damn hard, probably the hardest thing you've ever done in your life. Harder even than living with him in your pocket. Marsh is going to undermine you at every point. He's been inside your head before. He'll get in there again. You've gotta put up the walls, and keep them up."

Abby drew a long, shaky breath. "Harder than everything he's done already?"

"Yep. But here's the thing—when it's over, it's really over." Cade didn't tell her the other thing he knew. Abusers liked to lurk on the fringes of their victims' lives, find a new place to set the thin end of the wedge and get back in. It might not matter to Marsh whether he was controlling Abby from within her own life. It might be enough for him to plague her with slashed tires or running down her business reputation, vandalizing her house, making her spend money she didn't have to fix his messes. Stalk her, terrorize her.

"I can do it." She looked once more out the window to where the silver Honda was slowly backing out, with the other car following. The boys were leaving. "I can. I'm not going to live like that another minute."

Cade stretched out an arm and pulled her mug of beer across the table. He picked up his water glass, since his mug was empty, and held it up. "I'll drink to that."

Abby clinked glasses with him, her eyes growing

stern and dark. "Tomorrow I'm going to close the checking account. Marsh can get his funds somewhere else. And I'm going to change the locks." Then her stern expression changed suddenly to one of alarm. "Um, Cade?" Her voice was small and uncertain.

"What is it?"

"Do you think you could give me a ride home?"

Cade threw back his head and laughed. "Abigail McMurray, you are without a doubt the most brazen car thief I have ever had the pleasure to meet."

Then Cade learned what it was like to be the reason for her smile. When it came, it blazed brighter than the reddened evening sun. A ragged piece of himself lurched once, deep inside. He realized it was his heart, thumping strong and swift, and feeling remarkably whole, instead of an empty place like where a tooth was missing.

She might be delighted by the compliment he had paid her, but now that her meltdown over the silver Honda was fading, Cade's brain began ticking over their conversation. He thought about what she'd said as he told her how he had enjoyed the K-9 training and refresher course.

Fulfilling.

Rewarding.

Maybe fulfillment and a sense of accomplishment could be as good as an adrenaline rush—not as quick or sharp, but surely longer lasting. He wondered if it was what Abby felt when she worked with her clients. He looked at her again and saw she was still smiling. Her eyes weren't even tracing over the edges of his scar. She saw *him.* That was enough of a rush for Cade.

For now, anyway. For now.

"Look, buddy, I don't know how to be any clearer. We don't give out information about our guests." The desk clerk crossed his arms over his chest and took a step back from the counter. His dark eyes were narrowed and stern in his thin, seamed brown face. Grooves ran from his nose to the corners of his mouth. Only a few minutes ago, those grooves had been deep with a welcoming smile, but now they bracketed his frown.

Guests. Marsh grimaced. Is that what they called the kind of two-bit hustlers and johns who would rent a room in such a fleabag motel?

"I told you. I'm her husband. I just want to make sure she's okay."

"And I told *you.* I don't care who you are. If you don't have a warrant, you don't get jack." The man's quiet drawl grew even quieter, more determined.

Marsh's hands clenched. He itched to pick up the shiny silver night bell that stood at one side of the counter and hurl it against the wall, or grab the man by his collar and drag him across the counter. The desk clerk was a tougher nut to crack than the hipster at the convenience store. This man was older, harder—and he had laughed at the five dollars Marsh had first slid his direction.

Now Marsh slid over a twenty. The man looked at it, then up at Marsh. "You got a C-note in that mighty tight wallet of yours, buddy?"

Marsh flushed dark red in fury. "Is that what it'll take? A hundred?"

"That's right." The man nodded slowly. "That's what it'll take. Or a warrant, like I said."

A hundred dollars. It was sixty more than Marsh had on him, since he'd come away from the house without proper prep or planning. He'd gotten out of the habit of carrying much cash—everybody used plastic these days. He'd given half his cash to Abigail yesterday to pay for the emergency groceries.

Enraged, Marsh opened his wallet and upended it over the counter. Another five and a ten dangled out and then fell, joining the twenty-five already lying on the smooth wood. "There it is. Everything I've got in my wallet. What'll that get me? Anything? Anything at all?"

The clerk began to smile again. "Might buy you a couple gallons of gas across the road. What are you driving?"

Marsh slammed his hand down flat over the money and crushed it in his fist. "Thanks for nothing. I'll remember you. If something bad has happened to her, I'll remember you, how you could have helped and wouldn't. And I'll be back." He crammed the cash into his pocket with the wallet, heedless as he yanked open the office door and then banged out through the screen door, which shrilled on its hinges. He felt he could rip open the motel's walls with his bare hands, but he settled for stalking down the parking lot to the end unit—

—where the red pickup truck was gone.

While Marsh had been in the office grilling the clerk, Abigail and her lover had vanished. He hadn't even heard the truck drive out, he'd been so intent on prying information from the desk clerk. He turned and sprinted the other way, to where he could see the road and the ramps of the interstate, but the truck was nowhere to be found.

Marsh slammed his fist against the cheesy painted sign—Rest-n-Refresh Motel We're Air-Conditioned!—and let out a howl of fury.

He'd been that close, he knew it.

He turned around again, passing the office once more, and headed for the end unit, where the truck had been parked. The curtains were closed too snugly for him to see anything inside.

He has his hand on the doorknob when the screen door shrieked again.

"I wouldn't, friend," came the clerk's voice, carrying clearly to Marsh's ears. "I think I'd better let the sheriff know you're showing a lot of interest in damaging my property."

Marsh took two steps back from the door and showed his hands, palms out. The clerk had a phone in his hands, forefinger poised.

"I'm just really…concerned," Marsh said, trying to keep the breathless fury out of his voice. "I have to find her before she gets hurt." *And then I'll show her exactly how much trouble she's put me through the past day and a half.* "There's no need to call the law."

The clerk eyed Marsh with a narrow stare. "I think it's time you took your leave, friend."

Marsh came back to the Honda. The clerk gave Marsh's license plate a good long look, standing in front of the "Checkout time 11 a.m." sign. *Checking Marsh out,* Marsh thought, gritting his teeth. He tried for a sincere smile, but was sure it only made him look as if he was about to puke. He couldn't help it. "I'm going. No problems here, right?"

The clerk didn't respond, just stood there glaring as Marsh started the Honda and backed out of the parking spot. When Marsh looked in the rearview, the clerk was speaking into the phone.

"No!" Marsh pounded the steering wheel. Without a doubt the clerk was reporting him, and probably the description of his car, to the sheriff. He had to get control of himself. Going off half-cocked like that—when he wasn't even certain Abigail had headed north instead of south—wasn't going to get him what he wanted. He didn't even know for sure the red truck was the right one, but he believed it was. It felt right. Something had to break Marsh's way, soon. He was owed a win, he thought, a little reward. He loved Abigail so much that he couldn't lose her this way.

Marsh headed the Honda into the little town of Micanopy, trying to calm down, peering at the people in every car he passed. The truck, if it was here, wouldn't be hard to find. The town was too small to hide a vehicle that distinctive, and its image was burned into Marsh's brain. The truck had a square blocky red body sporting a few scoured spots with brownish primer paint sprayed to guard against rust. A white camper shell capped the bed of the pickup, windows on both sides, and a hatch window at the back. Big chrome gas cap cover behind the driver's door.

A few minutes later, having already passed through the town on its main street, he pulled into a convenience store with elderly gas pumps out front, the sort that didn't even take credit cards. He went inside to prepay, and bought a rock-hard burrito from under the heat lamp in the deli area. While he pumped gas and methodically gnawed at the burrito, he thought hard. It was not quite four in the afternoon. The day's heat was building to its apex. How many streets were there to this town? How long would it take him to scour them all? Were Abigail and her lover even still here, or had they climbed onto the interstate and driven away?

Checkout time 11 a.m.

Marsh stopped chewing.

Eleven. It was nearly four.

If Abigail and her lover were planning to check out, they'd have already done so. That meant the truck would return to the hotel at some point. All Marsh had to do was find a good place from which to watch.

His heart began to beat faster. He chewed rapidly. The bite of burrito went down like a stone, but he didn't care. Luck had turned his way at last.

Chapter 11

The ride back to the motel was short, but even so, it was enough time for Abby to begin questioning herself and her motives. The damage Marsh had done was extensive, subtle and pervasive. She could see it for herself now, but it was still too hard to fight it off every time it surfaced. At the restaurant she had agreed to spend another night with Cade at the little motel. It was selfish and greedy of her to grab for comfort with both hands.

"You know, Cade, if you'd rather, I could get my own room—"

Cade tightened his hands on the wheel and said nothing. The truck moved smoothly through the humid dusk. Above the dark tops of the pines, she could see a few clouds limned in fire from the beginnings of the sunset. The air didn't feel oppressive or stormy, as it had the night before, though it was steam-bath hot.

Abby tried again, her fingers knotting in her lap. "I don't want to keep imposing, presuming—"

This time Cade turned his head to glance at her before returning his attention to the road. "All your clothes are in our room," he said, as if that simple fact settled everything.

Our room. The phrase jolted Abby, snagged her like a fishhook in her brain.

Cade kept talking. "You used up most of your cash on dinner. All you have left is the credit card, right? You don't want to use that in case he's flagged it or closed the account."

"He can't close the account. It's *my* card—" Abby flared.

"I'm glad to hear you getting angry for a change. Honestly, Abby, you're so innocent. Haven't you ever thought about how the crooks in the world operate? Hell, not even the crooks—just ordinary, manipulative people. You have to think like them to stay ahead of them. You're a babe in the woods, you need a minder."

"And you think you should be that minder, or something?"

Cade's look was slash-quick, but he said nothing, gripping the wheel even tighter, and scowled. The motel was less than a mile away. Soon enough they'd be in the parking lot and he'd usher her into the stuffy little room, where the rumpled bed would make it all too apparent what had happened there earlier in the day.

As quick as her ire had flared, it burned away. He didn't deserve sharp words.

"I'm sorry, Cade, I shouldn't have—"

"Stop apologizing. Now that I've helped you decide to take your life back, I can't complain when you do exactly that." There was a short, tense silence. Cade pulled the truck into the motel parking lot and slowly edged up to their unit. He turned off the engine and spoke to the windshield. "Look. I know you think you're ready to make the change. I…guess I'm ready for you to do that, too. But…" Now he turned his head to look at her, the blue gaze burning like a lamp. The truck's big cab suddenly seemed too small, and oven-hot with the fan turned off. Abby found it hard to breathe, speared by that gaze.

"But?" she prompted, swallowing hard, heart pounding.

"I'll help you psych yourself up. We'll talk. Make some plans. I know those plans won't include a certain…um, ugly Marion County deputy, beyond getting a ride back to Wildwood. We'll talk, but, Abby—" Cade gritted his teeth, then somehow twisted the look into an uncertain, slightly bitter smile. "Abby…just… give me tonight. Please."

His plea snatched her breath and left her legs weak, too unsteady to support her if she climbed out of the truck. Her fingers twisted together for a moment, then she reached across the cab and touched his right hand, where it was still clamped on the steering wheel. Like lightning, his hand shifted to catch hers and bring it to his mouth, where his lips all but scorched a hole through her palm.

"Cade." Her shaken whisper lit a brilliant fire in his eyes. Her fingers trembled, then curved to his jawline.

"Tell me that's a yes."

She nodded, unable to speak.

"Thank you." He kissed her palm again, then gave a short laugh that was almost a bark. "An ugly guy like me doesn't get this close to gorgeous women like you very often. I have to enjoy it while I can."

"Stop that," Abby said. Cade's head tilted to the side and his mouth moved to her wrist, where she felt the tip of his tongue and his teeth at the spot where her pulse pounded. "You're not ugly."

"Mirrors tell me a different story."

Abby could hear the rough uncertainty in his voice, even as his lips moved against her skin and roused her nerve endings. "And I'm sure you think the eyes of strangers tell you that same story. But believe me, Cade—" She slid closer on the bench seat. "They just haven't met you yet. Don't listen to them. Listen to me instead."

"Keep talking." He nibbled at her wrist, then pushed the cuff of the borrowed shirt she was wearing up her arm, baring more skin to the exploration of his lips.

"You make it hard to think straight." Goose bumps rose over her entire body at the hot sweep of his tongue on the tender flesh of her inner forearm. "I think I ought to get out of this truck before things go too far—"

His gaze flicked up to meet hers. "It's a bench seat," he pointed out, voice roughened.

At that, Abby smiled and started to laugh. In the pickup bed, Mort gave a short woof at the sound. Cade let her go, fishing in the pocket of his jeans. He held out the room key on its plastic fob. "Go on in. I'd better walk Mort. Poor dog, he's not used to sharing me."

It was on the tip of Abby's tongue to toss back a lighthearted, "Then he'd better get used to it!" But she realized it wasn't true, would never be true, and even more than that, it wasn't right to be flippant about something she suddenly felt so deeply, like a stabbing pain in her body. By this time tomorrow, Cade would be well on his way to continuing his vacation, and she…she'd be somewhere safe, away from Marsh, but she would have begun the tasks necessary to remove him from her life. There was nothing for Mort to get used to. There would just be something for Abby to miss and mourn a little. For a relationship that had started out in such an awkward way, it had swiftly become unexpectedly sweet, something to be cherished during the hard and lonely times looming on her personal horizon.

She took the key, leaning forward to press a kiss on Cade's mouth. He was surprised, but only for a moment, before his arm snugged around her waist and pulled her torso against his. He deepened the kiss immediately with a soft, swift slide of his tongue. His hand slid to cup her buttock and half lift her into his lap, pulling her thigh across his own. Abby's knee found the edge of the bench seat, and she balanced there, feeling the bulge in his jeans growing beneath her.

Mort woofed again. This time Cade groaned. He kissed Abby fiercely for a long minute, then pulled away and banged the back of his head hard against the truck's rear window, repeatedly. "Go on, Abby. Go while I can still get out of the truck and maybe walk that mutt of mine without doing myself permanent injury."

Abby laughed breathlessly, opening the door on Cade's side, sliding out over his body, prolonging the moment as much as she dared. She felt exhilarated, brave and free, smiling so widely her cheeks hurt. Cade's second groan was the icing on the cake. "Have mercy, woman."

She ruined her sexy exit by bumping the truck's horn with her elbow as she slid past. The blaring of the horn made both of them jump, then they laughed loud and long. Cade reached out of the cab to touch her face, which was rosy with mingled embarrassment and laughter. "Go on," he said, when he could speak again. "Before the whole town shows up to see what the fuss is about."

Abby scampered to the motel room door and let herself in, giving Cade a saucy flip of her hips. He was standing next to the truck watching her. Even from several feet away, she could see desire burning in his eyes and twisting his face into a mask that would have been frightening had she not known it so well.

Thoughtfully, she closed the door and leaned against it, surveying the small, cheaply furnished room. The bed was still rumpled—they'd slept through checkout time earlier that day, and obviously maid service had passed them by. She took the few steps to the bed and flicked up the covers, smoothing out the biggest wrinkles, but not making too much of an effort. She and Cade would only be getting back into it, after all. The thought made her smile even wider, if possible. The white sheet and dull printed bedspread were curiously welcoming—there was a feeling of homecoming, a warm sweetness that spread through her as she looked around the little room. She could hardly believe in such concentrated happiness, and vowed to seize as much as she could in the little time that was left. By this time tomorrow, she was sure she would be at Judy's house, in the little guest room off the short hallway, making her break from Marsh. Cade would be on the road to somewhere else, and this savagely sweet interlude would end.

Abby shook her head. She could think about all that in a little while. Right now, there was nothing left in the world except this one small room, and the amazing man on the other side of the door. The least she could do was have the room ready when he walked in.

Mort took his own sweet time. It was as if the shepherd knew Cade was impatient to be back in that motel room with Abby. Cade sauntered along the edge of the motel's grassy verge that separated it from the roadway. Mort sniffed every weed and blade of grass.

Cade had no doubt Abby was already regretting her decision. She was probably changing back into her own clothing, folding his ncatly on the dresser, and would announce in her quiet way she'd reconsidered and thought she'd better get her own room.

Or, hell, maybe she'd tell him she was sure she wanted to be driven back to Wildwood right now, tonight, to implement whatever crazy plan she had in mind for getting rid of Marsh.

Cade shoved his hands into his back pockets, but the motion tightened the already too-snug fit of his jeans where his desire for Abby was still uncomfortably firm. He took them out again and hooked his thumbs into his belt loops.

"Come on, Mort, hurry it up! Do your business and we'll get you some dinner back in the room."

The shepherd flicked an ear in Cade's direction, but did not change his leisurely pace. Instead, he investigated every golden frond of a tall clump of love grass the motel lawnmower had missed. Cade decided to ignore the dog for a minute or two to see if that would work better. He half turned back toward the roadway, looking around him and keeping the dog in the corner of his eye.

There wasn't much to this part of Micanopy. Just the interstate exchange a couple of dozen yards away, with cars humming past at high speed, and a convenience store across the road. The gas prices at the store were higher than he liked, but it would be an easy stop in the morning when he and Abby headed back to Wildwood, assuming she would wait that long.

As Cade watched, an old VW bus pulled into the store parking lot, and a pack of high-schoolers got out, laughing and punching each other's arms as they headed inside. A moment or two later a silver Honda sedan just like the one at the restaurant earlier, the car that had triggered Abby's sudden and devastating reaction, turned into the parking lot.

Cade stiffened, turning to face the store more fully. The Honda slowed and stopped next to the coin-operated air compressor by the phone booth.

No one got out of the Honda.

That sixth sense, the one cops developed over time, tingled its awareness down the back of Cade's neck. He told himself it was just a silver Honda, the same car millions of people drove, and there was no reason why it, of all those millions, would contain the man who was undoubtedly searching for Abby by now. Abusers like Marsh didn't just let their women get away without a fight. He couldn't think of a way Marsh could have tracked her here; she wasn't using credit cards, she wasn't driving her own vehicle and she wasn't even traveling alone. Yet he continued to watch the car, his body taut and alert.

Mort pushed his nose against Cade's palm. Cade rested his hand on the dog's head. "Hey, boy. Gimme a minute. Go sniff another bush."

The office door of the motel opened with a hideous screech, and Mort's head turned alertly. Cade gave the hand command for Mort to stay. The motel manager, the same man who had rented Cade a room last night, came out onto the concrete walkway in front of the office and lit a cigarette. He looked over at Cade, who lifted his chin and a hand in greeting. The manager nodded back.

It can't be Marsh, Cade thought. He'd just been hypersensitized to notice silver Hondas since dinner with Abby.

Still, he waited. The driver didn't get out of the Honda, and now the daylight driving lights went off, and still the car waited.

The manager was watching the car, too, Cade realized, after a moment. Now Cade was on full alert, and called Mort to heel. The two of them crossed the blacktop, still hot from the day's baking sunshine, to the manager.

"Evenin'," said the manager.

"Evenin'."

"Everything all right with your room?"

"It's fine."

"Gonna stay another day? Sorry we didn't get to the maid service, but you were sleeping, and the maid had to get to her college classes up the road in Gainesville, so we skipped your room."

"No problem. But I think we'll check out in the morning. Thanks for your hospitality."

"Let me know if you need extra towels. We got plenty."

"Thanks." Cade waited a beat, then jerked his head

toward the car across the street. "Wonder what that guy's up to. Not really a parking place, but he's not airing up his tires or making a phone call."

"Yeah," the manager said. "He's been a pain in my ass today, that guy."

"Yeah?" Cade told himself to keep it light; the best way to get information out of people wasn't always to interrogate, especially in circumstances where he didn't have any legitimate involvement.

"He was here earlier, being a jackass, yelling and trying to get me to tell him about my customers."

Stay casual. "Must've been looking for somebody, huh?"

"Sure was. Thought he ought to show what a big man he was by turning doorknobs and trying to break our poor little ol' sign over there." The manager gestured with the cigarette at the Rest-n-Refresh signboard. "I called the sheriff, but he drove off before anyone came. He drove through my parking lot twice after that, 'bout once an hour. And now he's back again, waiting over there." A couple of deep drags saw the cigarette sucked down almost to the filter. The manager crushed the butt on the sidewalk's edge, then picked up the butt and tossed it into the trash container nearby. "I gotta quit those someday."

"Yeah," Cade said. "I hear they're bad for you." He kept his tone neutral, but the information about the silver Honda's repeated appearances shifted him from mild curiosity to hyperawareness.

"Bad, but so damn good." The manager offered a handshake, and Cade took it. "Well, I'm gonna go call the sheriff again. That guy just don't take no for an answer, looks like. You have a nice night, now."

"Thanks." Cade turned and went slowly back to his truck with Mort and opened the hatch to the pickup bed. He reached inside for the container that held Mort's kibble, and scooped out a handful. He leaned against the side of the truck, where he could keep an eye on the convenience store. He fed the dog his entire dinner bite by bite, giving Mort hand commands, drilling him in the basics. Mort, as always, was all business, even when he took the kibbles one at a time. Cade remembered afresh how much he'd enjoyed the weeks he and Mort went through K-9 training. Drilling kept them both sharp, and they did it often, but tonight it seemed especially meaningful, since he'd told Abby about the months after the task force pulled the plug on his undercover work.

It wasn't long before the sheriff's car pulled into the convenience store parking lot and blocked in the silver Honda. Cade watched in the gathering twilight as the deputy got out of his car and went to lean in the window of the Honda. He remembered stops like that, where all that was needed was a little demonstration of police presence to make someone straighten up and fly right. Shortly the deputy headed back to his patrol car. The silver Honda's lights came on, the car backed up and a few seconds later the car was on the ramp to the interstate, red taillights disappearing into the dusk.

Gone.

South, toward Wildwood.

Cade shook his head. He'd probably never know what that was about, but at least the crawly feeling of alertness was fading, and he didn't think there was any way the driver—if it had been Marsh—could have seen Abby getting out of the truck and going into the room. The timing had simply been wrong, which was in her favor, even if by some strange coincidence Marsh knew what kind of vehicle Abby had driven away from the Wildwood convenience store. Cade reached into the truck again, gathered up his duffel with the gun inside, put Mort's food container under his arm, locked up the truck and walked to the motel room door. He tapped softly on the metal door before turning the knob.

"Hi, honey, I'm home," he said to the quiet room, which was lit only by the light from the open bathroom door and the faint light from around the edges of the closed curtains.

"It's about time," Abby said, from where she sat in the bed, with the white sheet pooled at her waist. She was naked above it, and Cade's mouth went dry. In the shadowy gloom, the bruises on her breasts and torso didn't look so bad. She held out her arms.

Cade all but dropped everything he was carrying. Mort swished past him and headed straight to his blanket bedding with a put-upon sigh. Cade double-locked the door with every intention of falling into those soft arms. He knew it really would feel as if he'd come home, all humor aside. He had one more night, and he was going to make the most of it.

"What took so long?" Abby asked, grinning as he kicked off his shoes and fumbled at his belt buckle.

"Blame the dog." Cade decided not to mention the Honda and the deputy. He was here with Abby now, and with him to protect her, even if Marsh had been driving the Honda and might return at some point, there was nothing to worry about. Men like Marsh folded the minute an authority figure called them on their bad behavior.

"Poor Mort."

There was a soft sound from behind the bed, where Mort's tail brushed the wall as he wagged in response to her sympathetic tone.

"Traitor," Cade told him. "Never let a woman sweet-talk you like that."

"How about you? Could I sweet-talk you, Cade?"

"Baby, you never even had to open your mouth. Look at you." His jeans hit the floor, belt buckle clinking against the zipper, and he pulled his shirt off over his head without unbuttoning it. An opened condom packet lay on the bedside table next to the lamp, its contents ready and waiting. Cade crawled onto the bed wearing nothing but his briefs, and caught her mouth in a kiss. She'd brushed her teeth, which made him aware of his own after-dinner taste, but before he could think about a fast trip to the bathroom, her hands were sliding up his bare chest and all rational thought departed.

Abby sank back onto the pillow. Cade followed, never releasing her mouth. The bedclothes were between them, but he was content to take it slow and savor the sensations one by one. This time there wasn't a reason to hurry. She was warm and willing and there was nowhere they had to be except in the here and now. He knelt above her, elbows keeping his weight from crushing her, letting the tight-furled peaks of her breasts brush against his chest. Where they touched, scorching lines of fire followed. She wasn't as shy as she had been yesterday, or even this morning. Her hands explored more freely, slipping along his ribs to toy with the elastic at the top of his briefs, and then moving beneath, one cupping his hip bone, the other cradling his erection in her warm palm.

Now he did pull back, just enough to look down into her gray eyes as they opened, drowsy with desire. Her mouth pouted open softly, wet and reddened from his kiss. The fan of her hair on the pillow invited his nuzzling, but he restrained himself. "Abby."

"Mmm."

The sound alone nearly made him come, her voice was so filled with deep pleasure. Cade's heart pounded hard in his chest. He stilled for a moment, looking down at her. She took advantage of the moment to push his briefs down as far as she was able—not very far, given his position with his thighs straddling her own, but his erection bobbed free of the cloth. Her gaze moved downward to where she grasped him, and she smiled.

"I…uh, was going to take it slow," he managed to mumble. Her thumb stroked over the tip and circled there gently. Cade had to bite down on his lip to stop the grunt of pleasure rising in his throat at her touch.

"Okay." She kept her thumb moving, and now her other hand joined it, sliding over his belly, her palm flattened and hot against his skin. She looked up into his eyes again and he saw a mischievous look growing in her face. "Can I ask a favor, Cade?"

"Another one?"

"I know I've used up my quota. I'm counting on your generosity."

"Ask, and I'll decide. Baby, if you don't stop touching me like that—"

"Don't you like it?"

He gritted his teeth at her. "What do you think?" he asked, when she squeezed her hand, and his erection pulsed and flexed. "But if the goal is to go slow, you're going to have to stop doing—that—"

"About that favor."

"Anything." He swallowed hard as her hands stroked upward, not too softly, not too firmly, but with a strength and steadiness that nearly blinded him with sensation. "Oh, anything."

Her laugh was rich and happy. "Get these briefs off. They're in my way."

In less than thirty seconds, though he hardly had brain enough to count them, Cade was naked and Abby had rolled the condom on and flipped back the covers. Underneath, she was as naked as he, and as he turned back to the bed, she opened her legs and whispered, flushing red as she spoke, "Please come inside me. We can go slow, but I need you inside me now."

"Have mercy, woman," he said for the second time that hour.

She took hold of him one more time and guided him in where she was warmest and wettest. Her legs wrapped around his waist to lock him to her, and she arched upward in ecstasy at his long, slow push. "No mercy," she breathed. "Just...oh, *Cade*."

"I'm keeping my eye on you. You're causing trouble in my town, and I don't like that."

That's what the deputy had said as he leaned on the top of Marsh's Honda and smiled. The words rang in Marsh's ears as he pulled out of the convenience store parking lot. *I'm keeping my eye on you.*

Damn it. Damn it. Double and triple damn it.

Marsh had to concentrate to herd the Honda onto the interstate. He kept a watch on his rearview to be certain the sheriff's deputy wasn't following him.

He knew who had reported him. It could be only the clerk at the Rest-n-Refresh Motel, the one who didn't understand how critical it was for Marsh to find Abigail. It was a shame, too—the store's parking lot had a perfect view of the motel. Marsh's heart had pounded when he pulled in, because the red pickup was already parked at the end unit. The third time he'd come back to the motel to look for it had been the charm, hadn't it? He didn't see Abigail, but there was a man with the truck, a tall, fit-looking man with a German shepherd dog. That didn't make sense to Marsh. Abigail didn't know anyone who had a dog, as far as Marsh knew, but since she'd been keeping secrets from him, there was no knowing what she'd done, whom she'd met.

His gut told him Abigail was in that motel. If only he hadn't lost his temper and tried to open the motel room door so soon after he left the motel office. If only he'd waited a little, the clerk would have forgotten all about him, and he'd have had his chance to get into the room and see what he could find.

Too late now, too damn late.

His brain whirled. He turned off the radio because it was interfering with his driving. The last thing he needed right now was a traffic ticket. Usually he enjoyed country music. The songs were about the right things, women who understood that their men knew best, men who might have troubles but would win out in the end. Right now he had to think, though, think hard. Think how to find out once and for all if Abigail was there. But with the motel clerk shoving his nose into Marsh's business, how could he?

I'm keeping my eye on you.

Marsh hadn't even had a chance to get close enough to write down the truck's license plate number, just in case. The deputy hadn't been satisfied with Marsh's explanation that he was just taking a breather before he checked the air in his tires and headed out. Now the deputy would be watching for him. Marsh didn't like the idea of the law coming down on him—the law didn't understand how much Marsh loved and needed Abigail, or how she wouldn't listen and had to be made to pay attention.

Exits flicked by with Marsh on autopilot, driving

south, thoughts chasing themselves like crazed animals through his brain, biting and clawing.

By the time he reached the Wildwood exit, he had no better plan than catching a couple of hours of sleep at home, then getting up before dawn to drive back to Micanopy before Abigail left that motel, so he could follow her—follow *them,* Abigail and whomever she was with—to the next place.

The streets were dark at last as he pulled into the driveway, hitting the curb and popping it in his distraction. He killed the Honda's engine and sat staring at the house, imagining Abigail somewhere inside, maybe humming a little in the kitchen, or bent to pull clean clothes out of the dryer, putting a casserole in the oven for their supper, which they never cooked until the clients had all gone for the day. He liked watching her at those small, ordinary tasks, because she was making a home for the two of them.

A ragged gasp broke from him. He loved her so much. *So damn much.* Right now he was terrified she was being taken away from him.

His head swiveled back and forth to check the neighboring houses for onlookers, but it seemed as if everyone was inside, probably eating their own late summer suppers. Marsh got out of the Honda and went slowly up the front walk.

I'm keeping my eye on you.

Yeah, if he went back to Micanopy, even at three in the morning, he bet the deputy would be watching for a silver Honda. So would that lackey at the motel. Between now and dawn, he'd have to think about a good place to watch for Abigail to leave in the truck. Maybe the far side of the interstate from the hotel… But what if Abigail went the other way, into Micanopy, and took some miserable little back road…

Marsh groaned and let himself into the house. He was hungry, that's why he couldn't think straight. He needed some decent food, not gas station junk and too many sodas.

The house still felt as empty as a beach shell. Two days she'd been gone, and the scent of her was already diminishing. He gave the door a kick to close it, pleased when it slammed and echoed his bad temper. He stomped into the kitchen and banged open cupboard doors. Even a sandwich was too complicated, now that he was in this mood. He grabbed a box of cereal and ate it dry, roaming the house, checking for Abigail, even though he knew she wasn't there.

Marsh wandered into the living room, ignoring the shredded wheat falling behind him like bread crumbs in Hansel and Gretel's forest, and stopped dead.

Gary smiled at him from the picture over the television; Gary and Abigail in one of those stupid, hokey lean-on-the-fence-rail photos every professional photographer seemed to take.

Except Gary looked happy, and pleasant, and obnoxiously in love with Abigail, whose smile was wider than Marsh had ever seen it in person. Gary had never been handsome, but he had looked friendly and approachable, and girls had always been at ease around Gary in a way they never had with Marsh.

Girls bumped shoulders with Gary as they walked next to him, even girls who weren't his girlfriends.

I'm keeping my eye on you.

The cereal box fell to the floor and spilled as Marsh lunged for the photograph and ripped it from the wall. One good whack on the TV console was enough to shatter the protective glass and put a long white crease mark in the image, right through the fake autumn leaves behind Gary and Abby, and through the dark brown of Gary's shirt. Marsh's hand became a claw digging into the photo's surface, dragging away the colors, scraping across Gary's face.

I'm keeping my eye on you.

"No, you're not, not anymore," Marsh rasped, panting. When Gary's face was a scratched, scarred mess, Marsh let the photo drop and went looking for another one. Gary wouldn't be looking at him, not anymore. Not ever again. No more happy Gary. No more judgmental stares. Marsh would replace every photo of Gary and Abigail with a picture of Marsh and Abigail, better pictures, more expensive ones, taken by better photographers than the itinerant ones at cheap hometown department stores.

The richest source of photos of Gary was in Abigail's room. Marsh remembered where he'd found the wedding album the night before. He grabbed it, still breathing heavily, and took it to his own room, where he sat with it at his small desk, and systematically opened every album page, one after the other.

He used his pocketknife to scrape away Gary's eyes in every photo.

I'm keeping my eye on you.

I'm keeping my eye on you.

Now Gary would never look at Abigail again. Abigail would belong to Marsh from now on. He'd see to it.

Marsh didn't notice his own harsh, tearing sobs as he worked. He felt a burning hatred cleansing his soul.

At last he closed the album and put it in a bin beneath his bed. Abigail wouldn't need to remember her other wedding, because when he found her, they would have one to replace it.

Chapter 12

Abby lay staring at the dark ceiling of the motel room. Aside from Cade's breathing, and Mort's occasional snuffle or snore, the only sound was the intermittent rush of cars on the interstate outside the motel. Though she was tired and half-drunk on the slow ebb of pleasure, she wasn't ready for sleep. Her mind would not rest, churning with ideas and fears, and even foolish hopes.

She had been away from home for almost two days now, and the terrible compulsion to return was keeping her awake, long after Cade had fallen asleep. A glance to her left showed him sprawled on his back, his naked leg and hip exposed where the tumbled sheet pooled at his side. But even in sleep he kept his scar turned toward the pillow, as if to guard or conceal it. She felt a clenching of pity. He believed himself repulsive, but Abby knew a beast when she saw one, and Cade was not.

Marsh, however… She pressed her lips together and turned resolutely away from the man in bed with her. She refused to keep comparing the two men; it only tore her apart inside by making her doubt her own judgment.

It was harder to turn away from the memories of their lovemaking. Cade's determination to make that first time last had resulted in nothing short of devastation for Abby. Once he was inside her, moving gently and with great deliberation, he remained supported on his elbows and forearms above her, where he could watch her face. He laced his fingers with hers, pinning her hands to the mattress. She could not touch him, and yet the connection with him was more profound than if they had been in a thrashing, frenzied tangle. His gaze bored into her with each slow stroke, as if he was memorizing every expression crossing her face. He was staring into her eyes when she felt her climax splintering her control, and she could not look away. She couldn't even blink, much less close her eyes to focus on the sensation of his body entwined with her own. She lay beneath him, biting her lip and shuddering, feeling the hot sparkle of tears in her eyes. Tears of pleasure, tears of joy, tears of something vast and deep that frightened her a little.

It frightened her a lot, actually, because she recognized that feeling of connection.

It felt like love.

Two days was not long enough to have fallen in love, even with a man as unique as Cade Latimer, she told herself firmly.

She slipped out of the bed, careful not to wake him, and groped to the window to peer out a tiny slit between the curtain and the wall. The motel parking lot was lit by a couple of halfhearted streetlights. More light came from the all-night convenience store across the road, but aside from one other car in the motel parking lot, there was nothing to see except the pools of light and the darkness beyond. Somewhere out there, Marsh must be searching for her. He wouldn't sit home patiently waiting for her to turn up.

She shivered and let the curtain close. It would be dawn before much longer, and still she wasn't sleepy.

In the bed, Cade made a quiet sound, turning onto his side and pulling her empty pillow close to him. Abby bit her lip. Cade had proved to her he found something of worth in her, something more than the sex they'd shared. Even that tiny crumb gave her confidence and boosted her self-esteem, foolish and ephemeral as she knew it must be. She sat on the edge of the bed and watched him as he slept.

It wasn't fair or right for her to drag him any further into her mess with Marsh. She'd slid down that slippery slope by herself, and from here on out she ought to climb out by herself, as well. The sooner she did it, the better, and when better to start than right now, while she felt strong enough to make the decision and stand by it, no matter what Marsh tried to do? There were people she could call in Wildwood, friends she'd left behind because first she had turned to Marsh, and then in her shame had cut herself off from. Judy and Drew would help, and if Marsh was as angry and reactive as she thought he would be, she would call the sheriff. She didn't want to for the sake of Gary's memory and the fact that Marsh was Gary's brother, but she knew Marsh was likely to push her to it.

Sooner was better, and alone was better still. One more gauntlet to run. She just hoped she was up for it.

With a nod, Abby rose and prowled through the dark room to find some clothes. When she was dressed, she went to the dresser and unzipped Cade's duffel bag as quietly as she could, checking over her shoulder to make sure he was still sleeping. Her fingers slipped inside, seeking the truck keys. Her fingertips brushed over something hard and cold and heavy, and she realized she'd found Cade's pistol. Her fingers flinched away.

Then they crept back.

Abby folded the note into a tent, wrote Cade's name on the front and set it on top of the TV, where he couldn't miss seeing it when he wakened next. Her fingers were cold with nerves, and they shook as she placed the note and gathered up Cade's keys as quietly as she could, stifling their metallic jingle. Mort's head rose alertly at the slight sound, and she stared at him, willing him to settle and be silent as she backed toward the door.

Outside, it was not quite dawn. The morning was humid and sticky-warm on her skin. She closed the motel room door behind her as softly as she could. Though Mort had followed her to the door, he hadn't tried to go through it, and she couldn't hear anything from inside now as she pressed her ear to the wood panels. She turned her attention to Cade's truck, parked only feet away. Silence was critical. Cade's hyperalertness, cop training and quick responses might bring him out any moment.

The slight slope of the parking lot made her plans simpler. Abby shifted into neutral and released the hand brake, letting the truck roll backward slowly. She would be many yards away from the motel room before she started the engine, and hopefully Cade would keep sleeping.

Her heart stayed in her throat until she eased Cade's truck up the ramp to the interstate. The rearview was clear, no naked sheriff's deputy sprinting behind her, enticing as that sight might have been.

All the way south to Wildwood, Abby reviewed her plan obsessively. She would make a telephone call to draw Marsh away from the house. She was sure he'd leave. She'd be able to see him drive past in his Honda from her vantage point at the market and the mask of Cade's truck. Abby would have almost an hour to grab her important business files, the checkbook, throw some personal things in a bag, and then run.

For her life.

Back to Cade, if he would forgive her just once

more. Even if all she did was hand him his keys and watch him drive away forever. She wouldn't look further than that, not right now. Too much was in the way, and she couldn't imagine Cade wanting to spend more time with someone whose life was as out of control as hers. But maybe, down the road…maybe someday she could give him a call, invite him to dinner somewhere and see if that could ever lead to more.

Abby shook her head to clear it. She had to keep her eyes on the road and her mind on the tasks at hand. She couldn't see anything in the plan that would trip her up. The most important part was to be gone before Marsh got back.

Oh, how much Marsh and his fists had taught her about planning for every least contingency.

She reached the exit where the whole insane, terrifying but wonderful adventure had begun and parked the truck near the pay phone at the convenience store. Again she reviewed the plan: call Marsh, tell him she was at an all-night diner in Ocala and needed him to come and pick her up. She wouldn't have to fake panic or tears in her voice—both would be only too real. Abby felt herself shaking, her bowels cramping with tension and dread, her heart pounding out her fear.

She got out of the truck and walked the ten feet to the telephone. It was misery to fumble change from her pocket, and worse to lift the receiver, insert coins into the slot and dial her own number. Her hand shook so hard she could barely keep a grip on the receiver. *Please make him believe me. Don't let him see the number's here in town. Let him answer the old phone in the kitchen that doesn't have caller ID.*

"Hello?"

"M-M-Marsh?" She'd been right: no need to fake her reaction. His voice went through her gauzy composure like an eighteen-wheeler through a flimsy wooden fence. The shaking grew worse, and only by leaning against the small shelter of the phone could she suppress her involuntary movements. She hated how much control he had over her. But at least now she understood what he'd done to her. All she had to do was not let the insidious fingers of her own inadequacy pry at her resolve.

"*Abigail.* Where the hell have you been?"

How different her name sounded on Marsh's lips than on Cade's. It made her shudder. She tried to quiet her breathing enough to speak. "I…I…want to come home. Will you—"

"Where are you, you stupid fool? Do you know what I've been through? I almost called the cops!"

Oh, but you didn't, and Cade told me you wouldn't. You can't afford for someone else to see my bruises. "I'm…I'm at the Good Eatin' Diner in Silver Springs." She named a small town outside of Ocala. Maybe morning rush hour would delay him.

"You stay put. I'm coming for you."

I'm coming for you. The simultaneous terror and relief she felt at hearing this made her knees weak. She had gotten him out of the house. Her plan would work. "What about our day care clients?"

"I had to close it when you didn't come home, or

didn't you even bother to think about that before you left? Can't run the place by myself. I told the agencies you're really sick. You've put us in a bad place, a really bad place. I had to lie to cover up what you've done. I made a ton of phone calls the past two days to some angry and upset families."

The receiver shook in her hand. The house would be completely empty. She wouldn't have to face the clients, or feel responsible for them, try to explain where she'd been for two days. "I'm sorry. I…know it was wrong. I'm really, really sorry."

"Where exactly are you?"

"At the pay phone outside in the parking lot." It wasn't quite a lie.

"Right. You stay put. I'll be there in a half hour. And—Abigail—I don't have to tell you how relieved I am to hear from you, do I, sweetheart?"

The antelope knows lions do not purr when they're hunting. Abby felt the tears spurt hotly from her eyes, so salty they stung her cheeks. "You don't have to tell me, Marsh." Never before had she fully understood what his love-words actually meant. She had always been confounded by how he could speak with such sincere gentleness and then raise his hand to her. Now she realized the sweet words were meant to put her off guard and make her grateful for his kindness, even as she felt guilt at making him so angry he must punish her.

"Good. I'm glad you understand. Now sit tight. Go back inside the diner. I'm leaving right now."

Abby hung up, and such was her fear that she all

but sprinted away from the telephone to lock herself in the shelter of Cade's truck. Logically she knew Marsh couldn't see her from the house several blocks away, and it would be a couple of minutes before he'd drive past the market, but she couldn't help it. She huddled on the bench seat and peered out the back window through the camper shell's tinted glass and film of dust. It would be enough to camouflage her.

She was unprepared for the violent stab of hatred and fear that went through her when Marsh's silver Honda—moving far too quickly for the road—went past the market. She stared after him even after the car was out of sight, before she realized she was wasting precious seconds. There was a lot to do at the house, and little time to do it before he returned, enraged by her deception. By then she had to be long gone.

When she pulled into the driveway, the house looked somehow small and unfamiliar. *But nothing's changed, except maybe me.* She wiped at the tears, slid out of the truck and pocketed the keys. Then she leaned across the seat and opened the glove box.

Cade's gun waited inside, right where she'd put it.

I won't need it. Marsh isn't here.

She looked at it for a long moment.

I won't need it. I can leave it in the truck.

She took the grip in her hand.

I won't need it. She nodded to herself and tucked the pistol into the back waistband of her jeans—*Cade's jeans,* she thought, with a tiny bursting warmth and a surge of confidence. She pulled the hem of Cade's shirt over it.

Marsh had left the front door unlocked in his haste, though he'd taped a hand-lettered sign to the door: CLOSED UNTIL FURTHER NOTICE DUE TO ILLNESS. Abby stared at the sign for a moment, thinking of the day she and Gary had welcomed their first client over the threshold. The day care had been the culmination of Gary's social worker training, his wish to help others. Abby locked the door behind her and went quickly to her bedroom to get a tote bag to carry the most critical business files, and fill another with enough clothes to last for several days.

Her bedroom was a disaster. It was easy to see where Marsh had vented his rage at her disappearance. The pillows were torn and scattered, pictures yanked from the walls and some of the glass broken. Her bedding was flung everywhere, and worst of all, her lingerie was strewn over the mattress. When she stepped near for a closer look, she saw the stains of his sexual excitement dried or drying on the soft fabrics. From the look of things, Marsh had been back more than once to relieve his frustration and mark her most intimate clothing.

All over the bed she and Gary had shared.

With a moan, she raced for the bathroom and was just in time to be sick in the toilet. She shook and sobbed, flushing twice. Cade's gun was ominously cold and heavy in the small of her back. Finally there seemed to be nothing left inside her, and she rinsed out her mouth and spat, flushing one last time. If she'd needed a bigger two-by-four to hit her over the head and make her leave, she'd certainly found it.

Gritting her teeth, she returned to the bedroom, yanked open her closet, snatched two tote bags and filled one with socks, jeans, shirts and shoes before topping it off with sundries from the bathroom. She left the underwear—she'd have to buy more somewhere. She couldn't wear hers, not after what Marsh had done to them. Then she stomped into the little office—hardly more than a closet—and began grabbing business files from the day care. She unplugged the computer from the wall and coiled up all its cables. The whole thing must come with her—there wasn't time to decide which electronic files to keep and which to leave. She carried it out piece by piece and put it in the back of Cade's truck, protected in bright afghans from the backs of the sofas and armchairs.

When she opened the desk drawer to grab the business checkbook, it was nowhere to be found. Nor was her personal paperwork—marriage license, birth certificate—or Gary's. These losses triggered her to look for her wedding album, and it, too, was not where it should be on the shelf near the television.

It was the last straw. There could be only one place to look for those things.

Marsh's room.

Mort's kibble breath woke Cade. Out of long habit he rested his hand on the dog's head and sleepily rubbed behind Mort's erect ears. Mort pressed his chest against the bed and snuffled to indicate he needed to go outside. While Cade lazed there, half in and half out of one of the best sleeps he'd had in ages, he let himself daydream. With a smile he remembered the night just past, a second night of lovemaking in the worn little motel. He was running out of rubbers at this rate, down to a single foil package, already waiting on the cheap veneer nightstand. Not that he was complaining—a shortage of condoms was a happy problem to have, one easily solved. The sex with Abby was hotter than it had any right to be. He'd had better sex—more athletic, more adventurous in terms of positions, more technically perfect—but it hadn't had the erotic quality, that intensely personal link. It hadn't felt like a punch to his gut to watch his partner tip into orgasm and writhe beneath him. He hadn't wanted to gather the other women to him and hold them while they slept afterward. He had been overwhelmed by the honesty of Abby's response as she looked up at him, her gaze clinging to his and sharing every nuance of emotion freely.

The problem with this new kind of sex was that he was dangerously close to calling it "making love." What if it was only the intensity of the situation that was skewing his perception? They'd been thrown together in the oddest of circumstances, and Abby's unhappy tale was perfectly constructed to pluck at his conscience, his sworn duty and his pity. Perhaps he should distance himself a little, not continue to plunge down the rabbit hole with abandon, but he could get used to waking up next to her and thinking of the two of them as a set.

He dreamed further, imagining Abby in his own

bed, at home in Ocala. He pictured her asleep there, waking on a sunny weekend morning with a slow, sweet smile as he brought her breakfast in bed, good coffee, crisp thick bacon, more. Cade could think of a lot of things to put maple syrup on; pancakes were only the start. His body began to rouse at the thought.

His hand slid over the bed beneath the covers, seeking Abby's body. Maybe they'd rip open that last condom and put it to good use before they went out to find some breakfast and head for Wildwood to shove that bastard Marsh out of her life. Abby's side of the bed was rumpled but empty, the sheets cool. Cade frowned and opened his eyes. The motel room's anonymous ceiling greeted him, popcorn texture looking gray in the early-morning light from behind the curtains.

Seeing that Cade was awake at last, Mort pushed against the bed and snuffled more urgently. Cade sighed. Dreams of another session of sexy aerobics would have to wait. He needed to give Mort a moment's exercise. Cade swung his legs out of bed and reached for his skivvies and jeans. It was still early; he'd risk stepping out shirtless and shoeless. As he zipped, he glanced toward the bathroom and saw the door standing open a bare inch, but no sounds came from the room. His brows drew together and he strode across the room to push the door fully open.

The bathroom was empty, and Abby's jeans were still draped over the shower door.

Where the hell had she gone?

Cade didn't like the anxious feeling that knotted his stomach. He turned, Mort at his side, and scanned the room. Her shoes were gone, but her shirt lay over the back of one of the chairs at the tiny table. Wherever she was, she was dressed in his clothes. Something about that gave him an odd surge of relief, as if his clothing could transmit a touch between the two of them, protect her somehow.

Then he noticed the folded paper on top of the chunky old motel TV, with his name written tidily across it.

He dived for the note.

Cade,

Please don't be angry, but I've taken your truck again. I've really borrowed it, this time. I promise I'll be back later this morning. I just need to go home and get a few things so I can make the break we talked about. I was halfway there on my own, and now after the time we've spent together I think I can make it the rest of the way.

Thank you for listening and for giving me the strength to do this.

I promise I'll be back soon, then if I can beg just one more favor from you—a ride to Gainesville so I can start over, and an address so I can send you a check for all the gas I've used, and other things—I'll be on my way and you can finish your vacation in peace.

Thank you again. You don't know what you've done for me, but my life is mine again

at last. I don't think I'll ever regret my short life of crime.
Abby McMurray

"No. No. Oh, damn it, Abby. No no no. You can't just go back. Not without me to look out for you." Cade lunged for the door and flung it wide. The truck was really gone.

Mort pushed past him urgently and trotted to the edge of the parking lot, where he lifted his leg against some shrubbery. Cade was too agitated to call the dog back, and instead returned to the room and paced it furiously, raking his hands through his hair. How long had she been gone? Did he have a hope in hell of catching her, and if so, how? She'd left him without transportation, at a backwater motel where there wasn't even a decent-size town to get a cab. Not to mention what a sixty-mile cab ride would cost; cash he didn't have on him.

Cadc paced more, thinking hard. Mort returned to the room and lay down on his blanket.

Cade's gaze fell on his duffel bag, and once more he pounced. The little black book inside was just what he needed, and thirty seconds later he was punching buttons on his cell phone.

"Come on, Roy, pick up. Pick up, pick up, pick up." He paced while the phone rang and rang and rang at the other end.

"H'lo." Gruff, sleepy, pissed.

"How you doing, Roy?"

"Who wants to know?"

"Latimer."

"Aw, no way, man, *no way.*"

"Yeah. Know you wish I was dead, but I'm not. But hey, Roy, remember that little favor you owe me?" Cade could feel an unpleasant grin curving his mouth, and turned so that he wouldn't catch his demonic reflection in the mirror over the dresser. His smiles were not his best feature, not with the tug of the scar. It was a miracle Abby hadn't been scared out of her wits by his grins over dinner the night before.

"Screw you, Latimer."

"I love you, too, man. Listen, Roy, I need a favor. And then we're even."

"Even, huh?"

Cade could hear the cautious interest in Roy's voice. "Yeah. It's easy. I need a ride from Micanopy to a house in Wildwood."

"What the hell you doin' in Micanopy? You ain't workin' drugs in Gainesville no more."

"Will you do it, or do I give what I know to the sheriff?"

"Aw, man, don't be like that. I got clean. I stayed clean. I married her. We got two kids now! I done what you asked."

"That was half of what I asked. Remember I said I'd call in that favor some day. That day's here, Roy. I need you to get in your car and get over here—right now—and get me to Wildwood. There's a woman who needs me there."

"A woman. You foolin' with me? Face like yours, and you got a woman?"

"Come on, Roy. I can't yap with you all day. I gotta get there before she gets hurt."

On the other end of the line, Cade could hear keys jingling, and almost sagged to the floor in relief. Roy would come. The man could drive like a bat out of hell—just what Cade needed. It felt good to know he'd been right about Roy, after all. Roy was a prince in thug's clothing. He'd just fallen in with the wrong crowd and needed one chance—just one—to make things right, and he'd done it. Playing the sympathy card for Abby had been the right move.

"Yeah, yeah, I'm on it. Lemme make sure we're both clear—I get you to this house in Wildwood, and then I'm outta there, and I don't have you 'round my neck no more."

"That's right. I'm gone for good."

"I'm on it, like I said. Tell me where you're at, Latimer. I'll get your sorry ass to your woman."

Cade rushed the rest of his dressing—socks, shoes, shirttails jammed into his jeans. Belt. Then he went to his duffel again and checked his kit.

Cable ties, check. He pictured himself shackling Marsh—who in his head looked like a redneck, hypertensive slob in a filthy wife-beater undershirt with a gut that hung over his belt. It would be a pleasure to link Marsh's hands behind his back, and maybe, for good measure, his ankles—and clip his wrists to his ankles, hog-tying the man.

Flashlight, check. He never went anywhere without it; in a pinch, it made a damned fine bludgeon.

Mace, check.

Ammo, check.

Spare clip, check.

Beretta, missing.

"Oh, *God,* Abby. Baby, no." He rummaged a second time and did not find the gun tucked somewhere unexpected. As he lifted his head, he encountered his own face in the mirror, and did not recognize the man there. For a moment he'd forgotten about the scars; he'd been back on the job, prepping for a call. He had expected to see his uniform, belt hung with all the tools of his law enforcement trade, hat placed just so on his head.

Maybe it was best if he kept that perspective in mind. More officers were hurt or killed responding to a domestic violence call than any other kind of call. Gritting his teeth, he clipped on Mort's leash and waited outside the motel room for Roy to arrive.

It couldn't be soon enough. Not with Abby out there alone. God only knew what she had in mind for his Beretta, but it couldn't be good, and it wasn't safe. He prayed she wouldn't be adding murder to her list of crimes. That wasn't something Cade could overlook, no matter how brutally Marsh had treated her.

Well.

Maybe Cade could, but society could not. And Abigail McMurray was the first place they'd look if Marsh turned up shot or dead.

Chapter 13

Marsh's room was as neat as a pin, even though the rest of the house was a wreck. One thing Abby could say for him, at least until today when she learned how deep his obsession ran, was that he was never a problem to clean up after. She hesitated in the doorway, dark rivulets of dread threading through her guts.

What would she find here, in the place she'd never ventured, not even to dust or change the bedding, since Marsh pressed her hand to his crotch in the kitchen all those months ago? In some peculiar delicacy of sensibility, he hadn't asked her to. It was like the sex—it was all right to masturbate himself to climax in her palm or between her breasts, yet he had never tried actual intercourse with her.

He might be ready to cross that line now, though.

She swallowed hard and clenched her teeth against the nausea as she pulled open the top dresser drawer.

Drawer after drawer yielded nothing of hers, nothing of Gary's. She forced herself to move on to the nightstand, and again—nothing. The closet next, and except for a closed cardboard box filled with back issues of *Hustler* and *Penthouse,* still nothing.

At last there was only one place left to search. Trembling, Abby approached the bed and twitched back the bedspread. Nothing under the pillows. Nothing under the sheets. Heart pounding, she lifted the mattress—still nothing. She bent and peered under the bed, and there it was. A low-profile plastic storage box, one of the very ones she'd once kept Gary's and her winter clothing in. Reaching for it, she caught it by a corner and pulled it out.

Inside she found what she was looking for. The checkbook and personal papers went straight into the tote bag, but she couldn't resist opening the wedding album.

If the semen on her lingerie hadn't convinced her of Marsh's obsession, the album did.

Every picture of Gary had been damaged. Gary's face was either scratched out or excised altogether. She sat hard on the floor, tears filling her eyes, a lump choking her throat. If she'd had anything left in her stomach, it would have come up, as well.

Marsh had erased his own brother.

The sob that brayed out of her hurt her throat, but it wasn't loud enough to drown out the sound of the front door slamming open against the foyer wall.

Shocked to gulping silence, she scrambled to her feet, rushing to peek out Marsh's bedroom window, hiding her body behind the wall, moving the curtain the smallest amount possible.

Marsh's Honda sedan was parked at the curb. It looked almost prim compared with the boxy, clunky power of Cade's old pickup. It wasn't possible that he'd already been to Silver Springs and back. He'd known she was calling from in town, and he'd just *waited* for the trap to be well and truly sprung.

"I know you're home, Abigail," Marsh called from the living room. "What I don't get is why you brought company with you when you *know* we haven't had a chance to vacuum the house this week."

He sounded normal. Not angry.

Of course. He thinks there's someone else here besides me.

Abby clutched the wedding album across her breasts like a shield, and edged into the living room. She couldn't bear to be caught in his bedroom, with only the window for a possible exit, and the looming presence of his bed and the disturbed bedclothes.

Marsh's head whipped around. "Well, now," he breathed. His gaze took in everything, she saw—the photo album, her too-big clothes, the terrified, half-sick look of her. "Let me guess—your friends are here to help you with whatever it is you think you're doing."

"That's right." She swallowed hard. "They're helping me pack. I'm leaving."

"Leaving."

"Yes. I think it would be better if you waited outside. My friends are really angry with you."

"Why's that?" His head tilted alertly, and Gary's eyes looked out of Marsh's red, furious face.

"Because I finally told them everything."

He smiled sweetly. "Abigail, sweetheart. Don't tell lies. It doesn't suit you, and it makes me upset. Where are they? Call them in here, let me clear up the situation with them. Help them understand how much I love you, how you love me, too. This is just a little misunderstanding."

A cold dagger of fear plunged into her belly, and once again she fought down nausea, this time from the dread of his fury. His words were soft enough; emotionless because he thought there was still someone else in the house. The longer she could play that game, the better off she would be.

Marsh was between her and the front door. If she went out the back, he would easily beat her to Cade's truck. She couldn't escape that way, and she hadn't finished gathering up everything she'd come for. The tote bag with the business paperwork still stood next to the desk. If only she hadn't wasted so much time weeping over what he'd done to her wedding album, she might have been gone from here, even considering Marsh's early return.

She swallowed down a throat full of bile. "I saw your sign on the door. About closing."

"Who else is here, Abigail?" He took a few steps closer to her, and she sidled away, but that left him able to look down the short hallway into his room, and see the tumbled bed. His eyes grew more wary. "Who've you been screwing *in my bed?*"

"I—I—haven't! Marsh—" She stopped, realizing he'd managed to put her on the defensive already.

"You have. You're wearing his clothes, even. Look at you. Gary always knew you were a slut."

"Stop it. I know what you've been doing while I was gone." She slapped the wedding album with the flat of her palm. "Now you need to leave, while...we finish up a few things here. You can come back after we've left. I'll give you until tomorrow evening to pack up your stuff and go. If you do that, there won't be any trouble for you. You can put all this behind you, and—"

"Whore," Marsh whispered. "I can smell the sex on you."

"Stop trying to change the subject. You—you—just go, Marsh, before I call the sheriff."

"There's no one here but us, is there, Abigail?"

Abigail. How different it sounded when it was Marsh saying her name.

He saw her involuntary glance toward his room. "I called all your friends, Abigail. Nobody knew where you'd gone. They were as surprised as I was that you didn't come home from the store. They've all been helping me look for you. That's why I know they're not here with you now. So tell me, Abigail, before I have to beat the answer out of you, who is he? Where is he, and I want to know *right now!*"

Abby tried to gather her scattered wits. The truth was in her mouth, about to burst out of her lips if only Marsh would stop clenching and unclenching his hands, when she heard Cade's voice in her head, saying clearly, "He didn't call anyone. He can't afford for them to learn the truth."

Her chin lifted as she recognized the truth of the thought, and she put the wedding album on one of the activity tables that lined the living room walls. "I don't have to tell you anything, Marsh, except *get. Out. Of my house.*" She reached behind her to the waistband and brought out the pistol.

"Where's this gal's house?" Roy's car screamed down the off-ramp and squealed to a stop at the intersection. In the backseat, Mort had lain down out of self-preservation, and had his paws spread to brace himself. "Left or right?"

"Carson Street." Cade looked desperately for the name on the street sign. It wasn't Carson.

"Well, where's that, Latimer? I don't know this town."

"Hell if I know." He pointed in the general direction of the convenience store where he'd stopped to get some coffee and give Mort a little water two days ago. Abby had been on foot, therefore Carson Street couldn't be far away. "Go right. Slow down. I gotta look around."

"You've come to save your damsel in distress, and you don't know where the hell she lives?"

"Drive, damn it! That way!"

Roy gunned the engine, then braked abruptly and pulled into the convenience store's parking lot.

"What the hell you doing, Roy?"

"Asking directions, asshole. My wife would say if you need someone to do your thinkin' for you, just ask!"

Cade bailed out of the car with Roy, and thirty seconds later the startled and confused store clerk had gestured wildly to the south and muttered something about two streets over.

Mort woofed as the two men got back into the car. Roy hadn't been happy about having a German shepherd in his backseat; he'd had to take out his kids' booster seats and stuff them in the trunk, but Cade wasn't about to leave Mort behind at the motel, and a blue-steel stare at Roy had ended that discussion pronto.

Two rights and a left later, they were looking for the house number, but instead Cade saw his truck in a driveway, and the silver Honda parked at the curb. "Pull over," he instructed Roy.

"What, here? This ain't 302."

"We don't want to scare…her."

"Listen here, Latimer. You swear on your life you're not here to cause trouble?" Roy hadn't stopped the car. He'd gone past the house and was continuing down the street. "She don't need a restraining order against you, does she, man? What do you mean, don't want to scare her?"

"That wife of yours has done more for you than you'll ever know, Roy," Cade said. "Time was when you wouldn't have asked that."

"That time's past. Swear to me."

"I swear. I'm just here to help."

"How you gonna get back to Micanopy?"

"That's my truck right there. I'll drive."

Roy cut his eyes to Cade. "You mean that gal has your truck? She ditched you at a motel and took your truck home to her place?"

"Shut up, Roy."

Roy threw back his head and laughed while he did a three-point turn in the middle of the narrow street. "Man, you got it bad."

"I said shut up."

The car headed back up the street. Roy pulled to the side well back from 302 and threw the car in Park. His lean face stared intently out the front window, and he drummed his fingers on the steering wheel. "I don't like this, man."

Cade was looking at the silver Honda parked in front of the house. "Neither do I. Looks like she's not alone."

Roy turned an astonished gaze on Cade. "And you're just gonna walk in there. Look, man, how 'bout I just drive you back to Micanopy, you get your gear outta that motel and come on for breakfast. My wife'll be pissed—hell, she's already pissed I'm not there right now. You come on back with me, make her whole day. But think about this."

Cade grinned and took his duffel in one hand, and reached for the door handle with the other. "You're a prince, Roy. Head on out, kiss your babies for me."

Roy grinned, but looked uneasily at the house again. "You sure?"

"I'm sure." Cade opened the door. "Thanks, Roy."

"We're square, right?"

"Square."

Roy held out his fist for a bump. "Luck, man. Looks like you gonna need it."

Cade felt a grin twist his face, and bumped knuckles with Roy's big, bony hand. He let Mort out of the back, unclipped the dog's leash and closed the car door. With a thump to the roof, he dismissed Roy, that prince of men, and waited till Roy's car was out of sight around the corner before he and Mort crossed the street in the early-morning sunlight. They stayed well out of sight of 302. Mort lifted his leg once and briefly at the hydrant in the middle of the block, then came to heel.

Cade tried to walk nonchalantly, as though he belonged in this neighborhood of tidy houses and lawns. His eyes were constantly moving, looking for signs of Abby, signs of Marsh. Judging from the careless angle of the Honda sedan to the curb, he thought maybe Marsh had parked in a hurry.

Had Abby managed to lure Marsh out of the house while she was going to be there? Had he come back unexpectedly, or what? Cade paused at his truck and looked inside. The back had what looked like computer equipment wrapped in bright crocheted afghans, and in the front seat, the glove compartment gaped open. He opened the driver's-side door as silently as possible and, keeping one eye on the house, pawed through the glove box. Nothing seemed to be missing, not even the flashlight he kept there, but he thought he knew why it was open.

It was where she'd put his gun while she drove from Micanopy to Wildwood, wasn't it?

A moment later, his thoughts and his worst fears were confirmed when he heard the Beretta bark inside the house, a woman's scream and a second shot followed by the most awful silence he had ever heard. His bowels turned to liquid, but he wasted no more time on thought. He sprinted for the front door.

Chapter 14

"You're too stupid even to do this right." Marsh's voice was harsh and loud, but he was not yet shouting. "You left the safety on. It works like this." With a flick of his thumb, he toggled a lever at the side of the pistol, held his arm out at an angle and put a bullet in the floor.

Abby screamed, her hands flying up to her ears.

Marsh took hold of her arm with his left hand, the black barrel of Cade's gun still smoking faintly in his right. "Stupid bitch. Bet you didn't even know there was one in the chamber. Where did you get a gun?" He didn't wait for an answer; he pulled the trigger again, this time putting a splintered hole in one of the activity tables and the sofa behind it.

Then Marsh put the barrel up against Abby's temple. Cade's words blazed through her brain like a bolt of lightning. *The only way it'll end is with you in the hospital and him in jail, or one of you dead, probably you.* How right he had been.

Tears flowed, but she was too shocked to make a sound, not even a sob, not even a plea. This was it. This was where it all ended. She had pushed too hard, and when the gun hadn't fired when she pointed it at the floor in front of Marsh and squeezed the trigger to scare him away, he had taken the three strides between them and ripped it out of her stunned, foiled hand.

"You know what's stopping me from shooting you right now, Abigail? Do you?"

The front door crashed open for the second time in five minutes. Her first thought was that one of the clients had arrived anyway, despite the sign on the door, and fear spiked through her heart. But it wasn't a client—it was Cade standing in the doorway, looking like something out of a horror film, the left side of his face bright red and raw. The thought was fleeting and words wouldn't come for a moment. Her second thought was that Marsh's head was pivoting to point toward Cade, and with it the gun. Abby found words at last.

"No, Cade, *run!* He has a gun!"

She saw Cade's blue, blue eyes sweep the room, and then, unbelievably, a grin split his scarred face. "Hi, honey, I'm home!" Abby's mouth dropped open in her astonishment—was this really Cade, standing in her doorway as if nothing in the world was wrong? Her terror-addled brain demanded to know how he'd appeared, like a genie, just when he was most needed. She had left him sound asleep an hour's drive up the interstate and taken his only means of transportation! A split second later terror rushed back in to displace her astonishment.

Cade's grin was the most feral thing she had ever seen, and if it had been directed at her, she thought she would have fainted where she stood. Marsh took the gun away from her head and held it half behind him, as though Cade could somehow have missed seeing it.

"I don't believe we've met, neighbor," said Marsh. Abby strained away from him, looking wildly around the room, trying to find something within reach to strike at him, and had to settle for trying one-handed to pry his fingers loose.

"We haven't been formally introduced, no," Cade agreed, with patently false cheer. "But I know plenty about you." His chin jerked toward Abby. "Abby, baby, come over here."

Marsh was panting now, and sweat had sprung out on his face and throat. "You need to get out of our house, before I call the cops, friend."

Cade put out a hand and took two steps into the room. "I like my plan better. If you leave now, I might not tell the cops what I know about you—might even stick around to explain how I was cleaning my weapon there when it went off, twice, because yeah, maybe I'm just that stupid, too—when they show up, because you gotta know your neighbors have already called. Gunshots at a day care." Cade tutted.

"Let me guess. Those are your clothes Abigail's got on." Marsh sneered in Cade's direction. "Guess she really couldn't do much better than a sideshow freak like you. Look at you. She's desperate—she's got you fooled. You'll do anything she asks. All she's got to do is promise you a little tail, right?"

Now Cade's smile was truly awful to behold. Abby stared at the two of them, at Marsh mocking Cade's disfigurement, and Cade continuing to ease into the room. He hadn't closed the door behind him, leaving an exit if they could use it before Marsh could fire the Beretta again.

"Now, that's just not nice, Marshall McMurray," said Cade softly. Abby saw Marsh flinch at the sound of his name—Cade knew too much about him already, and the simple use of his name had changed all the rules of the game. "Abby's real special, the sweetest lay I've ever had. And the way I hear it, you can't get it up, not even for her."

Marsh's grip on her arm shifted as he clenched his fingers even tighter, grinding the small bones in her wrist together. Abby went to her knees, her mouth open in a gasp.

Cade looked right at her for the barest second, brows lifting slightly, his head inclining in what looked like a nod of approval, and it was as if he had sent a thought straight into her brain. She continued her slump to the floor, making herself as heavy as possible, pulling Marsh off balance, and in that moment Cade breathed, "Mort, *fass*."

From outside the house came a black-and-tan

streak, swift and silent as a wolf, the hunting stride and bared, eager teeth even more frightening than the gun.

The pistol's barrel lifted from its hiding place behind Marsh's back, and Abby screamed again, pivoting on her hip bone and pulling hard, wedging her leg between Marsh's feet as Mort came on. Cade threw himself to the floor behind his dog, and the gun spoke once more.

"You sick *creep,*" Abby screamed, kicking, striking with her hand, clawing at Marsh's fingers around her arm, drawing blood on the back of his hand. She was suddenly on her feet and aiming kicks at his midsection and legs where he lay on the floor. Kicks that hurt her feet in the worn sneakers, but obviously also hurt him, given his grunts. "You *bastard,* trying to shoot a dog!"

Cade stood to one side, his booted foot holding Marsh's right arm to the floor, and bent to pick up the pistol. His hands made a quick motion and now the gun was in Cade's hand, pointed at Marsh.

Mort stood with a front paw on Marsh's chest, his muzzle no more than one hot breath from Marsh's taut throat, ears pricked forward, tail motionless. The dog was unharmed and very, very focused on his task.

"Rip his throat out, Mort," Abby sobbed.

"Abby," Cade said.

"What's the command for him to kill, Cade? Give it!"

"Abby."

Marsh's chest heaved, but other than that he was

utterly still, his eyes wide and terrified, fixed on the pricked, eager and terrifyingly attentive ears of the shepherd.

Abby aimed another kick at Marsh, and Mort growled when Marsh's body flinched. A dark spot appeared at the front of Marsh's jeans, and spread slowly.

"Abigail," Cade said for the third time. Her head turned to him, but her gaze and attention were still on Marsh. Cade was holding out the gun to her, butt first. "If you want him dead, here you go. I won't stop you."

At last Abby turned to him, stared at the gun in his hand, then at Marsh, then at the wedding album lying on the table next to the bullet hole.

Then she reached out and took the gun from Cade. Her hands trembled, and she nearly dropped it. It took two hands to hold properly, but in a second she had it aimed, and a finger on the trigger.

"That's what you came for, isn't it?" Cade said quietly. "That's why you took my gun, to shoot him."

Abby shook her head, staring down at Marsh. Cade would have to call off Mort before she could fire the gun, unless she knelt down and put it to Marsh's head. She couldn't risk shooting the dog. "No, I… All I wanted was to get a few things, enough that I could…that I could…shut it all down, start over somewhere else."

"No, you want him dead for what he's done to you. That's why you took my gun. So why don't you go ahead? Do it now, before the cops come. We'll say it was self-defense. No one has to know except us."

"I...I took your gun because...because..." Tears welled and fell, blurring her vision, and she gripped the gun tighter. "I..."

"Shoot him, Abby. Do it now. If you shoot him in your house, it's self-defense. We can make that stick. You'll have to show the cops your bruises, and tell them what McMurray has been doing to you all this time. There'll be a mess in court, but in the end it'll be over, and he'll be dead. Isn't that what you want?"

Abby turned, the gun still held at the end of her rigid arms, pointing at Cade's hip. His gaze flicked down to the gun, then up to her eyes.

"Isn't it?" he prompted, shifting a half step to one side, out of the sight line of the muzzle, keeping his foot on Marsh's arm.

"Yes." Her mouth quivered loosely, and her own ferocity terrified her. She wanted Marsh dead, dead and bleeding, beaten to a bloody pulp right there on the carpet. But that meant killing the last part of herself, the one spark of hope and resistance that still burned in her heart. And it would obliterate any respect Cade might have had for her. "I mean no! Oh, God, Cade, no. I just didn't want him to h-h-hurt me, not ever again. That's why I took your gun. And your truck. I'd have given them back. I was coming back, just as soon as I could get there, only *he* came, and I was so frightened and I had the gun but the safety was on and I couldn't— I c-c-couldn't— I didn't— I just want it to stop. It has to stop, Cade. It has to stop. *He* has to stop." The words tumbled out, making no sense to her. The gun pivoted in her nerveless hands, spinning on her finger through the trigger guard as her hands unclenched. Deftly, Cade caught it, pulled Abby close and wrapped his arm around her.

Outside, they could hear sirens.

"I'll go," Marsh whispered, hardly daring to speak with Mort's teeth at his neck. "I'll go right now, and never touch her again. Just…just…c'mon, call off your dog—"

Cade looked down at Abby. She stared up into that blue gaze, the gaze that seemed startlingly new each time she met it.

"Tell me what you want, baby," Cade murmured.

Her mouth shaped into a square of awful grief, and a wail burst from her throat. "I want my life back, and I don't want you to hate me for everything I've done."

Cade nodded. "Then go out to the driveway and meet the squad car, Abby."

"W-what are you going to do?"

"Mort and Marsh and I are just going to wait here." His smile was bleak. "Marsh and I have a couple of things to talk about. Just so he's clear on where things stand before he goes to jail."

"Cade—"

"Go."

"Tell me you don't hate me. Please tell me you don't—"

Cade turned a dark look toward her. "Never beg, Abby."

Abby gulped hard, snuffled back a sob and fled the living room for the hot, humid, glare-bright morning outside her house, where the man she thought she might be in love with stood over her brother-in-law with a gun and a killer dog.

"Which way back to Carson Street?" Cade asked, aiming the truck for the parking lot exit from the sheriff's department, where they'd just spent the past couple of hours giving detailed statements to the deputies who'd arrested Marsh.

Abby pointed left. "I'm sorry about your gun, Cade."

Cade shrugged. "They need it for evidence. It's standard procedure when shots are fired. I'll get it back when this is over. If I really needed a gun, I could go home and get my service weapon out of my gun locker."

"You know, I've never even asked, in all this time. Where do you live?"

"Ocala. I rent half a duplex."

Abby shook her head. "It's crazy."

"A duplex in Ocala is crazy?"

"No, I mean…it's only been three days, but after all we've been through, I feel like I've known you for years. But I didn't even know what town you live in. We've talked about…"

Cade heard her voice choking up a little, and stole a glance. She was swallowing hard, getting a grip on herself.

"It's like you know my darkest secrets. And I know some of yours." She turned her head and caught him looking at her. "But all the little stuff…nothing." She faced forward and stared out the window, unblinking. Cade thought perhaps she was trying not to cry. She'd been strong while the deputies were taking her statement. Though tears had threatened more than once, she'd taken hold of her courage and followed through. He was proud of her. Marsh was in a cell and she was safe for now, but Cade knew that emotional walls toppled most easily when the storms were over.

"You know what matters most to me." Cade pulled out onto the street.

Abby was silent for a block, then spoke again, her voice husky with emotion. "Well. I'm sorry anyway. You've lost a lot because of me. Your vacation, your fishing reel and now your gun. I'm even wearing your clothes."

"Since we're counting, don't forget my spare condoms."

Abby turned an astonished face to him, and Cade laughed outright. She reddened, but then she let out a half-choked laugh. "I'm…um, not going to apologize for that, but I'll replace them, if you'd like. Turn right at the next corner. That's Carson."

Silence bloomed again as they approached Abby's house. Cade sensed their adventure winding swiftly to its end. With Marsh in jail for at least a few days until his arraignment and bail hearing and Abby in her own home again, there wasn't much reason for Cade to stay around. He would probably have to return to Wildwood when or if Marsh's case went to trial, but beyond that, he couldn't see a reason to stick around.

Except he desperately wanted to. But why would Abby want him in her life? Sure, the sex was great, and he'd been a help to her in the past few days, but was that foundation enough for anything more? Beauty and the Beast was a fairy tale. His appearance wasn't going to change. Being in a sheriff's department again today after the time away the past two weeks and more had only reinforced the feeling that staying in law enforcement was more and more the wrong choice for him. The officers had stared openly at his face, and a couple of them had even asked if he was the deputy who'd been at that bad meth lab bust they'd heard about. Some of the glances seemed judgmental, as if the officers thought Cade had been careless or sloppy in his job. He had briefly entertained the idea of asking if the Wildwood Sheriff's Department was looking for officers, but he'd abandoned that thought with the first negative reaction.

It hurt afresh. He was glad to be heading back to Abby's house to pick up his dog, the one creature in his life who didn't stare and wonder, fear or judge. He would move on. He still had a few days left of vacation, but maybe he wouldn't drive all the way to northern Alabama now. Maybe he'd just find a quiet Gulf beach town with a fishing pier and a case of cold beer instead, and think about what he should do next.

He pulled the truck into Abby's driveway and killed the engine. Mort's doggy face appeared in the front window, nosing aside the curtain. They had left the shepherd in the house while they were at the sheriff's department. "Let me give Mort a short walk and then I'll help you carry your computer stuff into the house."

Abby sat rigid in the passenger seat, staring at the house. "It looks like nothing happened here, doesn't it?"

Cade studied the ordinariness of the little house, its tended lawn, a few unwatered petunias wilting in the late-summer heat, its tight-closed curtains and the Honda at the curb with its rear half blocking the street. To his trained eyes, things looked not quite right. He was about to agree with Abby, nevertheless, when she spoke again, turning to look at him and putting her hand on his arm.

"You know I will never be able to thank you for everything you've done for me these past few days, Cade."

This is it, he thought. *The big kiss-off for the helpful but scary, ugly guy.* He gripped the wheel tighter, and her touch faltered and fell away as his muscles tensed beneath her fingers.

"I can never apologize enough, either. Not even for the c-c-condoms—" She tried for a laugh, but there were tears in her voice. "You were such a help with the deputies. I might have chickened out if you hadn't been there. They listened to you! You knew just what to say!"

"You wouldn't have chickened out, not a habitual offender like you, you're too tough," he growled. "So what happens next? Will you call your clients back for tomorrow?"

Abby gnawed on her lip as she stared out the windshield. Then she shook her head. "No. Not for tomorrow. I have a lot of thinking to do first. I'm not surc I want to keep doing what I've been doing. It's not only that Marsh has ruined everything. It's more than that. The day care was really Gary's life's work. I was just along for the ride, I guess. It was rewarding work, but I think… I think maybe it's time for a change. Another one. A big one."

Her words resonated with Cade. He was ready for a change, as well. Since last night, in the back of his mind was a tiny germ of a plan. Maybe the K-9 trainer team in Bushnell would be up for opening a branch office, say in Ocala…. Meanwhile, staying in Bushnell would mean he could be nearer to where Abby lived, while she put her life back together. He could check in with her, be around if Marsh decided to cause trouble. Maybe even get to know those little things she'd talked about, like her favorite color, whether she liked her Chinese food spicy or not. His heartbeat quickened. It was a big shift—he'd have to buy back Mort from the Marion County Sheriff's Department so they could train another deputy, and he might have to dip into his savings for a while, but it would be money well spent.

But first he needed to know if there was a chance she'd leave the door open for him. A crack was all he'd ask for. Had Marsh destroyed any possibility Abby would consider a long-term relationship again? The cab of the truck was heating swiftly, with the engine off. Sweat trickled down from his scalp. The place where he'd hit his head on the toolbox in the pickup bed still stung in the salty moisture.

The words jerked out of him. "I just have one question. Why the hell did you sneak off, Abby? Why didn't you wake me up, if you were ready to come home and face Marsh? Why'd you put yourself in so much damn danger? Why didn't you let me help you with that? He might have killed you, Abby. He was ready to do it." It wasn't the question he'd meant to ask, but maybe it would get him the answer he sought even more.

"That's more than one question," she said shakily, and he at last turned to look at her. Her gaze slid to his scar and he put up a hand out of a reflexive fury.

"You know what I'm asking you. Explain. Before we call this quits, you owe me that much."

"You. You always want *the story,* don't you?" But her voice wasn't angry, just exhausted and resigned. "I couldn't believe it when I saw you in my doorway. It was like… It was like magic. How did you even get here?"

"I called someone who owed me a favor. You're avoiding the question, Abigail."

Her lips tightened. "You don't have to interrogate me."

"Seems like I do. Go on." Despite his irritation, he was pleased to see her standing up for herself. People could and did change. Roy had; Abby had. Two lives to which he'd made a difference, hadn't he? Even as ugly as he was. He wanted to make a difference. It was the way to fill the voids in his life. He didn't have to do that by busting drug dealers, living like a spy supercharged with adrenaline and secrecy. He could give people the tools to change on their own, and whether that was training K-9 dogs and their handlers or helping this beautiful, haunted, glorious woman marshal the strength to take control of her own life again, it didn't matter.

She reached for the door handle. "Your dog must really want out by now—"

"I'm sure he does, but five more minutes inside where it's air-conditioned won't kill him. Come on, Abby, give."

She stared forward, not looking at him. Sweat trickled down her temple and beaded her upper lip. Cade thought about the salty taste it would have, if he could kiss her just once more. "You'd think we were back at the campground again. All right, you want me to bare my soul, here it is. I was embarrassed, all right? I got myself into this mess, and I had to get myself out of it. Prove to myself—and I guess to you, too—that I wasn't weak and useless and stupid and…and everything Marsh has made me into, since Gary died. I thought I'd only be gone a few hours. I'd get him out of the house, grab a few things and come right back to…" Her voice trembled to a stop, then she seemed to gulp and force herself to continue. She looked at him with earnest gray eyes and soft, sad mouth. "Come right back to you, in that crummy little motel room, if you'd have me after everything I've done wrong these past three days."

Cade thought his heart might burst. He reached

across the cab, and marvel of marvels, she didn't flinch at his sudden movement. He hauled her to him, never more grateful for the old-fashioned bench seat, and buried his hot, raw face in her sweaty neck. *Come right back to you.* Sure, she'd have brought back his truck, but he thought she was saying more, so much more, than that. It was just so hard to believe.

"Have you? If I'd have you?" He spoke against her neck. He wasn't sure he could look at her and keep his heart out of his eyes, but Abby wouldn't let him stay hidden. Her fingers crept to his face and lifted his head so she could look into his face.

Cade closed his eyes.

"I keep thinking about last night," Abby whispered. "There was something there, wasn't there? I know how stupid and Hollywood romance that sounds. But when we were—when you were—going slow, didn't you feel it? Something different? When we were looking at each other? It's what gave me the last bit of strength I needed. You gave me hope, Cade, hope for a future, even though I know I don't have a right in the world to ask you for anything ever again."

He replayed her words in his head, but it was hard to think, because her lips were soft on his cheek where his scar pulled at the corner of his mouth. Soft, too, on his temple where the scarring was rough and angry.

Hope. He'd done that for her. Her words stabbed the dark, ugly center of his heart, and burned fierce and brilliant, lighting the long-hidden corners.

Cade hoped, too, but what he hoped was that she meant what she'd said at dinner last night when she told him his scars didn't matter to her. He hoped she would listen when he spoke to her about his ideas for the future, leaving the sheriff's department, changing his life. He hoped she would think about being a part of that—her experience as a small business owner was invaluable, but he wanted her around for more than just her skills. Abby seemed to be offering him a chance at a full and complete life, and he wanted to grab at it with both hands, even though they'd known each other only a few days. He was afraid of rushing her, frightening her, and so he held his tongue. He could be patient. He could take it slow. She deserved that kind of consideration.

When he turned his head, her lips were waiting for his, sweet and open, and her skin tasted of salt and sweat and she twined her arms around his neck. She didn't complain when he held her too tightly and dragged her into his lap.

The furnace heat and stifling air of the truck cab finally drove them apart, panting and disheveled. They both looked at the house again, where Mort's head still showed in the front window, ears pricked and alert.

Abby shook her head. "I don't want to go back in there right now. It's a mess. I don't feel like cleaning up. I'm not ready to deal with the things Marsh did while I was away. Not yet."

"So don't go in." Cade shrugged, feigning nonchalance, though his heart was beginning to race. This much optimism couldn't be good for him, but he was too hopeful to push it back down. What if she really meant she was planning to walk away from everything Marsh had touched? Could he be a part of whatever followed in her life?

"But I don't know where I could go—"

His mouth quirked in a smile. He pushed her hair back from her sweaty face. "You've been dealing with a lot today. I don't expect you to realize what time it is."

Abby glanced at her watch. "It's almost two in the afternoon. You're probably starving. I know I am."

"It's after checkout time in Micanopy."

Abby blinked in confusion. "What?"

"Check-out time is eleven o'clock at the Rest-n-Refresh Motel. We owe that guy for another day's stay."

Understanding dawned on her face, making him chuckle. She fished in her pocket for her house key, and handed it to Cade. "Why don't you go get your loyal K-9 sidekick and lock up, while I move that damned silver Honda out of the street."

"You got it, baby." He opened the driver's-side door and stepped out, feeling the rush of cooler but still humid air into the sauna of the truck cab. Between the sun and the kissing, the cab had really heated up.

"Then we'll look for a drugstore."

Cade paused. Now it was his turn to look confused.

Abby smiled, a slow, sexy smile that turned his guts inside out with a mix of happiness and hope and desire. "I believe I owe you some spare condoms."

"Why, Abigail McMurray, I believe you do. Remember to pay for them, please."

"Oh, I will." She scooted out of the cab on his side, wrapping her legs around his waist when he reached to help her down. She slid her arms around his neck and bent her head for another long, deep kiss. Cade braced his legs and folded her tightly in his arms, only letting her feet down slowly as the kiss ended, supporting her as she staggered. He leaned his forehead against hers, watching her desire-drowsed eyes open. Desire for *him.* He believed in that at last.

Abby pulled back just far enough to prevent her eyes from crossing as she looked at him. A smile crept across her lips, one of those rare smiles that bathed him in happy delight. It changed from sweetness to devilish mischief. Her fingertip traced along his bottom lip for a moment, then she leaned back in his arms and outright grinned. "Besides, I think I should stick to stealing trucks, don't you?"

"As long as it's just one particular truck, I think I could live with that."

Abby looked at him a long time, serious once more, twining her fingers with his. "I think I could, too," she said. "Now, let's ride off into the sunset, just the three of us, what do you say?"

"Baby, I like your style."

* * * * *

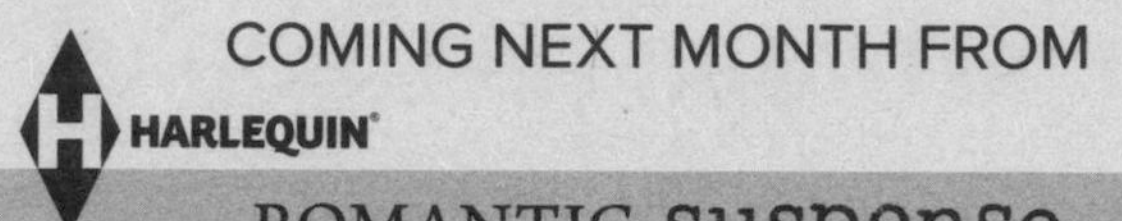

Available June 3, 2014

#1803 OPERATION UNLEASHED

Cutter's Code • by Justine Davis

Drew offers to marry his brother's widow and care for her son, though he never expects to fall for Alyssa. But when the child is kidnapped, Drew will do whatever it takes to make his family whole again.

#1804 SPECIAL OPS RENDEZVOUS

The Adair Legacy • by Karen Anders

After surviving torture, soldier Sam Winston sees threats everywhere. When his politician mother is almost killed, he teams up with his psychiatrist, the mysterious Olivia, to find the assassin. Except Olivia is keeping a secret....

#1805 PROTECTING HER ROYAL BABY

The Mansfield Brothers • by Beth Cornelison

As Brianna Coleman suffers amnesia, Hunter Mansfield vows to protect her...even when her baby proves to be royalty hunted by international assassins. But can he protect his heart?

#1806 LONE STAR REDEMPTION

by Colleen Thompson

When Jessie Layton arrives seeking her missing twin, rancher Zach Rayford defends his mother's lies. Together, they confront dangerous secrets, including the parentage of the "miracle child" holding Zach's family together.

When Drew offers to marry his brother's widow and care for her son, he never expects to fall for Alyssa. But when the child is kidnapped, Drew will do whatever it takes to make his family whole again.

Read on for a sneak peek at

OPERATION UNLEASHED

by Justine Davis, available June 2014 from Harlequin® Romantic Suspense.

"We did this."

Her voice was soft, almost a whisper from behind him. He spun around. She'd gone up with Luke to get him warm and dry, and set him up with his current favorite book. He was already reading well for his age, on to third-grade level readers, and Drew knew that was thanks to Alyssa. "Yes," he said, his voice nearly as quiet as hers. "We did."

"It has to stop, Drew."

"Yes."

"What can I do to make that easier?"

God, he hated this. She was being so reasonable, so understanding. And he felt like a fool because the only answer he had was "Stop loving my brother."

"I'm not Luke," he said, not quite snapping. "Don't treat me like a six-year-old."

"Luke," she said sweetly, "is leaving temper tantrums behind."

He drew back sharply. Opened his mouth, ready to truly snap this time. And stopped.

"Okay," he said after a moment, "I had that one coming."

"Yes."

In an odd way, her dig pleased him. Not because it was accurate, he sheepishly admitted, but because she felt confident enough to do it. She'd been so weak, sick and scared when he'd found her four years ago, going toe-to-toe with him like this would have been impossible. But she was strong now, poised and self-assured. And he took a tiny bit of credit for that.

"You've come a long way," he said quietly.

"Because I don't cower anymore?"

He frowned. "I never made you cower."

For an instant she looked startled. "I never said you did. You saved us, Drew, don't think I don't know that, or will ever forget it. I have come a long way, and it's in large part because you made it possible."

It was a pretty little speech, a sentiment she'd expressed more than once. And not so long ago it had been enough. More than enough. It had told him he'd done exactly what he'd intended. That he'd accomplished his goal. That she was stable now, strong, and he'd had a hand in that.

And it wasn't her fault that wasn't enough for him anymore.

Don't miss
OPERATION UNLEASHED
by Justine Davis,
available June 2014 from
Harlequin® Romantic Suspense.

HRSEXP0514

ROMANTIC suspense

SPECIAL OPS RENDEZVOUS
by Karen Anders

The Adair Legacy

Heartstopping danger, breathtaking passion, conspiracy and intrigue. ***The Adair Legacy*** has it all.

After surviving torture, soldier Sam Winston sees threats everywhere. But when his politician mother is almost killed, he teams up with his psychiatrist, the mysterious Olivia, to find the assassin. Except Olivia is keeping a secret....

Look for *SPECIAL OPS RENDEZVOUS* by Karen Anders in June 2014. Available wherever books and ebooks are sold.

Don't miss other titles from ***The Adair Legacy*** miniseries:
HIS SECRET, HER DUTY by Carla Cassidy
EXECUTIVE PROTECTION by Jennifer Morey

Heart-racing romance, high-stakes suspense!

www.Harlequin.com

HRS27874